continued on next page . . .

Whose Death is it, Anyway? A lively family reunion turns deadly when a young relative of Peaches's disappears—and an unidentified body turns up not long afterward . . .

> "Peaches is back, and she's better than ever . . . absolutely the best in the series!"   —*The WordShop*

Is There a Dead Man in the House? When Peaches's father and his new wife renovate the old family home it's a fascinating process—until the discovery of century-old buried bones brings not only mystery but a foreshadowing of more danger for the current occupants . . .

> "Squire goes for a realistic approach with her charming character who should provide fodder for a long series."   —*Fort Lauderdale Sun-Sentinel*

Where There's a Will: After they come into a hefty inheritance, several members of a wealthy family meet untimely deaths. Hired to investigate, Peaches joins the rest of the clan on a glamorous—and dangerous—cruise . . .

> "A delight from start to finish. Can't wait for the next in the series."   —Dorothy Cannell

FORGET ABOUT MURDER

Elizabeth Daniels Squire

BERKLEY PRIME CRIME, NEW YORK

This is a work of fiction. Names, characters, places, and incidents are either the product of the author's imagination or are used fictitiously, and any resemblance to actual persons, living or dead, business establishments, events, or locales is entirely coincidental.

FORGET ABOUT MURDER

A Berkley Prime Crime Book / published by arrangement with the author

PRINTING HISTORY
Berkley Prime Crime edition / February 2000

The Penguin Putnam Inc. World Wide Web site address is http://www.penguinputnam.com

ISBN: 0-425-17343-7

Berkley Prime Crime Books are published by The Berkley Publishing Group, a division of Penguin Putnam Inc., 375 Hudson Street, New York, New York 10014. The name BERKLEY PRIME CRIME and the BERKLEY PRIME CRIME design are trademarks belonging to Penguin Putnam Inc.

PRINTED IN THE UNITED STATES OF AMERICA

10 9 8 7 6 5 4 3 2 1

ACKNOWLEDGMENTS

I'd like to thank the wonderful people who helped with know-how for this book. If any mistakes have crept in, they are my own.

Thanks to all the Western North Carolina community newspaper folks whose suggestions have enriched this book, including Hugh Koontz of *The News Record* in Marshall; Sandy Sox of the *Tryon Daily Bulletin*; Lynn Hotling, Rose Hooper, and Lisa Duff of the *Sylva Herald*; and those whose newspapers inspired me, too, from *The Mountaineer* in Waynesville to *Mountain Xpress* in Asheville and *The Blowing Rocket* (my favorite name) in Blowing Rock. Also thanks to Sally and Jack Sanders, Betty Grace Nash, Helena Caston, and the other folks with whom I once worked on *The Redding Pilot*.

Richard S. Dillingham, Regional Specialist at Mars Hill College, and Peggy Harmon, Special Collections Supervisor, Renfro Library, Mars Hill College, made sure I had access to all the material about moonshine and stills in their archives and even steered me to an old still in the Rural Life Museum in Mars Hill, North Carolina. Also, thank you to some former moonshiners I interviewed about the way it was. More information about moonshine can be found in *Mountain Spirits* by Joseph Earl Dabney (Bright Mountain Books, Asheville: 1984), and the late winter 1999 issue of *Appalachian Voice* in Boone, N.C., which has an article by Nathaniel H. Axtell.

The great Dorothy-L Mystery Listserve can furnish information on any subject known to man. It told me what type of guns one particular suspect would own, even down to the machine gun by his bed.

Kenneth Reeves, of the North Carolina Cooperative Extension Service, provided background on the history of the use of DDT in the region.

Terry Bubar of Radio Shack explained the ins and outs of illegal use of scanners to listen in on car phones.

Dr. Geraldine Powell furnished information on post-traumatic stress syndrome.

As always, I am grateful to my writing group: Jan Harrow, Dershie McDevitt, Peggy Parris, and Florence Wallin for good suggestions—especially to Peggy Parris for last-minute creative thinking.

Thanks to my editor, Judith Stern Palais, and my agent, Luna Carne-Ross, for all their help.

Thanks to all the people who contributed memory tricks, including Frank Wallis, who kindly supplied the "old sock on the television" rule, and Seymour Sheriff, who keeps me abreast of the latest research on memory.

Thanks to Sammy Vasquez of the Opryland Hotel staff, who was so friendly and helpful as I cased the joint.

Thanks to Betty and Ralph Chamberlain for the use of their house, with a few changes, as Isaiah Hubbel's home.

Thanks to Lisa Franklin for teaching me about upright hollows; to Julie Burns and Bonnie Kettner for invaluable help and moments of hilarity; to my son Worth Squire for valuable suggestions, and most of all, to my husband, C. B. Squire.

CHAPTER
1

THURSDAY, LATE APRIL

A woman with demanding blue eyes, as sharp as knives, stood in front of my desk, staring at me as if she expected something. I would have wondered why if it hadn't been Thursday.

"I'm very busy," I said. "If you have news for next week, put it in the basket there."

A wry smile twisted her mouth as if my instructions could be funny. This gal wasn't young, but she was full of it. She plunked herself in the chair across from my desk.

"Tonight," she said, "I'm going to put on my U.S. Government falsies and go out and start to prove that the King of the Mountain killed his wife!" That got my attention. She reminded me of someone. Someone I had good and bad feelings about, both at the same time. But I couldn't think who.

I didn't want that woman messing up my day, even

though she sure knew how to pique my interest, and looked arresting in her gaucho hat. Very few people here in the mountains of Monroe County, North Carolina, wear gaucho hats. Beneath a fringe of gray-streaked dark hair, her face was square-jawed but attractive. Her blue eyes were dead determined. And she had backup—she'd helped a small dachshund into her lap. The dog eyed me as if it might bite if I didn't behave.

"Look," I said, "I'm close to deadline. The paper comes out on Thursdays. This is Thursday. I've got enough to do to choke a horse." I waved my hands at the papers on my desk. "If you can't prove murder yet, come back tomorrow."

She hunkered down in the chair, glancing up at the fake wood walls that divide the *Weekly Word* office into cubicles. As if dissatisfied, she glanced out my one window, then back at me. She picked up a brass letter-opener from my desk. Ah, so that's where it was, behind a stack of papers. Next to the sign my cousin Mary sent me which says "If a cluttered desk is a sign of a cluttered mind, what is an empty desk a sign of?"

"You're Peaches Dann, and you're supposed to be a reporter," she accused. "I'm Belle Dasher, and I have a story." She still eyed me as though I was missing something.

I should think of a way to remember her name. I didn't intend to let her ring my *bell*; also, she was slightly *dashing*, though she was no spring chicken, and dressed in blue jeans and a red shirt. And that hat.

She ran her finger down the blade of the letter opener. "Not very sharp." She looked me straight in the eye and said, "That man killed my beloved husband." She paused, and tears came to her eyes. She pulled out a handkerchief and blew her nose. She squared her shoulders, narrowed her eyes, and spat out the next words bitterly. "He also killed two more of your subscribers, six ducks, and a pig. And nobody will call any of this murder."

O.K., she had my full attention, though I still didn't know who she could be. She had my sympathy, but with reservations. I would never mention losing my wonderful husband in the same breath with six ducks, and a pig.

But I was curious. I'd have to listen, even though it was press day. Even though I took this job to put myself at one remove from murders.

"Do you have any hard facts?" I demanded. I'm fifty-seven and new at this. I have to act professional. The publisher is taking a chance on me because I've written a book, *How to Survive Without a Memory,* about mnemonic strategies. What did I need to remember now? Her eyes said *plenty.*

This Belle and her little brown dog kept their gimlet eyes on me. "You want facts? My husband died of lung cancer a year ago. I got breast cancer three months ago," she said. "My neighbor Lem Wilkes on one side got a brain tumor and died. My neighbor Miranda Snow on the other side had a tumor in her throat, her daughter was sick, too, and her pig died. And farther around our mountain there's a guy named Sam Mound whose ducks have begun to die. They had tumors, too. Now, that's not normal. So I had my well tested."

That made sense. But what did it have to do with murder? I had begun to take notes. Well, I'd need them to pass this on to Martin. He's my editor. Belle still eyed me as if I was missing something big.

"They found DDT in the water," she said. "DDT causes cancer. It's been banned for years, but there it was. When I got my neighbors to test their wells, they found the same damn thing." She said that so angrily, the dog growled.

"Have you been able to prove where the DDT came from?" I could ask that much without getting involved.

She snorted. "If Isaiah Hubbel up on his mountain had an outhouse, the seepage downhill could pollute our wells—right? The man from the Health Department did admit that. But Isaiah says this is all just me making trouble because I like to. I say he tells lies."

Isaiah Hubbel was big *Trouble*. That's what this Belle Dasher thought. And she said, "I say he tells lies." *I say* was like "Isaiah." Belle was full of *I say* and anger at the King of the Mountain. I could remember that!

"Does Isaiah have an outhouse?" I asked. "Is that still legal?"

"They didn't find any damned outhouse," she fumed, "but there's some source of DDT at the top of Isaiah's mountain. There has to be. And if the man from the government who came to inspect hadn't been Isaiah's second cousin, he would have looked hard enough to find out what it is."

I nodded. In our mountains we do protect kin. "So of course you're upset and angry," I said. "I see where you're coming from."

"No," she said, "you don't." She leaned forward as if she might jump across my desk. "Or you wouldn't sit there so cool. I don't take it lightly that I lost my husband and then my boobs," she cried, slapping her breast, or—whatever. The dog winced.

My guest smiled broadly and narrowed her eyes. She radiated irony. "See? The U.S. Government kindly gave me a prosthesis for each side." She patted each one. "Because I'm sixty-five, I got a lovely matched pair. My U.S. falsies. They even get warm like the rest of me when I wear them. They're even soft like real breasts. Oh, the miracles of science. You can't tell when you look at me. You wouldn't know if you squeezed me. But they didn't give me a new husband. Nobody squeezes me. I lost my Ernie." She was red in the face with anger and looked like she might cry.

I felt I ought to say something kind. I also felt that she'd throw the letter opener at me if I did. She wanted me to be as angry as she was. Even the dog let out a low, unhappy growl and readjusted his position in her lap. At least she had the dog.

I knew this woman from somewhere. Why didn't she tell me where?

She preferred to give a lecture. "One in three people die of cancer of some kind. Did you know that? And one in eight women have breast cancer before they die. One in eight! But who cares? Not enough to stop polluting."

She had a point, though there are other causes of cancer, too. But I felt cornered. I felt as if she was going to whip a false breast out and wave it at me. I almost touched my own breasts to be sure they were still safe. But I don't weep with people who can obviously take care of themselves. She was one of those. And I still had a deadline. I needed a way to ease her out of there.

Maybe she sensed that. "As for you," she said with a sudden, accusing glance, "you're too hipped on Thursday. You don't even remember me," she crowed. Behind her, a flyer on the bulletin board—next to the one about the weekly square dance—said YOU CAN BE PERFECT.

Not me. So I really was supposed to remember this woman? Her face rang some kind of faraway bell. That square jaw, those piercing eyes. I am not good at faces or names. But I'm not bad at detecting. If she'd just give me hints.

Finally she came out with it: "When you were a kid you saved my life!"

Wham! The details came back to me. I stood up, amazed. How could I forget! "You're that Belle!" Yes! A teen who found homes for stray dogs and cats. Who adopted birds with broken wings. Who socked a bully. She'd been a friend in a way, though I was six and she was fourteen. I'd looked up to Belle.

"You were trying to save that cat." I saw it now. "You made me hold onto your feet while you leaned down over the edge of a scary drop-off to get a cat off a ledge." Where was it? On a school picnic?

She smiled, but with her jaw still set in anger. "That's me."

We should have gone for grown-up help, but the cat was on a narrow ledge and crying, and it looked like rain. The drop was steep. And Belle was a real persuader. All of that came back to me now. She'd said she just wanted me to hold her feet in case, because she didn't have to reach that far over. Ha!

"And then you were so far over you couldn't get back up, and I held onto your feet for at least half an hour, which felt like a year, and screamed for help. Finally someone heard us and came and saved you, and you saved the cat."

She nodded looking a little sheepish. "We did take a chance." She'd said *We*! I was only six years old. Goodness knows how I held on. Except of course I didn't have her full weight, thank God. I was just a balancing force. She stood up now, shifting the dog into the crook of her arm. "You were a true friend." She reached out across my desk and touched me with her free hand. Her eyes said, So be one now!

I went around the desk and put an arm around her, complete with dog. "It's been so long!" Fifty years.

But even as a kid I'd known that Belle was dangerous. Wonderfully dangerous. Because she'd felt things so. Because she'd acted first and thought afterwards. Like the time she hit the class bully when we were way off at the edge of the schoolyard. Luckily he was a coward. Belle had never bored me.

She'd moved away shortly after the bully thing. Her mother, who'd been sick, was better, so she left her grandma's and went home, out of my life. And now here she was, a little gaunter, with gray-streaked hair and that dern gaucho hat. And demanding my help.

When you've saved someone's life by holding on until first your hands and then your whole body aches, you have an investment in that person, even if she wasn't a close buddy.

"It's good to see you still alive," I said, "after all these years."

"No thanks to Isaiah Hubbel," she announced. Back to that.

But now it seemed to me that the clock on the wall was ticking more loudly than usual. My deadline creeping up. You can't stop the presses for personal reasons. Even for someone you admired in first grade. I gave her an extra squeeze for old times' sake. The dog under her arm began wagging his tail. "I really want to see you," I told her. "Let's get together when it's not a Thursday," I said firmly, "and I'll pass everything you've told me on to Martin, our editor."

She stiffened. "Is that a brushoff?" she demanded.

"It's not a brush-off, Belle. I have a job to do." And then, remembering her proclivity for dangling from cliffs, I let my curiosity get the best of me. "So what are you going to do now?" I asked. I bit my tongue. I must stay out of this.

She let the words rush out. "I'll find out the source of the DDT, even if Isaiah does have those damn Dobermans and that No Trespassing sign." She slapped her leg with the end of the dog's leash as if she absolutely had to hit something, even if it was herself. "I also intend to find out what happened to Isaiah's Joan. A man who'd kill his neighbors and not care would never hesitate to kill his wife!" She plunked herself back down with the dog in her lap. I'd blown it.

Joan, I thought. That almost rhymes with *gone*. And whatever happened to *Joan,* she's *gone*. I have to use tricks like that to remember names.

"You said your husband and two neighbors died." I had to be accurate. "I'll tell Martin," I repeated. "He handles this kind of story."

"Three people dead so far," she emphasized. "And don't forget the ducks and the pig. Animals suffer, too."

I said, "What makes you think Isaiah Hubbel killed his wife?" I did not sit back down, except on the edge of my desk. But I didn't make her leave, either.

She smiled. She thought she had me hooked. "Nobody has heard from that woman for three weeks. Nothing. And she was a person who kept in touch. Nobody has seen that woman since April first."

"You know the exact day?" I glanced at the calendar on the wall. The one from the funeral home. Today was April 21. I'd been at work here for a month.

"That's what they say around town," she said. "He lost his

wife on April Fool's Day. Some people don't like Joan. They think that's funny."

Yes. *Joan* who was *gone* and didn't *phone*. Appropriate rhymes help capture names.

"And how do you know all that?" I asked.

"Why, everybody in town knows that," she said. "You know this town."

I didn't know the town yet, except superficially.

"And Joan wasn't a loner like Isaiah," Belle pointed out. "She'd write or call. He says that she drove off to Georgia, but he killed her. Now, the whole place is his. And any man who will pollute his neighbors' wells and swear their cancer is none of his business, any man like that is perfectly capable of murdering his wife." She pounded my desk. Really mad. My coffee cup bounced. If someone had come in just then to place a birth announcement or a Girl Scout story or an ad for a lost dog, they'd sure be amazed. Nobody did. Everybody knew it was Thursday.

But Pat from Advertising heard and came over to my cubicle. She must have been listening for a while. "You want to see justice done," she announced. She stood in my doorway and patted her blond hair pulled up on the top of her head. Pat's no dumb blonde. She gets passionate about injustice. She came in and stood next to me.

"No," Belle cried, "I want to get even! I admit it. I'd like to see him rot in prison for the rest of his damn life. He's a reptile. He should be locked up." She took a deep breath and seemed to pull herself together. She patted the dog.

I thought of putting a sign on my desk: *Free scream therapy, but not on Thursdays.* Not even for old friends.

"You've had editorials against polluters," she said. "They're evil! You've got to understand!"

I nodded. She'd had more than her share of trouble. My nod led her on.

"I might just go buy some hamburger and something to drug those Dobermans the King of the Mountain keeps up there." She shook with anger. "I'll go to search that place myself and find out what's wrong or die trying."

Pat and I both cried, "Be careful!" like a Greek chorus. And I added, "Don't do anything so dangerous, Belle. Please! You can't drug that man's shotgun. Let the sheriff handle this. And come back tomorrow. Martin will want to hear your story. I want to see you."

She lifted the dog out of her lap, stood up to go, and gave me a scornful glance. "I live with danger. I gamble. My doctor told me the odds are fifty-fifty the cancer will return. And I'll be careful. I have more than a fifty-fifty chance of not getting shot if I search that mountain at night. Or in the early morning when Isaiah is still asleep. But don't worry, I won't get you involved," she said, glancing from Pat to me disdainfully.

I bet she had never been careful in her life.

She stood for a moment, holding the small dog against her—well, I guess against her U.S. falsies. At least she had something to hug. She stared out the office window. There's a redbud tree outside.

"Beautiful," she said. "Every tiny blossom up and down each bough is perfect. Have you noticed there are two kinds of bees collecting nectar, small ones and a few big ones, buzzing round?"

Boy, could she change gears fast. I looked at the redbud, something I wouldn't ordinarily stop to do on Thursday. Yes, it was lovely. I found myself smiling.

Meanwhile, she set her dachshund on the floor, attached

his red leash, gave him a pat when he wagged his tail, turned on her heel, and stalked out, leaving me disturbed.

Pat sighed. "Back to furniture-store ads. Poor woman. I hope she'll stay off that mountain." She started to leave, then turned to me and said, "April first. That's the day they found the body of the Good News Man."

I all but groaned. How could a small rural county have a murder and suspected murder all in the same month? And I was honor-bound to stay away from murders. Pat didn't help. "The Good News Man had been passing out leaflets at the bottom of Hubbel Mountain," she said. She turned and looked at my bulletin board. "Like that one you have that says 'You can be perfect.'"

"Passing out flyers in a lot of places," I said. I didn't have time to worry about that. I didn't have time to dwell on Belle Dasher, either. I had to work fast.

As I put together a story about roaming dogs, an odd thought slipped through my mind. Why think of searching Isaiah Hubbel's place at night when the man was at home? Why not go when he was off somewhere?

I finished a piece about the Town Council, and another about a loose pig that walked down Main Street and into the jail. I E-mailed the last-minute news to Martin, who was over at the print shop. The paper got out on time, and I drove home to my comfortable, square-cut-log house over in Buncombe County and to my wonderful husband, Ted. To my good luck.

Ted and I have only been married a few years. It's the second time around for both of us, but we fit. He's naturally logical. I'm naturally intuitive, which is a help to a reporter—though I have to double check that I've included all the *who what when why where* and *how.*

But to get back to Ted, he's also great to look at. Though maybe I'm prejudiced. He has a twinkle in his eye and streaky gray hair and a wry smile. Also, he's kind. When I came in the door, he gave me a hug. He smelled good, too. Like aftershave and soap, and just like himself—Ted, who had asked me to stay away from murders. You see, I solved a family murder, more by luck than good management, and nearly got killed in the process. My relatives and friends decided I was a volunteer detective. Better to be a real reporter and detect the news than to be expected to risk my neck. Ted says he needs my neck. Now he has high blood pressure, so I shouldn't scare him to death by getting into danger, right?

I thought of Belle and hoped the husband she'd lost had been as kind and warm. How wretched for her to lose him, then have cancer surgery herself. I hugged Ted extra hard. And had she been alone? She hadn't mentioned children. What had her life been like since I looked up to her way back when?

"A friend from long ago came to my office today," I told Ted. "She said she could prove murder. Don't worry. Martin will handle the story," I added quickly, as I placed flounder fillets and a little butter and white wine in a casserole. "Her name is Belle Dasher," I said. "She told me there's a fifty-fifty chance her breast cancer will come back and kill her, so she's going to gamble on danger. And she's lost her husband, so I don't think she feels she has much to live for." I went over and gave Ted another quick hug. Then back to fixing supper. "The strange thing is, she reminded me that fifty years ago I saved her life. Now I hope she doesn't get shot. The whole thing makes me feel bad."

I told him Belle's story as he made a hollandaise sauce for the fish. On press night, we celebrate getting the paper out.

He's the sauce chef. A sauce chef with good legs! That may sound silly to say about a man, but his legs are straight, and he plants his feet so firmly on the ground. His legs make him seem powerful in a quiet way. High blood pressure doesn't show. I want him to stay strong!

So, I reminded myself again, Belle Dasher's problem had to be a spectator sport for me. I could sympathize with her. I could tell Ted her colorful story. But I must not get involved in a possible murder.

"And when was this Joan Hubbel last seen?" Ted asked.

"On April Fools' Day," I said.

He frowned. "What an odd coincidence."

I knew what he was going to say next. "That's the day some kid found the body in the woods, isn't it? The body of the man nobody knew except he was going from door to door."

"Yes," I said. "Giving out religious flyers. Some said 'Here's the good news' and some said 'You can be perfect.' He was shot in the chest, and the sheriff still doesn't have a clue as to why. Although the man did tend to shout about how the damned would be pulled down to hell if anyone refused his flyers. He was from over in Jackson County, and his family said he didn't have an enemy in the world. But he couldn't have anything to do—could he?—with Joan Hubbel's disappearing, if she did.

"The strange thing is," I went on as I washed salad, "that with Belle so upset about 'murder,' with anger hanging around her just like a cloud of hornets, she stopped to admire the redbud tree outside my office window. She showed me something I hadn't even noticed, working in sight of that tree all day. We have two kinds of bees, large ones and small ones, buzzing around the redbud blossoms. It's as if she thinks in terms of loneliness and dying, so she has to grab hold of beauty. Belle worries me, but I still admire her."

"She also told you she was ready to be reckless," Ted said. "Remember, you decided to become a reporter because that seemed like a safe and useful way to snoop. And you said you didn't want me to have to worry about you. And I did worry about you."

"So I intend to stay out of this," I promised. He walked up behind me, as I stood at the sink, and put his arms around me. "Watch out," he said. "You're valuable."

I turned and hugged him tight. "And so are you."

A picture floated through my mind: The poster on my bulletin board that said, YOU CAN BE PERFECT. It reminded me of the unsolved murder. Why had I saved the poster? I told myself that in the morning I would throw it out.

CHAPTER
2

THURSDAY NIGHT

We took our coffee into the living room. I sat down in the comfortable chair near the table with the phone. Ted sat across from me in the rocker he favors by the fireplace. Immediately the phone rang. Ted grinned. "I bet I know who that is," he said. "The woman who has to know everything that happens in this county first. Your brain-picker and news source: All-ears Suzie."

Suzie always calls as soon as the paper is out. She makes sure before it hits the newsstands that there's nothing in it she doesn't already know, and nothing upcoming that she can't put her two cents' worth into. She's such a good news source that I play along.

She used to be a reporter herself, but she doesn't want to work full time. That's why she was a matchmaker between me and my job. I'd only written a book, never worked for a paper, but Ted is a journalism professor if I need advice, right? Suzie knew that the publisher needed a reporter, and weeklies don't pay enough to make it easy to find a good one. I won't get rich. Still, I owe her. I answered the phone. Yes, it was Suzie.

"Peaches," she said, "there's a rumor that Joan Hubbel, who lives on Hubbel Mountain, has been murdered."

Ha! I heard it first! About *Joan* who didn't *phone*. "Murdered?" I said, letting Suzie tell all. I was aware of Ted watching me closely. I could see he didn't trust Suzie not to get me involved.

"Of course, that place is not really a mountain," she was saying, "more like a great big steep hill, but that's what we call it. And nobody around there has seen Joan for three weeks, and her husband, Isaiah, is strange. You've heard how people in our back coves have intermarried and turned strange?"

"Yes," I said to encourage her to go on.

"Well, that's highly exaggerated," she said firmly, as if I'd accused her friends. Long pause. "But in the case of those Hubbels, well, maybe not. In fact, all those Hubbels who originally come from Winn Cove are peculiar, to say the least. Charming, but peculiar. Their money came from moonshine whiskey, back when we respected that. It was a man's God-given right to make it. Isaiah's grandfather was a state senator, but he took to hellfire preaching. He ran off with the church organist and shot her husband in self-defense." I could tell by Suzie's enthusiastic tone that she was enjoying this seamy history.

"So there's a violent streak in the family," I said. Boy, that was putting it mildly! "Who thinks Isaiah Hubbel killed his wife?" I asked. I glanced at Ted. He shook his head no. He meant, don't get involved.

"Her neighbors are all in a state," Suzie said. "This kind of talk just spreads like wildfire once it starts. But you've already heard about this because Belle Dasher came to see you this morning."

Sometimes I think Suzie has a spy satellite over Monroe County. I don't even bother anymore to ask her how she knows who comes to see me. I waited to let her tell all before I chimed in.

"You have to remember who's who in Monroe County to understand what's going on," she said. "I know I've told you this before, but it's important. There are the old-time reliable folks whose families go way back, mostly farmers, craftsmen, and a few of the lawyers and preachers." I knew Suzie counted herself as one of those people even though she'd gone off to the next county, married a millionaire, and then divorced him and come back. That's why she didn't need to work.

"There are some back-cove crazies and hotheads, of course, and also the new people the others don't quite trust yet. The Hubbels are a mixture of everything but the new. Belle Dasher is new. Her family came here when she was fourteen years old, and she never has really fit in yet. Watch out for her."

"I knew her before she moved here," I said. Ha. One up on Suzie. "And I'm worried about her."

"Oh," she said, "you mean because she's spreading bad stuff about the Hubbels. They don't take well to that. About how Isaiah Hubbel has polluted wells and contributed to Belle's cancer and her husband's death. Belle says that anybody who would do that wouldn't hesitate to kill his wife.

That talk makes the Hubbels livid. And furthermore, Joan disappeared. So some folks half believe it."

"Belle said she wanted to search Isaiah Hubbel's place at night or in the early morning," I said. "Poor Belle. She sure seems reckless." Then I realized I probably shouldn't have told Suzie that. So I added, "But I trust she won't actually do it. That's a good way to get shot." My curiosity rose up. "If she did search, why wouldn't she want to wait until Isaiah goes out—not that either way wouldn't be trespassing, and therefore . . ."

"Because he never leaves his hill," Suzie interrupted. "You've still got a lot to learn about this county."

"I know I do," I said, and felt defensive. "But it's not so different in Buncombe County."

"But with more old feuds, more family secrets. Why, even the land can be secret," she said, "with steep, hard-to-get-to spots like Isaiah's place and back coves and nigh ways and even upright hollows."

I knew what back coves were: narrow valleys that reached between steep places the way ocean coves reached into the land. Nigh ways were back-country shortcuts.

"I bet you've never known an upright hollow," she said. "That's where the sides are so steep that you can only see the sun when it's directly overhead. There's one over in back of Indian Head Rock. Certain kinds of plants grow there. Jewelweed, ferns, things that live with less light. A few folks might go there to gather ferns," she said "but not often. So if you fell down and hurt yourself in an upright hollow, no one might find you until it was too late. They used to be good places to make moonshine, if there was water."

I shivered, and pulled myself back to the subject. Suzie

meanders. "And why won't Mr. *Trouble* Hubbel leave his mountain?" I asked.

"Something about the war," she said. "The Vietnam War. He saw things that he didn't have the strength to bear. He came back with that post-traumatic stress syndrome. If you're odd to begin with and shocked on top of that, it's too much. They tried to help him, but he won't leave his mountain. He won't budge. You couldn't get him off it with a gun at his head."

"What did Isaiah Hubbel see that screwed him up?" I asked. Ted fidgeted with curiosity. I was glad he couldn't hear Suzie's end of the conversation.

"The Hubbels won't talk about that," she said. "Something dreadful. I don't know what."

I shivered again. I guess war turns some men insensitive to horror and leaves others unable to shake it off. But if Isaiah Hubbel was the sensitive type, how come he didn't care about his neighbors?

"It annoyed Joan," Suzie said, "that he would never leave the mountain. Maybe that's why she took off—if she did take off. She said a man who stayed on one hill all his life got boring. So she needed to be the one who got out and brought life back to that mountain. She sells real estate, or did till she disappeared."

"And Isaiah never leaves that mountain at all?"

"Not in over twenty years," Suzie said. "He says he intends to live there and raise fruit trees, and die there where it's safe. He watches TV and plays solitaire and takes care of those fruit trees as if each one was an only child. And I hear he surfs the Internet. I'm not into that yet. He has a buddy that he talks to every single day via E-mail. Somebody he knew in the war. Joan complains about that. I think she's jealous."

Imagine relating to your closest friend only by E-mail and your wife being jealous. The sadness of that got to me.

Suzie went on: "And some say that women slip up the mountain to visit Isaiah. That being lonesome makes him sexy. You hear names, but I doubt it. Joan would have killed them. Everybody in this county knows where he lives." Then Suzie told me how to get there as if I wanted to visit the man.

"Tell me more about Joan," I said. If someone is murdered, the seed of that murder is partly in that person. I believe that.

"That woman could drive a man to murder," Suzie said. "Joan wanted to be in charge. And of course when Isaiah couldn't come down the mountain, Joan could say what that man got to eat, except for what he raised—what he got to drink or read or wear. She controlled the part of his life related to the world below."

I tried to imagine being so much in someone's power.

"And Joan put on airs," Suzie said, "wearing silk blouses and black skirts."

"Didn't she work part-time over in Asheville, sell some real estate there?" I asked. Black skirts would be just fine in Asheville.

"Not to speak of," Suzie said, "and she smoked those menthol cigarettes and acted as if the menthol made them good for her. She drove a Range Rover. I guess she made good money to pay for that red Range Rover, but you sure could see her coming."

I wanted to ask if Joan Hubbel's car had disappeared. I told myself I must let Martin do that.

I could see that Suzie didn't like Joan. "But if Isaiah killed Joan, how would he get stuff from down the mountain?"

"Oh, she stocked up," Suzie said, "on corned beef and tuna fish and toilet paper and things like that. She had to be away some to see about her mother, so she bought stuff wholesale. Besides, his family would never let him starve."

"I write stories about his brother, Jake Hubbel," I said, "the one who's a county commissioner. He keeps giving money to worthy causes."

"Of course," she said, "so everybody likes him. And he serves on committees. If you want something done, ask Jake Hubbel. But watch out. He's a fixer. And sometimes he drinks. Not always. But at the worst times."

"What a strange family," I said. "And you think Isaiah killed Joan?" O.K., I admit it. I sounded curious.

Ted raised his eyebrows.

I pulled back. "I did take this job to stay away from murders," I said, maybe a little plaintively.

"Oh, don't worry about that," Suzie said. "Martin won't let you loose on this one. Your editor's a little bit old-fashioned about a woman's role, and you are the same age as his mother, who knits afghans for church sales and tends her garden. In that family they have kids at a young age. You notice Martin watches his language around you. That boy can have a dirty tongue when he puts his mind to it. But only with the boys. Well, he is just twenty-nine. He'll look into the rumors about Joan Hubbel all by himself. Just like he covered that poor kid who got killed trying to save souls last month. A dark back road is not the place to save a soul in Monroe County."

Suzie loved to warn me about dark back roads and boys with too much to drink.

"I imagine Martin will have you covering that high school fair, and the annual meeting of the Friends of the Library and that sort of thing this week. Not a possible murder."

I was annoyed. Is that what Suzie had intended? She said goodbye and hung up.

The phone rang again. It was Martin. "I suppose Suzie has already called you tonight just like she called me," my trusty editor said with a chuckle. "This time she may actually be onto a murder. Or not. You know Suzie."

"Yes," I agreed. I told him about Belle.

"Well, I'll nose around a little," he said. "It's probably all a rumor. Three weeks is not too terribly long not to write home. We covered the pollution story a while back." His voice got businesslike. "Tomorrow morning on your way to work, go by the high school and get some good pictures of the kids getting ready for the fundraiser. We'll also get some pictures of the fair in progress on Saturday. We'll do a big spread."

"O.K.," I said.

I wrote "high school on way to work," in my portable calendar, and put the calendar in my shoulder bag, ready to go. I wrote myself a Post-it® note and went into the bathroom to put it on the mirror where I look at myself while I brush my teeth in the morning. It pays to be primed.

I looked at myself now. Curly short brown hair, determined chin, snap-to-attention eyes. I thought about what I'd wanted to say to Martin.

Listen, sonny, I'd wanted to say, *I can do features about nice kids and teachers—why not? While you're off looking into murder. But I could nose around just as well as you can, except I'm new here and still learning the ways of this county. But the folks here can't be any rougher or slipperier than the ones in my own Buncombe County, where I've actually tripped over killers.* Except now I've sworn off.

CHAPTER
3

THE FOLLOWING DAY

Friday was one of those early spring days that thinks it's summer, warm but windy. The wind seemed faintly moist and friendly. Bits of green and red leaf peeped out from trees along the road as I drove toward the high school. I passed maples with faint clouds of red buds and a tulip poplar with furled buds of leaf. In fields, the grass was getting longish. Dandelions were out like stars. Belle would savor all that because she had a fifty-fifty chance of dying. I made up my mind to enjoy it just because it was there.

At the high school, kids were out in teams helping adults put up tents for booths. I also noticed a tall pole as thick as a tree peeled of bark and yellow-naked, that looked as if they might be intending to burn a witch at the stake. But high school students don't go in for that sort of thing at nine o'clock in the morning.

Going up to a woman with dark hair in a bun and granny glasses who seemed to be in charge, I explained that I was from the paper and we wanted to do a picture spread and story on the fair. I gave her a copy of this week's paper in case she hadn't gotten hers yet. She eyed the headline on the front page. HIGH SCHOOL FAIR SATURDAY. "Too bad you couldn't do the picture spread ahead of time," she said. "To publicize the fair." A complainer. One of those.

"I'll just go around and take pictures of the preparations," I said. She nodded. "And what's that pole for?" I asked.

"One of the contests," she said. "Climbing a greased pole." Oh, yes. One of our mountain sports, for special occasions. The person who keeps trying the longest wins, because the others have wiped off the slippery stuff with their efforts. Life is sometimes like that.

I introduced myself to three boys and a man putting up a tent. I snapped them struggling against a gust of wind, then took down their names. "I'm a volunteer from the Boosters Club," the man said. "A lot of us are here to help." He had long hair and wore a tie-dye shirt and didn't look like my idea of the Boosters Club. He was probably one of the ex-hippies who came to the county in the sixties. They made for variety.

I'd noticed a number of pickup trucks and cars parked near the edge of the field. Volunteer transportation. Complete with gun racks and guns. I turned back toward the field and snapped a man putting up a grill.

The sun was downright hot. I happened to glance back at the row of cars and trucks. One large white pickup was parked under a tree as if the tiny leaves could provide shade. I realized someone in the truck was waving. I looked around to see who he was waving at. It must be me.

Me as the Press, no doubt. Maybe he wanted to give us a story. Maybe he wanted to complain.

I figured that I had enough "before" pictures so I wandered over to the truck. Three hounds in the back got up and barked at me. I took their picture.

The rather good-looking man in a red shirt behind the wheel eyed me as if he expected the worst. He looked like George Washington on a quarter, same straight nose, but with curly black hair and an angry mouth. George Washington wearing a John Deere cap. O.K., this was going to be a complaint. Maybe we got the telephone number wrong in his ad about a lost dog. Maybe . . .

"Listen," he said before I was even close. "Don't mess with me or my brother." His voice was so loud I could hear him clearly over the yapping dogs. His eyes were fierce. What had I done? Was that his brother sitting in the far seat of the truck, leaning over as if he were listening to the dashboard? That second man had white hair, and I couldn't see his face. But then he wasn't the one who'd called me over. I waited. Man number one had a voice with momentum. He intended to tell me his complaint in fulsome detail. I was sure of that. Behind his head were two guns in a gun rack. I was glad one wasn't in his hands.

"My brother is a veteran," he said. "He served his country and he can be proud of that. If you listen to some fool woman who's made up some crazy story about how he poisoned his neighbors and killed his wife, you'll be sorry. If you hurt my brother, I'll personally see that you get hurt worse. I have some influence in this county. I don't fool around."

Good grief, he must mean Isaiah Hubbel. How would he even know I'd heard of Isaiah Hubbel? "If someone tells us a story, we check it out before we run it," I said. I sounded prissy in my own ears.

The second man in the truck couldn't be Isaiah Hubbel. He never left his mountain. Number Two with head turned away was listening to some sort of radio. I could hear a lot of static.

"You listen to that Belle Dasher," Number One said to me, "and you'll hear nothing but shit. That woman makes trouble. And you folks printed what she wrote about guns, about making it harder for law-abiding men like me to get guns." Unexpectedly, he smiled. George Washington as a charming salesman. The corners of his eyes crinkled. "You're too smart to let that woman dupe you."

"That was a letter to the editor," I said, going back to the gun bit. "People are entitled to express their own opinions in letters to the editor, about gun control or anything else." Personally, I would have felt more comfortable if this man had found it harder to get guns. He was still smiling. He was so good-looking when he smiled that I had to concentrate on not being swayed by that. Even serial killers can be handsome.

"Look," he said, "in Monroe County we protect our own."

"Which Hubbel are you, sir?" I asked, trying to sound unmoved and professional.

"Jake Hubbel." He spit it at me. Mad, I guess, that his charm didn't sway me. The dogs could tell how things had changed, and they began to snarl between barks. Jake Hubbel, good citizen, Suzie said. And a county commissioner. Not a good enemy, I could see.

So this was *Trouble* Hubbel number two. Jake Hubbel, which rhymes with *Make Trouble*. He thought I would, and it seemed that, for me, *he* would. Jake Hubbel, big man around town.

"Thank you for explaining how you feel," I said to Jake *Make Trouble* Hubbel. When I'm feeling threatened I get sickeningly polite. Which annoys people. But that's O.K. They are annoying me. "If there is anything to this accusation against your brother, you can be sure someone from the paper will cover the story," I said, "and if there's nothing to it, you don't need to worry. You will admit that Martin is fair."

Jake shrugged. Why did I let that make me so mad that I turned on my heel and walked away? I shouldn't have done that.

CHAPTER
4

LATER THAT DAY

My wonderful husband truly feels that I'm my own person, and I can lead my life however I want to. I've nearly scared him out of his wits several times, however, and now, with his high blood pressure, that would be no joke.

I reminded myself of that. *I'm working for this newspaper to keep so busy I won't get drawn into danger.* Yes! *Because I love my husband and I don't want to be the reason he has a stroke.* No! I drove almost all the way to work. But I was dying of curiosity about the Hubbels.

Perhaps, I thought, it wouldn't hurt just to look at the foot of the mountain—the one Suzie said was really just a steep hill. I could drive by and not even get out of my car, before I went to the office. That was almost in the line of duty. I looked in the rearview mirror. Jake *Make Trouble* Hubbel, with two guns in his gun rack, was nowhere in sight.

Suzie said the road onto Isaiah's mountain looked like a gravel driveway but I couldn't miss it. I wasn't even going on that road, just on the one around the mini-mountain. Mountain View Road. I'd actually remembered to bring a map.

I turned into Mountain View. A part of me felt guilty and cautious. Another part said it couldn't hurt just to look. I raised my eyes to the very top of the hill-mountain. I could just see a house there, a gray, weathered-wood house. The source of death and sickness? Water can carry those. But did Isaiah Hubbel really pollute the wells below?

Down on my level, the first house I passed was actually a doublewide with tulips and daffodils all around and a whirligig in the shape of a duck with wings that circled when the wind blew. A cheerful house.

I rolled my window down. I wanted to hear as well as see what went on at the foot of the "king's" mountain. Only bird calls. *Would-you, would-you.* High and shrill, but sweet.

I came to a field with the first green grass just coming up, then a bit of woods, skeletons of trees, still largely bare. The next house was an old one, not large but with graceful porches and all painted white. A big old tree in the front yard had one of those rubber-tire swings hanging from a branch, so children must live in this house. I remembered Belle Dasher had said there was a child with cancer. I shivered. A blue Volkswagen Bug, looking brand new, was parked in the driveway.

Which one was Belle's house, where her husband had sickened and died? I didn't even know that.

Beyond the house with the tire swing, there was a field with ridges in even rows as if it had been plowed the year before. The third house, where the road curved, looked neglected. The white paint was peeling here and there. But there were curtains in the windows. The flag was raised on the mailbox, indicating mail to go.

The Good News Man had left his flyers in the mailboxes of all these houses because nobody was home. That's what the sheriff had told Martin.

I looked in my rearview mirror. Oh, my gosh! Was that Jake *Make Trouble* Hubbel's pickup behind me? I continued to drive at the same speed, squelching the impulse to put my foot on the gas and vamoose. The pickup passed. It was white, but it wasn't Jake's. Fear can sure create illusions. I had a right to be on a public road, I told myself firmly. But a little voice inside me said, *Get out of here*. It didn't speak loud enough.

I passed a gray-brown house with a weathered-wood porch rail made of peeled logs from young trees.

I should be coming to the road up Isaiah Hubbel's mountain before too long. Then what would I do? Drive on, of course, I told myself. The woods were rocky here. There were even several huge boulders. Just beyond a stretch of woods with a few pine trees among the new leaves, I came to a gravel drive. That must be the Hubbel drive.

I heard a dog yipping frantically. At something in a tree? I slowed, promising myself again I wouldn't stop. The yipping was high pitched, as if it came from a small dog. Small but frantic. Then I saw him, a fair distance in from the road, but with the leaves on the trees still about the size of a mouse's ear, I could see a long way into those woods. I saw a dachshund, long and thin with short legs and a sharp nose. Then, just beyond the dog and near a large rock, I saw what at first looked like a pile of brush and dead leaves. The dog ran toward me as I leaned out my car window. He looked just like Belle Dasher's dog. Same breed. I stopped to figure out what was going on. He jumped up on his hind legs and yelped, then looped back toward the pile, short legs fast as pistons. He was comic. I all but laughed. He was demanding that I come with him in dachshund sign language. But as I stared at that pile off in the woods, my laughter died, and I felt a chill. That could be a person dressed in brown, lying on the ground. Lying there under the branches of a tree. Yes. Once the idea took hold, a human shape leaped out. Dead? Fear hit me in the solar plexus. I had to stay out of this. I couldn't stay out of this. I called 911 on the car phone. I also called Martin at the paper. I got Pat, and she said she'd try to reach him.

But, damn, I still had to go make sure whether Belle Dasher—I had this strong hunch now that it was Belle Dasher—was alive. I felt a pang of sadness. I hadn't even had a chance to ask what she'd been doing the last fifty-odd years. This very determined dachshund sure looked like the dog that she'd brought to my office. The same color, a reddish brown.

If Belle or whoever was alive, she might need a tourniquet to stop bleeding, or need CPR. I was the only one on the spot and might be for ten or fifteen minutes. *I'm sorry,* I said to Ted inside my head. I got out of the car and walked toward the small dog. He ran over to me in a fit of joy, licked my leg, and raced back toward—yes—it definitely was a person. I shivered. The dog was still asking for help, but his bark became less frantic. As I got close, he wagged his tail as if to say thank you.

But I may be too late, I thought. I fixed my eyes on Belle. Yes, it was Belle. She lay, pitched forward, head to one side, face away from the road, with a big egg already forming on top of her head, poking up the hair. I watched for the slightest movement, and, thank God, I saw it. She was breathing. Great surge of relief. I could see no sign of bleeding except what was oozing from the bash point, so I stayed back from the unconscious woman, not wanting to disturb any evidence.

Thank God, I thought, I did not find a dead body. I found a live person who could be helped.

The small dog dashed over and licked Belle's face. He felt he was her keeper, I realized with a start. I wouldn't have been surprised if he'd been a German shepherd. But I found myself again on the verge of laughing at so much nurturing from such a small dog.

What was Belle Dasher doing here in the woods that got her hit over the head? And who hit her? If Isaiah Hubbel never came down off his mountain, it couldn't have been him, could it?

But if she was here, Isaiah *I Say* Hubbel would be the one to be angry at her, wouldn't he? So would Jake *Make Trouble* Hubbel.

I searched the woods with my eyes. No other human beings or human leavings in sight. The land tilted upwards gradually, then sharply, thick with tree trunks and branches, faintly colored by beginning leaves. You couldn't see Isaiah Hubbel's house from here.

The dog ran over to me again and whined. He wanted me to do something. I reached down and patted him, and he wagged his tail, then ran back over to Belle. "I mustn't touch her or move her till the ambulance and the sheriff come," I told the dachshund. I've always found that talking to dogs in a reasonable tone of voice calms them down. They get the impression you know what you're doing, even if they don't know what that is.

Finally I heard a siren, and everybody arrived at once, the medics, the sheriff's deputy, then the sheriff, then Martin.

"I was passing by, and the dog alerted me," I explained to the sheriff. The dog was now confused and upset and growling.

"Get that damn dog out of the way," said one of the medics.

"Let me take him," I said quickly. I picked him up and tucked him under my arm. Handy size of small warm dog but full of nervous shivers. He whimpered and struggled to get down. "We have to stay out of the way," I told him, "so they can help Belle." I adjusted him to a more comfortable position, and he calmed down.

Meanwhile, as soon as Belle was placed on a stretcher, she opened her eyes. "Good God," she said, "did I cause this?" She tried to sit up.

"Lie still," the medic said. "You may have a concussion."

"From running into a tree branch?" she asked in an incredulous voice. She wasn't as incredulous as I was. I didn't believe she could get an egg that big from running into a tree. I believed she was lying.

"Where's Bailey?" she asked. Then she spotted me.

"He alerted me that you were here," I said. "I just happened to be driving by."

"In a pig's eye," Belle said. She didn't believe me any more than I believed her.

"I'll keep Bailey till they let you loose," I said. "Don't worry about him." That dog deserved a reward, not to be put in a cage somewhere. As the stretcher passed by, I took him over to give his mistress a lick goodbye.

"Stay out of the way, lady," one stretcher-bearer growled.

"Thank you," Belle said with a smile. She always had a warm smile.

"I need you over here to give me a statement," a deputy called. I went right over with Exhibit A: the dog who'd sounded the alarm.

"Have you ever seen this woman before?" he asked. I told him about her visit to my office and that I'd known her when we were kids.

"And you say you were just driving by?" he asked suspiciously.

"Well, of course I wanted to see what the place she described looked like," I explained. "Just idle curiosity. I do not want to get mixed up in whatever is happening here. If there is a story, Martin will handle it. I don't do crime," I said firmly. "I do features about community events. Like the fundraising fair at the high school." My tone of voice said, I'm just a harmless old lady, the kind who knits afghans for church fairs.

CHAPTER
5

FRIDAY, LATER

When I finally got to the paper, Martin came over to my desk, sat in the visitor's chair, and asked me even more questions than the sheriff's deputy had. My editor is not good-looking, but he has lively quizzical eyes. He always wears a conservative tan corduroy jacket with patches on the elbows, but he collects wild shirts. Today's shirt had baseballs and baseball hats and baseball bats all over it. At least Belle Dasher probably wasn't hit with anything as big as a baseball bat. That could have been fatal. "How did you happen to be near Hubbel Mountain?" Martin asked.

I told him about Jake *Make Trouble* Hubbel, with his gun rack and threats, and how Jake said that Isaiah *Trouble* Hubbel up on the hill was his brother and a veteran who should be treated well. I said I was curious. Well, that's me. I explained how the dog actually summoned me to help

Belle and why I took her dog. Bailey, meanwhile, fell asleep in my lap, draped as if he had no bones at all. Good. That way he wouldn't make more than a tentative yap at anybody who came in to place an ad or a birth announcement. I hoped.

"So what do you think happened to Belle Dasher?" Martin asked.

"Somebody hit Belle over the head, and she has some reason to hide that fact," I said. "Very strange. Jake Hubbel says she's an activist with enemies, but you wouldn't knock someone out because they believed in a cause, would you? Or bang up someone who believed that you shouldn't be allowed to have a dump on your property or a gun in your closet, or whatever?"

"Anything is possible," Martin said, slanting his head to one side the way he does when he's mulling something over. "Belle has been arrested for getting violent herself. I'll look into this case. As you know, Jake Hubbel is a county commissioner," he added. "He's not dumb. He married the sheriff's niece and owns the Ford dealership. He gives money to popular causes. I don't think he'd do anything to get himself in trouble. But Belle is unpredictable."

I did not offer to help or even ask questions. Martin assigned me a human-interest story about people who were angry that the high school's soda pop machines might be removed. Seems the machines were too close to the cafeteria to comply with state and federal guidelines for the lunch program.

"This county can get het up at the drop of a hat." Martin sighed. "They hate it that the state folks and the feds won't send money if it's too easy for the kids to get sugar drinks before lunch."

As my mother used to say: "Don't spoil your lunch."

I called the principal.

"Listen," he said, "the money from those machines helps with field trips and prizes and all that. It wouldn't be worth having the machines if they had to be locked up till lunch is over." He sounded mad.

The chairman of the Boosters Club called the proposed removal "another incidence of the feds sticking their nose into stuff that is none of their business. We should tell them to go to hell."

If folks got this hot over soda pop, maybe they would hit a woman over the head for sticking her nose in their affairs. *Stop it*! I told myself. That was not my business.

"The fools want to get us kicked out of the lunch subsidy program," a school-board member fumed. This was not a county of nice Nellies. People raised angry voices. But Bailey slept through every phone call, zonked out after whatever had happened this morning. I could write on the computer fine with the dog in my lap.

But the dog didn't stay quiet. Not when a pretty girl with wild curly hair appeared at my desk with a news release in hand. She was a knockout in an offbeat way with a slightly snubbed nose and blue eyes too large for a perfectly regular face. She was someone you noticed, especially since she wore silver earrings in the shape of snakes—complete with fangs—a bright orange T-shirt, and blue jeans that fit like wallpaper. She was put together so that the jeans looked good. The news release was about a production of *Charley's Aunt* by the Monroe Players. Bailey reared up in my lap and let out joyous yips.

So the rescue dachshund knew her well. She must be a friend of Belle's. But Belle was sixty-five, and this girl was maybe twenty-two. So how did she fit into Belle Dasher's drama?

"Hello," I said, "I'm Peaches Dann." I figured that would inspire her to name herself, but she merely nodded and got down on her knees and patted the dog, who leaped into her arms. Then tears ran down her face, which he busily tried to lick away. What on earth?

Well, this was Friday. My deadline was not for nearly a week. "Is something wrong?" I asked.

She began to sob. "If you're nice to me," she said, "I won't be able to help crying." She hugged Bailey with one arm and pressed the back of her other hand hard against her mouth.

"Well, sit down in my chair and have a good cry," I said. "On Fridays I double as a psychiatrist, and any friend of Bailey's is a friend of mine." At this point I figured I'd just let things unfold.

She sat down in the straight chair across from my desk, the dog now in her lap, and took me up on the good cry. "It's not news," she sobbed. "It's just that today my life is ruined."

For some reason people feel free to tell me things like that. Maybe because I'm really interested. What does it mean to be a human being? Facing life's ups and downs? That's the question I need to answer for some strange reason. That's the question that has lured me into solving murders. What makes a person kill? Murder is the dramatic down. And how do people who've been close to murder get past that and find some good creative way to go on? I've seen some people do that, too.

But I could listen to troubles without trying to solve them, couldn't I? There was no law against that. I said, "If it would help you to talk about whatever happened, I'm here to listen. If it's not news, I won't repeat it."

I guess she was ready to explode, so she talked. The story came pouring out. Bailey sat up and gave her a quick lick from time to time for moral support. Amazing how dogs seem to know what people need.

"George is a good, kind person," she said. "I love him and I know he loves me."

George who? This hardly seemed related to the dog, and it didn't sound sad. But tears kept falling down her face. "George's mother has this thing about cancer," she said. "About how it's her fault George's father died of cancer, and Isaiah Hubbel's fault for letting DDT leach down the mountain. She thinks DDT caused her cancer, too. She kind of goes off the deep end. And she hates all the Hubbels. But we were friends at first when she knew me by my married name. We were good friends! Now she hates me, just because I'm a Hubbel."

Oh! "She" must be Belle. She was "George's mother?" Did Belle have a son she hadn't even mentioned? He should be keeping the dog! And what did this poor girl mean by "married name" if George was her boyfriend? My head whirled.

"I would be less confused if I knew your name," I said.

She looked up, startled. "Oh. I forgot. I'm Maureen Hubbel. I went back to my family name after my divorce. Jake Hubbel is my uncle. You've met him, I bet."

Hubbel! Hubbels were coming up around here as thick as new leaves in April. And Belle sure didn't like Hubbels.

I was still confused. Had this Maureen in my chair not heard about Belle's "accident"? Too soon, perhaps.

I figured I better just listen and see what came clear.

"You said you were married!" I blurted.

"Oh, that," she said. "Just for a year. It didn't work out. But I liked his name. It went so well with mine: Maureen O'Conner. And he didn't mind if I kept it. So I did for a while. I lived over in Asheville. Belle was selling a house, and our firm handled it. It was about a month before Belle found out my real name. We were not friends anymore after that."

I handed Maureen a tissue, and she blew her nose.

"My family doesn't want George and me to get married, either, and I guess it's hopeless."

Poor Maureen Hubbel, in love with the son of a woman who hated Hubbels. So maybe we had Romeo and Juliet here, and Romeo was welshing out.

"Now let me get this straight," I said. "Jake Hubbel is your uncle, and your father is—"

"Herbert Hubbel," she said. "He's the one who runs the nursery. I bet you've bought his plants. I have an uncle Jake and an uncle Brad, and my father's sister is Mabel Wallen, who teaches third grade in the elementary school. Last year she was Teacher of the Year."

They were prolific, these Hubbels. And they'd done well. Yes. I'd bought some impatiens from Maureen's father, a quiet, intense man with lovely plants, and I'd meant to get my next car from Jake.

"Talking to someone does make me feel better. Thank you," Maureen said, blowing her nose again.

I said she was most welcome. "So Isaiah Hubbel is your uncle," I said. "What is he like? I understand he never comes down off his mountain."

Two frown lines rumpled her smooth brow. "In a way, he's a love," she said slowly. "He's so pleased when anyone comes to visit. I've been staying with him a lot since his wife is—" She hesitated, and then said, "Away." She added, "We've all been taking turns." She kept frowning. "But he kind of makes me nervous. He's jumpier than he was."

I waited for the reason. She was in no hurry. Perhaps she felt guilty telling a stranger. "Uncle Isaiah has guns all over the house," she said, her brow still creased. "Well, I was raised with guns and can shoot pretty good myself. But he keeps them loaded, and there's one in every room, even in the bathroom, taped in the top of the toilet tank. That one's a handgun. He's afraid of break-ins. I hope no kid is ever let loose in that house." She stroked Bailey briskly as if that might neutralize the guns. "That silly story about how he killed his wife could come from people hearing about all those guns. I guess you've heard that story?"

"I may not have heard it right," I said.

"There's no 'right,'" she said. "My aunt Joan is just off somewhere, and people say he killed her because nobody knows where she is. But Aunt Joan has a mind of her own. She might act contrary." Her voice trailed off, a little doubtful. "Since she left, Uncle Isaiah's kind of"—she groped for the right word— "withdrawn. Which upsets my whole family. And then, on top of that, Belle Dasher is out spreading rumors." Maureen blew her nose hard, like a trumpet of anger.

Then she crumpled. "But I still want to marry George. This is not his fault. But he—" She wept some more. "He can't take his mother and my family all being so—Why can't they . . . ?

"All my uncles, even my father—I don't want to be like them! It's them against the world. If somebody hurts one, we all have to hate that person and that person's kin. I don't want to be like that! Even Belle is like that!"

She looked down at the current issue of the paper on my desk. "You're a reporter!" she said in a shocked tone. "How could I forget? I shouldn't tell you all this! I just got—carried away."

"People do," I said. "I won't repeat what you've said except in some very unusual situation. Such as, if it became part of a murder investigation."

She gasped. "Nobody's been murdered!"

"Did you know Belle Dasher got hit over the head this morning?" I asked. "Who do you think might have done that?"

Maureen flinched. "Is she all right?"

I explained she was in the hospital, and I repeated, "Who might have done that?"

Her face closed. "I have no idea." Her eyes went dull with what I guessed was despair.

She got up quickly and put Bailey down, giving him a goodbye pat.

She hurried out, leaving no trace behind except tear-sodden tissues in my wastebasket. Bailey went back to sleep in my lap. Being young can be hard. I wished it wasn't so.

I finished the soda pop tempest-in-a-teapot story and wrote a piece about the United Methodist Women's flea market and hot dog lunch, not to mention three birth announcements and a golden wedding anniversary. All the while I wondered about Joan, who disappeared. Maureen wanted to think that was all, that Joan would be back. I wondered about Belle Dasher, who was sure that Joan was murdered. I wondered if there was any way the Good News Man was connected with all that. I did not allow myself to call Suzie and hear the latest rumors.

At ten of five, Ted called. " A fan has sent you a bumper sticker," he said. "I thought you'd like to know. She loved *How to Survive Without a Memory,* especially the part about how laughing improves your memory. The sticker says 'Mind out to lunch, back in ten minutes.' Well, that should scare the other drivers!

"Don't forget, we're going over to have supper with Pop," he reminded me. "It's closer if you go straight from work."

Yes, it was, but what was I going to do with the dog?

"Would you bring a length of clothesline or cord of some kind?" I asked. "I have temporarily acquired a dog without a leash." Then I had to admit about finding Belle Dasher. "I can see," I said, "that I don't even dare drive by a neighborhood where a murder might have taken place. I won't do that again. But I can't help being curious about poor Belle."

"No," Ted said, somewhat dryly, "you can't. And I get the impression you are under the thumb, or paw, or whatever, of a dog that's all mixed up in the plot."

CHAPTER
6

LATER THAT AFTERNOON

I was about to lock the office door and leave, when one last visitor arrived. The nice young deputy with the curly red hair and the face of a pixie came in with a story on a firehouse fundraising supper. He was a volunteer fireman in his spare time—he'd brought me news before. Most of our firemen were volunteers, God bless them.

"I saw you this morning," he said, bouncing on his feet, "and it did scare me."

He looked so friendly with a big grin that I couldn't imagine what he meant.

"I was relieved," he said, "that it was just a case of hit-over-the-head, because I hear you're murder prone." He sat down in my chair as if he was going to stay awhile.

I opened my mouth and then shut it. What could I say?

"I mean, you just naturally turn up at murders and even

figure out who did 'em. That's what my friend Tom Estes over in the Buncombe County Sheriff's Department tells me. So I was glad Belle Dasher wasn't dead."

"So was I," I told him. "But, listen, some of the things that happened to me were coincidence and some were because of who I know."

He shook his head no. "Look, Miz Dann," he said, "I've got a cousin, Jane Jeetem, over in Skunk Run Cove, who's accident prone. That woman will fall down and break a leg, or sprain an ankle, or even knock a tooth out at the drop of a hat. From what I know about you, you're murder prone."

I wanted to say, Thanks a lot! I refrained.

"But I guess it's in a good way, because you're likely to figure the thing out."

I must have looked skeptical, because he went on explaining. "Now, how many people do you know who come upon bodies? Even once. My granny says we all have powers that we don't understand. Like my cousin Howie, who can answer the phone with your name before you speak, and Miz Justice over in Chestnut, who can put her hand on a woman's belly and tell her if the baby's a boy or a girl. Cheaper than the hospital. She does it free.

"And you wrote a book, right? They have it in the library. My aunt Flo is the librarian. You wrote that book because you can't remember things. Now, if you can't remember, you have to develop other powers, right? The way blind folks are good at music."

"You have to develop intuition," I said, "and you have to be inventive. You have to use strategy to get around what you don't remember. That helps you figure things out. But that's not being murder prone!"

"But sometimes we have powers given to us," he said.

"Not what we develop, but just what comes! That's what my granny says. Her mother had the Sight."

I could see by the way he kept smiling that this whole idea pleased him a lot. So I didn't argue. I took his news item and thanked him.

CHAPTER
7

FRIDAY EVENING

Ted's car was already in the driveway when I arrived at Pop's place on Town Mountain Road and parked under an apple tree that was lacy-white with half-open blossoms. The late afternoon cool made me glad I had a sweater. The white Cadillac that belongs to Pop and his ever-cheerful wife, Azalea, stood in the driveway, too. Also, a new blue Volkswagen Bug. The second blue Bug I'd seen today.

Ted met me at Pop's door with a piece of thin rope in hand. He looked at Bailey clutched under my arm, wagging his tail in greeting. Ted laughed and kissed me on the tip of the nose. He said, "What will you turn up with next?" We fixed a makeshift slip-knot leash for Bailey. "I hope he's well behaved," Ted whispered. So did I.

Inside, I found Pop at the round table near the bookcase where he likes to hold forth, smiling broadly like the frog that swallowed the fly. Except for that grin, which I took to be an ominous sign, Pop does not look a bit like a frog. More like an ancient but noble eagle. Yes, he gives himself airs. But noble eagles do not have shocking-pink Post-it® notes plastered to the middle of their chests. Pop did. Too far away for me to read. "If that's a dog," he said, "I hope you'll keep it quiet. What we enjoy here is good conversation."

Azalea, on his right, smiled benignly. She's got smile lines all over that heart-shaped face, so you look at her and it's catching. She wore a T-shirt that said Think Positive. Behind her, the view of blue-green mountains through sliding glass doors looked like endless peace. The room inside was warm with Persian rugs and furniture that said Relax.

But the thin, earnest man with glasses who jumped up from Pop's left and shook our hands was plainly uptight.

"This is Professor Albert Bright," Pop said, waving his hand grandly. "He is writing a book on memory. I gave him a copy of your book on how to remember."

I must have blushed. "I'm no scientist," I told the professor, "just a collector of what people do that works."

And I thought: Albert Bright. Maybe almost as *bright* as *Albert* Einstein. And Albert almost rhymes with *Halibut*, and he did look a little like a fish, with almost no chin and a small mouth and large eyes behind glasses with tortoiseshell frames. And, come to think of it, Einstein looked the least little bit like a wise fish, didn't he? All that would help me remember *Albert Bright.*

Why was Albert Bright so tense, as if something was going to happen that was more important than our small talk? His hands fidgeted. He fingered a red macramé chain attached to his eyeglasses. Odd. Someone he loved must have been into crafts. He fidgeted, but his voice stayed calm.

"My book will be quite academic," he said, "but as I read yours, I was fascinated by how you've collected what might be called folk memory aids, and how they fit with the new technical knowledge. I imagine you are aware that more has been learned about how memory works in the last ten or fifteen years than in all of history before that. Also we have more electronic memory aids," he said. "That is one of my areas of specialization."

Plainly, Pop had invited the professor to improve my mind. But then why was Pop wearing that ridiculous pink note? I knew he'd tell me. I waited. "Actually," I said to Albert Bright, "I look forward to your book. I like to learn the technical stuff."

Meanwhile I headed for an empty chair next to the professor, whose hands still fidgeted in his lap. Fortunately the dog was behaving well, trotting along at my side. Maybe he was awed by all the people. I explained that an emergency had come up for a friend of mine and I had to keep the dog. I sat down, and Bailey jumped up on my lap. Either sleeping on me was his favorite form of recreation, or he was still zonked out from his adventure with Belle. Ted sat next to Azalea.

"Have you noticed anything unusual about me?" Pop demanded. He knew that I had if I wasn't blind.

"You have a note on your chest," I said. "What does it say? 'Return to this address if found lost'?"

"It's for you," he said testily.

So I put the dog under my arm, got up, and went over to read Pop's chest. The shocking-pink note said, "Tell Peaches Cousin Chester's memory trick." Oh, for heaven's sake. Why couldn't Pop just do it? And why plaster himself with a note? Pop thinks you should never admit you have a bad memory. He's told me so a hundred times.

The dog and I sat back down. "Yes?" I said. "I'm ready."

"This is it!" he said triumphantly. "You know, Chester is a poet. Plays the guitar and calls himself the Bard of Monroe County. He can be pretty vague. When he absolutely has to tell his wife something, he doesn't put it on a stick-em thing on the wall that he might forget to look at. He puts it in the middle of his chest, so the minute she sees him she knows."

"Hey," I said, "that's a new one. Thank you."

"Actually, I was in Monroe County today," the professor said, and he stopped fidgeting. Whatever he was so impatient to get to, this must be it. "I understand you work on the paper over there."

I was startled. "You weren't on Mountain View Road, were you?" That's where I'd seen a car like his, a blue Volkswagen Bug. I blurted out the question without thinking. One mention that I found someone there who'd been hit over the head, and Pop would be on my case. Never mind— he'd be on it soon anyway. He must have had the phone off the hook or he'd know already.

"Well, yes, I was there," Professor Bright said. "If you work for the paper, I bet you know what the sirens and the ambulance and the deputy's car were all about." His eyes burned with curiosity behind his glasses. "We heard somebody was hurt in the woods."

Pop smiled even more broadly. "And killed?" he asked.

"It was a freak accident," I said quickly. "The woman claimed she had been running in the woods and bumped into a tree branch and knocked herself out."

"Who was she running *from*?" Pop demanded.

That's what I should have asked her. But I'd been so sure she made the whole story up. Drat!

"I believe she was exercising," I said to calm Pop down.

"Exercise is wonderful for people our age," Azalea said. "I do water-aerobics three times a week and yoga every day."

Our age, ha! Azalea must be seventy-five—a lot older than me. But spry. She left us and came back with a bottle of white wine and glasses, and a dish of nuts. Ted got up and poured the wine.

"What were you doing on Mountain View Road when all the cars with sirens arrived?" I asked the professor.

He took a large sip of wine, and shifted in his seat. "I have a relative who lives near there."

"And who is that?" Pop demanded. "Did your relative know the woman who got whacked?"

"My sister Joan lived at the top of the mountain," Professor Bright said, as if he didn't like to admit it.

I noticed he used the past tense. Was that the Joan that Belle thought was murdered? "Isaiah Hubbel's wife?" I blurted. "I heard she'd disappeared."

He spilled his wine and quickly mopped it up with his handkerchief. He was back to nervous. "I haven't seen her for several weeks," he said. "I can't reach her and I haven't been able to track her down. So I was worried."

"So maybe there's been foul play?" Pop suggested eagerly. He twirled his wineglass.

"People just need some time to themselves," Azalea said. "Some retreat from the busy world. I hope you found out she was fine."

The professor seemed to shrivel. "She went to Georgia and she hasn't written. At least that's where she said she headed." He frowned, and his hands fiddled with his eyeglass chain until I expected it to break. "She went off to be by herself to think. That's what she told her husband. But she didn't say to think about what. And she never called me or anyone else in the family, not once after she left town.

"I have been rather busy," he said with a sheepish shrug, "so I didn't worry right away. But then I couldn't reach her. I was on my way to see Isaiah, to find out anything he'd heard."

If half the county was saying his sister had been murdered, as Belle and Suzie believed, he sure was up in an ivory tower not to go confront Isaiah until now.

"And what had he heard?" Pop demanded. He looked as if he might jump right up out of his wheelchair with excitement. Oh, he was loving this!

"I never got there," the professor said. "I stopped to see a friend nearby who knew Joan, and asked him if she'd been acting strangely before she left. He said he hadn't noticed. By the time I came out, there were all those flashing blue lights." He took another sip of wine.

"Did they block the road up the hill?" I asked.

"I didn't want to get mixed up in whatever was happening," he said, squirming. "I don't like to admit it, but I have asthma, and stress can bring on an attack."

I glanced at Ted. Speaking of attacks . . . He looked O.K. This conversation didn't seem to bother him.

Was this Albert *Halibut* Bright scared of the law? I wondered. If so, why?

"How did you happen to come to meet us?" Ted asked him.

He shrugged his shoulders. "I had a doctor's appointment yesterday," he said. "I met your father"—he nodded at me—

"in the doctor's office, and we got to talking. He mentioned your book, and I mentioned mine, and he invited me to dinner to meet you."

"First he couldn't come," Pop said. "Then he called today and asked if it was too late to say yes."

"A happy coincidence," Azalea said.

This was too much of a coincidence. "Did Pop also mention that I work for the paper in Monroe County?" I asked the professor.

He flushed slightly. "I admit I did hope you'd have some information about what happened today."

"I want to hear all about the woman who disappeared!" Pop cried. "How lucky that you could join us tonight."

How odd that Professor Albert Bright hadn't just stopped and asked the deputies what was going on. How odd that he hadn't gone on to visit his brother-in-law Isaiah Hubbel on his mini-mountain. Was there something about his sister that stopped him when he saw flashing blue lights near her house?

I was dying to know. I glanced at Ted. He winked at me. He meant just listening probably couldn't hurt me.

"What is your sister like?" Ted asked the professor.

"Determined," he said. "Ambitious. And loyal. Her husband won't leave that mountain. He hasn't been quite right for years, but she sticks by him no matter what. My sister has a hard row to hoe." Now he was using the present tense. "Oh, she has enemies. She's sharp when she closes a deal. She beat out several other real estate agents when she sold the old glove factory for a mail-order-catalog headquarters. But she looks after family. She always stays in touch."

"So where could she be now?" Pop asked. "And did she

know the woman who got hit in the head?" Hey, Pop was sharp today.

"Belle Dasher," I said. Belle deserved the dignity of a name.

The dog sat up in my lap and looked around. I said, "This is her dog." Bailey lay back down as if he'd only wanted to be introduced.

"So Belle's a friend of yours?" The professor gave me a suspicious glance.

"I knew her back when we were kids," I said. "I met her again this week. Now I guess you'd say I'm a friend of the dog's." I patted Bailey's velvet head. He let out a sigh. "Nobody else was there to take him when they took her off to the hospital, and he seemed such a gallant little dog."

Pop pointed toward me. "Peaches is a sucker for animals."

"So you were there. What did you see?" Bright asked. His breath quickened.

I told him briefly and asked how well his sister knew Belle.

"Everybody knows Belle," Bright said, with a shrug, "and she lived near my sister. But Belle became very strange, well, really dangerous, after her husband died."

Pop grinned broadly and leaned toward the professor. "What did she do?"

Albert Bright's eyes seemed to grow in size behind his glasses. "That woman accused a man of killing kids! She threw a brick through his shop window." The professor flushed red. He clenched his fists on the table in front of him. I could see this made him angry, even now.

Oh, brother, I might be looking after the dog of a real nut. I didn't want that to be true. Belle was a helper, not a hurter, at least when I was a kid. I saw her in my mind's eye. She looked so grown-up to me then. She had braids around her head and she was pleasantly plump. Sad stories made her cry. Funny how when something begins to come back to you, more and more comes. I saw her leaning over the edge of the cliff, with me desperately holding on to her ankles. She had on brown loafers. And we survived.

"This shop man didn't kill kids?" Pop asked in a disappointed tone.

"He was selling cigarettes to kids over the legal age, but selling them more than they could smoke. Those kids were selling cigarettes to younger kids. Belle demanded he be made to stop selling tobacco. She said he was addicting young kids, and some of them would eventually die of lung cancer or emphysema. That woman exaggerates." Mr. Professor glowered.

"That tobacco shop was run by a poor sick man who needed that business," Bright went on. "Nobody would stop him from selling cigarettes, so she threw a brick through his window."

"And this Belle woman went to jail?" Pop asked.

"She was put on probation," Bright said. "I think she deserved more than that!"

I wanted to confront him and defend my long-ago friend. But I needed to know the details. This story would be in the newspaper's back file. I could look it up.

Right at that moment, Sandy, Pop's sitter-on-duty, motioned to Azalea, who went out to the kitchen. There's always a sitter on hand because Pop is so physically helpless. Azalea came right back to say that dinner was served. "The dog can eat in the kitchen," she announced. Sandy came and carried off Bailey, who wagged his tail when he heard the word "eat."

We all filed into the dining room, Ted pushing Pop in his wheelchair. A large platter of sliced tenderloin with an herb crust, a platter of marinated thin asparagus, and a bowl of assorted roasted potatoes were set out on the table. Also hot rolls. Azalea had outdone herself. My mouth watered. "Laurey's Catering," Azalea whispered to me. "Why cook when you don't have to? And save room for a wonderful meringue dessert."

We all helped ourselves, and Ted poured more white wine into our glasses.

I was savoring the tenderloin and asparagus when the professor turned to me, quite pleasant now, and asked if I truly had trouble remembering what I needed to know. I figured he wanted to change the subject. I still didn't trust the man.

But I told him how I have to work to get around my Swiss-cheese memory, and he handed me a brochure. On the cover was a picture of a hand holding a small gray object with what looked like a minicomputer screen. "Get one of these," he said, now bubbling with enthusiasm, "and you'll remember everything."

I put the folder on the table in front of me and continued to enjoy my dinner. Perhaps I looked doubtful. When something sounds too good to be true, it usually is.

"You are not making the most of technology, Peaches," Pop chimed in. "It's hardly necessary to have a brain anymore. You can buy one. In fact, that thing"— he pointed at the folder— "is a portable brain. Professor Bright told us all about it. It's called a Palm Pilot. It will keep track of everything from addresses and phone numbers to notes you want to write to yourself to meetings you have to attend."

I could see how pleased he was at knowing more about this portable brain than I did. I buttered a dill roll, and considered. "Thank you," I told Bright. "I'll look into it."

"It will even keep track of how to get to places you might have to go," Pop added. "It could save your life!"

"It rings bells so you won't be late," Azalea told me, fork in midair.

Once I had a portable organizer, but I admit it couldn't do all that. It was heavy, and I lost it.

"Whatever is in the Palm Pilot can be moved to your computer, and what you've put in your computer can be moved onto the Pilot," the professor said, still pleased with himself and his device.

So, O.K., the three of them had been talking about how to replace my brain before I came. I was both annoyed and touched.

"Make Ted buy you one," Pop said. He leaned over and took the brochure away from me and handed it to Ted. "She'll forget to get one," he said. "She'll get into trouble. She has a talent for that!"

I was considerably more annoyed than touched. I concentrated on the asparagus, one of my favorite foods.

Meanwhile, Azalea tactfully changed the subject and reminded us that her birthday party in Tennessee was on Sunday, and Ted and I had promised to come.

Azalea's granddaughter Alice and her husband were living in the 1795 house that Azalea and Pop had renovated, while Azalea and Pop were up here in Pop's house in the mountains.

Azalea winked at me. "Alice's birthday is next week, so this will really be a double celebration."

I said that Ted and I would get there just in time for the

party Sunday, since he had an important meeting at the college on Saturday. Also I had to be in my office Saturday morning. Ted would remind me of the party, God bless him. A loving buddy is a brain extension.

The professor, meanwhile, had turned off his good cheer. His eyes said, You folks don't get it. His mouth said, "When someone disappears, you don't know *what* will happen next."

"We'll be right near your office Saturday, picking up a present for Alice," Azalea told me, ignoring his gloom, "and you can join us and go right on to Tennessee."

I said I'd talk to Ted and see.

I wanted to look in the newspaper's back files on Saturday and read all about my friend Belle Dasher's past. That way, I could satisfy my curiosity and not get into any kind of trouble at all. That's what I told myself.

CHAPTER
8

Suzie barged in and caught me looking in the newspaper back file. I'd stopped by the office after taking some big-day pictures of the high school fair, which was going great guns. Maybe I'd drop by later and take a few more. Now I was looking at the story about Belle and the brick.

The back file is actually a collection of huge bound volumes with black covers, and there's a table in the back room to lay one out so you can see newspapers full size. I'd found a story about Belle just as the professor said I would. The story was from May the year before, and it included a picture of a smashed storefront, with jagged shards of glass still in place.

I was reading that story as Belle's dog, Bailey, lay nearby and watched me. Belle was due to come by in about half an hour and collect him—Belle, who'd maybe gone round the bend. She'd called the night before and said she was out of the hospital and feeling much better but in need of her dog. He lay calmly on the floor, head on front paws, eyes following my every move. He seemed to sense that something important was due to happen. He wagged his tail when Suzie arrived, all dressed in red, her usual color. This was informal red, a sweatsuit, just right for Suzie, who has aged gracefully with a well-tended face. I remember that when I met her I decided she had a Ronald Reagan smile. For some reason it didn't make her look less feminine.

She gave me that contagious smile and a squeeze, then read the headline on the Belle Dasher story out loud. " 'Local woman arrested for vandalism.'

"It caused a furor," she said. "Read on."

Of course I did. I read how Mrs. Ernest Dasher had been arrested for throwing a brick through the window of the Great Smokes Shop on Main Street. How she claimed she'd done it because she couldn't get the place closed down. She said she wanted to call attention to the fact that the owner, Bradley Hubbel—what, Hubbel again?—had been selling tobacco and cigarettes to older teens who were reselling them to kids below the legal age. The sheriff was quoted as saying he hadn't been able to take any action, since there was no proof that Hubbel sold cigarettes directly to kids under twenty-one.

Boy, I could imagine how that would inflame my volatile friend Belle! "Belle liked to protect small creatures," I said to Suzie, who stood there with a quizzical look, waiting for my reaction. "That would include kids. But I can't see her throwing a brick. She must have really changed."

The story quoted Belle: "You want little kids to get addicted to tobacco before they are old enough to understand it could kill them? Some of them who can't stop will die of lung cancer or emphysema some day, and nobody cares."

"So Belle threw a brick through the smoke shop window," I said to Suzie. "I'm sorry, because I like her. And I don't think kids should smoke. But if every person takes the law into his own hands, a lot of us will wind up dead."

Suzie raised an eyebrow. "Don't be judgmental," she said firmly. She pointed at the picture of the smashed window. "Belle's Ernie died of lung cancer a month before she threw that brick. She was crazy about him. Ernie started to smoke when he was ten years old. She told me all about it. When he died, she took to drinking for a while. She was drunk when this happened."

Judgmental, was I? "Listen," I said, "you certainly left the brick out of the story you told me. And a lot more. You never told me about her son. And are there other kids? Some reporter you are! And the son dates a Hubbel girl. I can't believe you kept that fact a secret. Why, that's downright juicy. And I gather you are Belle's friend," I said. I don't know why it annoyed me so that Suzie, who I thought told all, was keeping her mouth shut—that, and defending people who threw bricks.

"Actually," she said, looking away from me, "there's more to the story than that. The Hubbels have had a bad time, too. Isaiah and Jake and Herbert's brother, the one named Bradley, has mental problems." She said "mental problems" in a hushed tone, as if they were severe.

Bradley? Oh. The one with the tobacco store.

"Isaiah has troubles because he was in a war," she said, still looking away, and patting her blondish hair into place. "They wouldn't send Brad off to war. He's off his head half the time." Now she looked me in the eye again. "Brad's all right if he takes his medication. But when he doesn't . . . He thought a street lamp on Main Street was a bugging device put there by men from Mars, so he shot it out. I'm afraid he may hurt someone."

"He has a gun?" I was shocked.

"They took it away," Suzie said, "but it's mighty easy to get hold of a gun in this county if you don't mind stealing, and he doesn't always know if he's stealing. His brothers have guns handy. We enjoy our guns," she said, and pointed to an ad for a gun show in Asheville, right on the same page with the story about Belle.

"Anyway, when he took his medication he could run a little shop. It gave him something to do. Kind of an anchor to reality. That and his computer. He's a whiz about that sort of thing. His brother Jake owns a building on Main Street and let him have the space for the shop."

"Which led to disaster!" I said.

Suzie gave me her you-don't-understand-but-I-love-you-anyway smile. "In a small friendly town like this," she said sweetly, "we can make allowances for people who are not quite right, as long as they don't hurt anybody. So people bought tobacco from him and he felt he had a normal life."

"Except for shooting out street lamps," I said.

"Oh, that was later," she said with a shrug. "He got worse because he did have to close the shop. All that bad publicity about Belle and the brick and killing kids embarrassed Jake so bad that he took back the space for the shop. Brad lost his anchor."

I shut the newspaper volume and put it away on its shelf. Those books are heavy!

"And suppose," I asked, "no matter how much we wish

Belle's husband had lived, we now suspect that our friend is about to do something else wild and extreme? What now?"

"I don't know what I might do!" Belle announced. She walked through the door, in black shirt and pants, like the prophet of doom. Even her boots were black. Bailey let out a string of yelps, flew through the air, landed on a chair, and then jumped into her arms. He licked her face till she craned her neck back. She shifted the dog to cradle him in her arms, wildly wagging tail and all. That's the advantage of a small dog.

"I intend to find out what happened to the King of the Mountain's wife, no matter what it takes," Belle told me, eyes focused like a hawk's. So strange, those angry eyes, when she was one who also wanted to defend the helpless. "I don't care what it takes," she said. Bailey let out one final yelp of joy as if he didn't care either. Suzie put her bright red arm around Belle's black shoulders and said, "Be careful."

"For God's sake, be careful, Belle," I repeated, thinking of the brick, and also the Dobermans and the guns she'd said were on Isaiah Hubbel's hill. "Don't get yourself in trouble. And, please, don't get me mixed up in this," I said firmly, thinking of Ted. "I am not the crime reporter on this newspaper."

Belle sat down heavily in the green plastic garden chair that had somehow found its way into the newspaper morgue. I will admit she looked unhappy when she said, "You *are* mixed up in it, Peaches—and there may not be anything at all I can do about it."

Suzie stared at Belle raptly. Whatever she was about to reveal, even Suzie didn't know. I was pretty rapt myself.

At that moment Azalea appeared in the doorway. Oh,

great! Azalea, all dressed up in ruffles to go with Pop to Tennessee.

"We're just hearing about a problem," Suzie told her firmly, meaning shut up and listen.

Azalea said—what else?—"I'm sure we can find a way to get around it." She came over and stood by Suzie and me, smelling of lily of the valley perfume.

Belle said, "Isaiah Hubbel's brother Brad has been let out of prison." She gripped the arms of her green plastic chair. "Unfortunately."

"Prison!" I said, amazed, turning to Suzie. "The brother who wasn't quite right?" Yes. *Mad Brad.* "Why did he go to prison? Why didn't you tell me about that?"

"I was about to," Suzie said indignantly, "when Belle arrived. But it wasn't prison. It was the prison ward at the state mental hospital in Morganton."

"What does that have to do with me?" I demanded.

"A while ago he tried to shoot me," Belle said. "Fortunately he missed. He missed two times and just grazed my arm the third time." She glanced at her right arm. Her short-sleeved black shirt showed a scar on her forearm.

"He thought Belle was one of the Martians," Suzie explained, as if it was up to her to make excuses. "He said Belle had a ray gun and was going to shoot him. You see, they left him on the loose after they arrested him for shooting out the streetlight."

"This is an amazing county!" Azalea cried. "I'm sure you never lack for news."

Belle just sat there hugging her dog and let Suzie tell the story. "Jake swore he'd see that Brad took his medication. But Brad worked out a way to pretend to take it and fool

Jake. Brad said he was afraid to take the stuff, because then he couldn't see the Martians."

"With their ray guns," I said dryly. My head whirled with all this crazy stuff. My heart sank. "Again, what does this have to do with me?"

"You see," Belle said, "Brad heard about how I was hit over the head and you called for help. In this place, everybody hears everything, especially the Hubbels. And, damn Jake—he must have let Brad get away without his medication again. So Brad thinks the government has sent us both to spy on him."

To think all this could hinge on a pill.

"Who does he think hit you over the head?" I asked Belle.

"Someone on his side." She shrugged, as if to say, I know that doesn't make sense, but what do you expect?

"And they can't put him back in a mental hospital? They can't make him take his medication?"

"They can't even find him," Belle said. "He wrote a goodbye note with that stuff about us being government spies. He stole Jake Hubbel's gun right out of the gun rack in his truck. To protect himself, Jake says." Belle made a wry face. "At least Jake had the decency to call and tell me. Or maybe he wanted to scare me. Jake can be ruthless."

"What does Brad look like?" I asked Belle. "I need to recognize a man who might shoot me! What kind of car does this man drive?" I was appalled at this development. Ted would certainly be upset.

"If Brad has a car, it's borrowed or rented," Belle said. She leaned forward in her green plastic chair. "But you can recognize his face even from a distance. And the way he walks. He has a scar all the way down the right side of his face. One long seam of scar. He was in an automobile accident once. And he walks with a slight limp. In spite of that scar, he's kind of good-looking. He has a classic Roman nose and an oval face," Belle added. "Oh, and he looks young, although he's in his late forties.

"But his hair is snow-white," Belle said, "and he has green eyes." She reached in her pocketbook and pulled out a smallish head-and-shoulders picture in a silver frame. It matched the description—an eerie face with something odd about the eyes.

"You stole that picture!" Suzie cried. "Brad's sister Mabel keeps that picture of her brother with all the family pictures on the living-room table. She'll have a fit."

So Suzie was on visiting terms with the sister. She walked over in front of Belle and glared. "Belle, you're going too far." Bailey let out a low growl.

"I borrowed it," Belle explained meekly. "I drove by Mabel's house, but the car wasn't there. I knocked on the door, and nobody answered, and then I discovered the back door was unlocked. I had to show Peaches what this man looks like since he wants to shoot her."

"That was certainly thoughtful," Azalea said. She could put a happy spin on anything! But then, if she couldn't, would she ever have married Pop?

"I have met some wild characters,"—I tried to sound calm and normal—"but this takes the cake." That applied to Suzie and Belle, and even Azalea and the dog, as well as to *Mad Brad*. How was I going to get out of this mess?

"Listen," said Azalea, beaming, "this may be a blessing in disguise. For me, at least."

We all turned and stared at her. She went right on beaming.

"You two government spies can come to Tennessee with

Pop and me! Then you'll be safe, and I'll enjoy your company. We're going down to the house in Tennessee for the family birthday party—mine and Alice's. It'll be wonderful to have you at the party!" Azalea said to Belle. "Any friend of Peaches is a friend of ours. Oh, I'd be so pleased if you'd both come with me now!" She smiled at Belle. "You'll love our place."

Belle would certainly never go to Tennessee—that's what I told myself. Belle would stay home and make trouble, and maybe be killed by a madman. I felt bad about that. Under all that anger there must still be the caring girl I knew as a kid.

"Thank you. I'll come for a day or two," Belle told Azalea, as politely as if she were responding to a wedding invitation. "And I'll get you to return the picture," she said, reaching out and handing it to Suzie. For once, Suzie was speechless.

I was amazed, even aside from the bit about the picture. Why would Belle agree to go to Tennessee? Was she really scared of *Mad Brad*? This new Belle didn't seem to be scared of anything. What was she up to?

I'd told Azalea that I'd wait to come with Ted. But now I really wanted to go with Azalea and Pop, not just to be safe but to find out more about Belle. She claimed to have run into a tree when I was sure someone had hit her in the head. She believed in taking justice into her own hands. She had a son she'd never even mentioned, a son who loved the daughter of the man Belle thought had caused her husband's death, whose brother wanted to shoot us. This was beginning to sound like that old children's rhyme: *This is the house that Jack built*—with everybody and everything in the house causing cumulative disaster. And here everybody was also related somehow.

I suddenly thought of a TV show I'd seen, of all things, about the biggest plant in the world. About a mushroom that looked like an acre of mushrooms, but when you dug down, the roots were all attached. Suzie made Monroe County seem like that. It wouldn't have been a surprise if she'd announced that Belle was related to Isaiah Hubbel, or his missing wife, Joan, or both. Suzie kept springing surprises about Belle Dasher, dern her. What was it with Suzie?

I was mad at Belle for getting me mixed up in this. At the same time I was wildly curious. Why did she want to go to Tennessee?

"Ted would want you to come with us," Azalea said to me. "You know he wants you to be safe. And you and Belle can help me with last-minute party details. I'd be thankful for that."

"But I have to write the story about the fair at the high school," I said. "I promised Martin. I have a camera full of film and a lot of stuff on my tape recorder."

Suzie stepped in. "I can do your job for a week, beginning with the high school fair," she said. "Martin won't mind. I think you ought to get out of here until they find Brad Hubbel. He may not be a good shot but he might hit one of you while he aims at the other!" She thought that was funny. I did not. "And we need to protect poor Brad from himself," Suzie added. "He's a lovely boy when he takes his medication."

"But he's ready to kill you when he thinks you're a Martian or a government spy," Belle reminded her.

"I'm not packed," I wavered.

"Ted can meet us down there and bring you clean

clothes," Azalea told me triumphantly. "The car is parked outside."

"I can buy some extra underwear and a toothbrush in Tennessee," Belle said. "I'm ready to go." She stood up and hoisted the dog onto her shoulder, like a baby she was going to burp.

I plunked myself down in the green chair, still warm from Belle. I tried to think clearly. Yes, as a former reporter, Suzie could easily do my job. She'd probably enjoy it. And a little vacation would be fun, if not safe. I also loved Alice and her husband, who worked at the Hermitage.

I led Suzie and Belle back into my office. I called Ted and told him about *Mad Brad* and the goodbye note that mentioned me.

Maybe it was fate that everything just fell into place. Ted said that, hey, I should go on. He didn't want me shot. "Be very careful." He agreed to come join us and bring some things for me, and bring the birthday presents. All of this was happening so fast that it seemed unreal.

I went to the closet and got the dress I keep on hand in case I have to go out straight from work. Thank goodness I had that extra dress. I gave Suzie the camera with half a roll of film left and the tape recorder, and the clipboard with my stories in progress and my to-do list on it, in case we did stay on. Also Pop and Azalea's Tennessee address and telephone number and their car-phone number. I looked at the bulletin board to see if there was anything I should point out to Suzie. The YOU CAN BE PERFECT flyer was still there. I'd sure meant to throw it out. Oh, well, not now.

Suzie stared at it. " 'Be perfect,' " she read. And then she said, "How boring." Which might help explain why she didn't condemn Belle for throwing rocks through shop windows.

I gave Suzie a hug, said, "Thanks, and take care," and went out with Azalea and Belle to join Pop and the sitter in the car, still feeling part of a dream.

Azalea told Pop the news, and he cried out, "Welcome! Great to have two lovely ladies along. Why, this is exciting. A chase!"

"Not a chase," I said firmly from the back seat. "No one but Ted and Suzie know where we're going to be, and they won't tell."

CHAPTER
9

SATURDAY, 10:30 A.M.

Pop says his big, sedate Cadillac has a smooth ride that goes with his arthritis. Since it's so roomy, we didn't feel jammed in. I sat next to Belle on the back seat. Sandy, the quiet sitter, sat on her other side. Azalea drove.

"Maybe this will confuse them all when we vanish for a few days," Belle said. "Maybe they'll do something foolish and expose themselves."

"Who do you mean by 'they'?" I asked.

"The Hubbels, of course. I wouldn't trust any of them as far as I could throw them."

I thought of Maureen (as in Romeo and Juliet) and felt sad.

Was that really why Belle had decided to come? To throw the Hubbels off kilter? I was sure that there were layers to Belle that I didn't understand. Reckless Belle, kind Belle, angry Belle—what else?

At least Pop hadn't said a word when Belle got in the car complete with dog. He'd met Bailey before, and I guess the nature of the rescue and possible chase pleased him so much that having a dog along more or less didn't matter. I could tell by his cheerful tone that he refused to believe that Brad wouldn't know how to follow us.

"We must be wily," he said, "and watch for any suspicious car in the rearview mirror. I assume this Brad will be carrying a gun."

"He'd be in a rented or stolen car," Belle said again. "Young-looking, with white hair and green eyes, a scar, and a slight limp."

I made a note of that, even though I told myself he wouldn't find us. I wrote it down in a little notebook that lives in my pocket whenever I remember to put it there.

We drove along the curvy road beside a river, and then by woodsy roads up toward the interstate. A boy of about sixteen was getting letters out of a green mailbox.

"I understand you have a son named George," I said to Belle. "Do you have other children?" I was annoyed that she'd led me to believe she had faced her troubles alone.

"I have one son," she said sharply, "and he doesn't speak to me. He stopped last Thursday at three P.M. I don't talk about him." So the son was as volatile as Belle.

"I would never stop talking to Peaches," Pop said from the front seat.

Nope, I thought, not even when I want him to.

Belle didn't seem to mind that Pop horned into the conversation. Nor did she remind him that they'd met when I was six years old.

"Did you talk to my son?" Belle asked me.

"No," I said. "I met the girl who thinks he's wonderful. She came to my office with a news release."

"She's the problem," Belle declared, not seeming to care who heard her. "Imagine my son saying he loves the niece of the man who helped to kill his father."

"Tell us about it," Pop begged. I could see this would make his trip, even if we weren't chased. "But I can't hear too well up here. Let's stop, and I'll change places with Sandy."

We pulled into the first gas station we came to, a convenience store with a few pumps. With folding wheelchair unfolded, and much ado, Pop moved into the back seat. "I certainly will enjoy having your company on this trip," he told Belle. "Now, tell me all about your son."

If I had been Belle, I might have said, *Mind your own business.* Tactfully, of course.

But she seemed pleased at Pop's invitation. "My son, George, is wonderful, or he used to be wonderful. He went to the law school at Chapel Hill. He was near the top of his class. He graduated last year and is with a law firm in Asheville. He used to listen to what I said. Then he fell for this girl who is two years older than he is." Belle said this as if it were a heinous crime to be two years older. "And she's convinced him that the Hubbel family is not a nest of vipers, but a lovely group of possible future relatives. Including her uncle Brad, who wants to shoot me and Peaches."

Pop nodded. "Why did your son stop speaking to you?" he asked. His eyes sparkled with approval.

"I told him what I thought," Belle said. "I told him I could never be friends with a member of that sorry family. I told him I thought he was a traitor to his father!" Then Belle filled Pop in about her husband's death, the DDT, the neighbors, six ducks and the pig, and her own operation.

Even Azalea couldn't think of anything upbeat to say except, "Let's stop and have lunch." We pulled into a Shoney's.

"So what is the Hubbel girl like?" Pop asked as he munched on his cheese sandwich. "Is she a looker? Did she seduce your George with her beauty?"

Belle shrugged. "Oh, she looks good, but you never know. Even Brad Hubbel seemed perfectly normal as a kid. He went berserk in college, and now they say he's schizophrenic. I say those Hubbels have all got seeds of craziness in them waiting to sprout."

"I liked Maureen," I put in. "She said it was hard loving a man whose family doesn't want her."

Dern, I shouldn't have said that. Belle glared and shut up. So, O.K., a quiet time wouldn't hurt.

But Azalea had to smooth things over. "Sometimes," she said, "we expect the worst, and it doesn't happen." With that, she led us out to the car to resume our trip.

We passed a sign by the road next to a small stone house. It said Hand-made Quilts and Taxidermy.

"Belle," I said, "what have you been doing all these years? What do you work at?"

"I'm a photographer," she said. "I do people's pets and their children. My big seasons are before Christmas and before Mother's Day." That sounded right. And it could leave her time to get into trouble if she wanted to.

"In Monroe County," she said, "people give pictures of their kids to all their relatives."

I thought about relatives and I pulled out my little notebook. We claim so many kinfolk here in the mountains, and

I have trouble keeping them straight. I made a little chart of the Hubbels. Not that it was really necessary. I wasn't making a suspect chart. But a who-was-who list would make it easier to keep straight what Belle might have to say about them.

There was sad Maureen with the snake earrings. Her father was Herbert, who had sold me some pansies and impatiens. Her uncle Jake owned the Ford dealership and was a big wheel around the county and gave away money as if it was going out of style. Uncle Isaiah never came down the mountain and had a gun in every room. Uncle Brad thought we were spies, and Aunt—was it Mabel?—taught school and was Teacher of the Year.

Maureen had never mentioned spouses except for Isaiah's wife, Joan, who sold real estate and had vanished. But somebody had said Jake married the sheriff's daughter. Maybe the Hubbel men were such strong characters that their wives faded away. By contrast, Belle never mentioned any relative, except her late husband and, finally, one son.

"Belle," I said, "who are you related to around here?"

"No one!" she said firmly. "My mother and father came here from Kentucky. And they're both dead." So the dog and her son, George, who didn't speak to her, were her family. I shivered. I hoped she had friends.

Sometimes I could crown Pop, but he sure keeps track of every relative, even the difficult ones like Cousin Jeeter who's in Craggy Prison for stealing whiskey.

Pop was sure we'd be followed. He was right that we should be super-alert to that possibility, although it's hard to tell on winding country roads. The leaves weren't far enough out to hide the far side of curves, but here in the mountains the land itself can hide whatever is far behind or far ahead. The road was in a valley by a river with steep hill-sides to the left and right. A couple of times when the road straightened, I thought I saw the same car in the distance, but even that wouldn't prove it was more than someone going the same way. When we got to I-40 we'd be able to see long stretches and be sure. I was thinking about what we'd do if it turned out we were being followed, when the car phone rang. We had just come to a straighter, flatter stretch of road.

"I bet that's for me," Pop said hopefully. So Azalea handed the phone back to Pop. He answered, and there was silence while he listened.

"Spiders," he said. "What do we care about a few spiders?"

Another long silence, then: "In the closet and in your shoe?" He sounded scandalized. More listening, then: "Brown recluse spiders can do that? You mean a bite could even kill you?"

To Azalea, he said, "Alice says the house is overrun with brown recluse spiders. She says they like our part of Tennessee. They hide in nooks and crannies and come out at night. It's lucky she shook out her shoe this morning, because there was a spider in it."

This news was greeted with an appalled silence. It seemed too bizarre to be running from a man who thought that Belle and I were dangerous spies, only to find our safe-house was overrun with deadly spiders. All that while I was desperately trying to mind my own business and stay out of trouble. Maybe I'm jinxed.

"Alice says the spiders have bred like crazy. They're thick as thieves," Pop told us. "The exterminator can't come till day after tomorrow. What shall I tell her?"

Short silence, then: "Why, this is a great opportunity!" Azalea cried. "Tell Alice and Ed to come and join us at the Opryland Hotel in Nashville. They have hundreds of rooms and seven or eight restaurants and even a canal and a boat ride all under one great big glass roof. It's the biggest greenhouse in the world, and much more than a greenhouse. That's what my friend Marsha says. They have memorabilia from the Grand Ole Opry. She went to a convention there. I've always wanted to go there. Oh, this will be exciting. That Brad Hubbel will never find us!"

"But what about the birthday party?" I asked. "What about meeting Ted?"

Pop dutifully relayed the birthday party question. "She's had to put it off a week," he reported, "so the guests won't be bitten by the spiders."

"We'll have a little party at the Opryland Hotel!" Azalea said. "We'll have it at Beauregard's. That's the most elegant restaurant. In a Southern mansion built right under that glass roof with everything else."

Pop relayed that to his step-granddaughter, Alice. "Oh, I'm sorry," he said. "Well, we'll do it again when he feels better." He ended the phone call and announced that Alice's husband, Ed, was sick to his stomach. They were already in a local motel. "Too bad," he said. "The Opryland Hotel will be more fun."

I should have had my mind on danger right then, but I was diverted as I tried to picture a hotel under glass. It sounded sort of like a live-in capsule on the moon. I could see that it would sure make a change from Monroe County, where the most popular restaurant is Milton's Barbecue. It would even make a change from my own Buncombe County, where the Grove Park Inn is large enough so that a small truck is needed to bring the huge yule log to the big stone fireplace in the lobby at Christmastime. But we don't have mega-acres under a glass roof.

I heard Pop getting the Opryland Hotel number from Information, then calling for rooms and a reservation at Beauregard's. Hey, maybe this really would be fun. I stayed diverted.

"But what will I do with Bailey?" Belle asked.

Azalea told Pop to call the hotel back for the name of a trustworthy place to board a dog for the night.

"Hey, we need gas," Azalea announced. "I didn't notice we were getting so low." She turned in to the station coming up on our right. I got out and stretched my legs while she pumped the gas. There was a pay-phone booth, and I figured that if I called Ted from there I could be a little franker about what was going on than if I called him in front of Pop and Azalea and Belle. He agreed to meet us at the Opryland Hotel and made me promise to stay alert "no matter how safe you think you are."

In spite of Pop's hope for a chase, we arrived safely in Tennessee—even heading west on I-40 where the traffic is sometimes quite exciting. There was no further sign of anyone following.

I was looking forward to an elegant dinner at a hotel under glass in Nashville, Tennessee, when I should have been thinking ahead about what could go wrong.

CHAPTER
10

SATURDAY, 4:00 P.M.

The recommended boarding kennel in Nashville turned out to be full, but the gal at the desk suggested another nearby. So we dropped Bailey off at the Pet Motel. Belle and I went in to register him. The motherly looking woman in charge made a big fuss over him. The Pet Motel was actually in an old house, and the amazing thing about it was a sign on the check-in counter that said "Two rooms for dog lovers. $50 per night. Inquire if available." We did not inquire, but I told the others when we got back to the car. "We could board some of us as well as the dog," I said, "if we really wanted to hide." I thought I was joking.

We drove past the Music Valley Museum of Stars; past a lot of outlet stores, taking advantage of the tourists, no doubt; past the Nashville Palace, which advertised Live Entertainment on a huge sign. Finally we came to a smaller sign that said Opryland Hotel.

It seemed to me then as if we weren't just escaping from danger—we had escaped from reality. As we drove between the gate pillars toward the hotel, the whole landscape was pure dream. Blooms flourished on each side of the entrance drive and on the median strip. Flowers seemed to burst forth from every available square inch. No dead or wilted blossom scarred the perfect tableau. Some of the blooms were in gargantuan flowerpots. Trees lined the median strip. Their leaves were as slick as magnolia leaves, but the shape of the trees was more compact. We passed an artificial pool and waterfall. The drive curved toward a huge building with arches and pillars, partly red brick, partly painted white. The building was shaped so that you couldn't see where it ended or if there was the beginning of another building.

We drove up to the entrance, and after we helped Pop out and into his wheelchair and Sandy removed Pop and Azalea's luggage, a uniformed valet took the car. We went inside to register. The lobby was huge with red velvet chairs and couches and a flowered green rug. The brass chandelier was so big and splendid that I was impressed until I thought of the *Phantom of the Opera*, in which a falling chandelier is a murder weapon. So, O.K., I was still nervous.

A sweeping staircase with white railings led up to another level. Walt Disney, meet Scarlett O'Hara and Tammy Wynette. Pop was in an expansive mood and said our stay was all on him. Also, I think Azalea nudged him.

"This is the luxury we deserve to cheer us up about the spiders," Pop said. "That madman will never find us here. Nobody even knows we're here except Ted and Alice. And

that man doesn't even know what Peaches looks like, I bet."
He paused and smiled. "At least, not that we know of."

I didn't remind him that my picture was in the paper when
I started work there.

"Don't worry," Azalea said to Belle and me, "the poor
young man who believes you two are spies sent to hound
him doesn't even know that Opryland exists. Staying in this
fun place is going to be a lark!"

We agreed to meet at Beauregard's at six o'clock, after we
washed up and rested.

Our rooms were down long corridors and through exotic
gardens, with fountains both indoors and out. Gardens with
banks of palmettos, for example, where a man with bad in-
tentions could certainly hide, all under the high glass roof. I
had to keep my imagination from running wild! Thank
goodness the person at the front desk had given each of us a
map.

I stopped gawking and realized I was separated from Pop
and the others. Take one wrong turn in this maze of flowers
and you were lost. I hoped I hadn't lost Azalea and Pop and
Belle for the duration. As I took out my map and studied it,
one of the bellhops noticed, asked if he could help, and
pointed me in the right direction, into a corridor. The out-
doors seemed to wind into the indoors here. All surprising as
a dream that I hoped would not turn into a nightmare. Something was gnawing at the back of my mind. Some disquiet-
ing fact that I couldn't quite dredge up. Dern my flaky
memory. If I stopped trying to force the thought, it would
come, I told myself. I took an elevator up to a corridor dimly
lit with flickering candles, or at least electrified lamps with
bulbs that resembled candle flames.

My room was absolutely grand. It even had its own brass

chandelier. Not large enough for a murder weapon. I hung my one dress in the spacious closet and sat down on a red couch flanked by Chinese urn lamps. Comfortable. I faced two wing chairs with a glass-topped coffee table between them, and a small mahogany dining table with four chairs. If the crazy man showed up, I could invite him to lunch. Of course there was a bed. King-sized. Plenty of room for Ted. I felt a sudden pang. Let this threat from *Mad Brad* not hurt Ted. Amen.

There was a sudden movement between the bed and a huge armoire against the wall. I caught my breath. Who was in my room? Whatever it was moved again, and I saw it was a sheer white curtain flapping in the breeze. Whew! I made myself go over and examine it. Two glass-paned doors opened out onto a balcony. One was open, and its curtain billowed. I pushed the curtain back and went out on the balcony. I looked down on gardens and paths. The path leading past my balcony was red brick. I was on the second floor. Someone could climb up on my balcony. My heart beat faster. Someone could have already been in my room and left the door to the balcony open. *Stop it!* I told myself. *The maid probably did it.* The moon must be full. That gooses my imagination.

I lay down on the bed and thought. I could call Ted on his car phone and see when he was going to get here. Then it hit me. That elusive thought came crashing down around my ears. It's possible to listen in on car phone conversations if you know how. I knew that! But certainly *Mad Brad* from Monroe County wouldn't be sophisticated enough to know how to listen in, would he? How could I be sure? I left the phone alone. *Mad Brad* could already know where we are!

I couldn't nap. I freshened up, put on my one dress, a

pretty blue but with no pockets. I stuck my flat plastic room key in my bra for safekeeping. Much easier to find than in my purse. I set out to explore. Could you put things in the cup pockets of U.S. Government falsies? I thought about Belle and wondered how many ordinary things she couldn't do and how that fed her anger.

I made my way back to the lobby where we'd started, and got directions to Beauregard's marked on my map. I had an hour to explore the inner landscape of the hotel. My senses reeled. Which was more overwhelming? The huge central gardens under glass, one so big that large houses built inside didn't seem out of place? The fountains? There was hardly a spot out of sight or earshot of a spurting fountain. I passed an orange tree in a huge pot. All the big flowerpots would make good places to hide behind. Black wrought-iron street lamps were entwined with artificial flowers. Odd when there were so many real ones. A girl passed me dressed *à la* Scarlett O'Hara. A family walked by in shorts and T-shirts, all the kids licking big lollipops.

I was admiring life-sized sculptures of marsh birds in an artificial pond when I began to worry about the hundreds of balconies above me. The edges of the tremendous indoor garden I stood in were part of the building. Rooms overlooked the central court and the buildings in it, and each one had its own balcony. A watcher could easily see me without being seen. Could kneel and look down. I felt vulnerable. I reminded myself that even if *Mad Brad* somehow found out where we were, he'd have trouble smuggling Jake Hubbel's shotgun from that gun rack into the hotel. I hoped.

Still exploring, I found myself on an open terrace with tables and chairs where a few people were sipping drinks. The terrace overlooked a stream. A boat with about twenty people in it passed by, and a kid waved. This place really did have everything! The terrace where I stood had a view up to another restaurant terrace that was part of a Southern mansion. That must be Beauregard's. It was on top of a bank sporting not one but two waterfalls. Heck, with all this falling water, somebody could slip up in back of me and I'd never hear them. I turned quickly and looked behind me. Just a mother and child standing next to a bed of flowers.

Soon I found myself in a corridor off the central court—a corridor filled with shops and restaurants. Even here, there was a fountain, a fancy one with layers of falling water. Did all these waterfalls and fountains fill the air with negative ions? I'd heard moving water did that. Did negative ions put you in the mood to spend cash? So many little shops wanted to sell me things—cards, candles, teapots, paintings, a relief map of the Opryland Hotel.

Wandering into another corridor, I passed a plain wooden pew with a plaque that said it was from the Ryman Auditorium, home of the Grand Ole Opry (and not for sale). I noticed a flower shop, which seemed to be competing with the flowers on every side of the court—exotic blooms that would never have survived in Nashville without that glass roof.

Back out in the central court, a man with a pushcart wanted to do my portrait in charcoal. No Face Too Ugly, his sign read. At least he had a sense of humor.

Why did I feel someone was staring at me? I tried to laugh at myself for being paranoid. That's the trouble with a good imagination; it's hard to tell when it's going too far. I walked up a path bordered with flowers, past a stupendous fern with fronds big enough to conceal a man.

As I glanced up at a walk on a higher level, I drew in my

breath. A man looked back at me. Intently. His white hair was striking with that young, haunted face. I couldn't be sure his eyes were green from this distance, but I thought so. His face was turned, perhaps on purpose, so I couldn't see the scar. I forced myself to keep walking, and tried not to change my expression. Maybe he wasn't sure it was me. My heart was beating so hard I thought I might faint. I hadn't seen a gun.

He hurried off as if I'd scared him. Of course. He thought I was a government spy. And, God help me, he limped. Not much, but he did limp. He bumped into a fat woman in shorts, hurried past an Asian couple, and managed to disappear around a curve in a garden walk. He became more frightening when I couldn't see where he was.

Where was the rest of our group? Where was Belle? I looked at my watch. Ten of six. Time to meet the others. Would I lead *Mad Brad* right to them? And what about Ted? He was due to arrive here at some point. Ted who was supposed to avoid shocks. I'd left word for him at the desk that we'd be at Beauregard's at six in case he arrived after we left our rooms. I'd be so glad to see him, but I wished he wasn't coming. What should I do?

I reminded myself I wasn't positive I'd seen *Mad Brad*. I hadn't seen the scar. Two men could have white hair and limp. I wasn't sure the man on the walk had green eyes. Was it *Mad Brad?* If Belle saw him, she would know. I was standing in a small courtyard with many wrought-iron street lamps garlanded with artificial flowers. If I walked across the courtyard and down a path, I'd be at the restaurant. I wondered what to do next; then part of the problem was solved for me. Here came Sandy pushing Pop's wheelchair.

Next I spotted Azalea and Belle. All heading toward Beauregard's. They called out to me in great good cheer.

I tried to be calm and reasoned. "I saw someone who
might possibly be Brad Hubbel," I said when they were
close. "He was young-looking and he had white hair and he
limped and he was staring at me and I think he had green
eyes. I couldn't be sure and I couldn't see the scar. I didn't
see a gun." I described exactly where he'd been and how
he'd acted.

Azalea reached out and touched my shoulder. "You had a
scare."

Belle tensed. "You must all watch out."

Pop chortled. "I told you there'd be a chase!"

He could at least have worried about me.

Azalea said, "We must enjoy our dinner and pray it
wasn't him. Also remember that everyone says he's a very
bad shot."

On that happy note, we arrived in front of Beauregard's.
Two ornate iron street lamps flanked the entrance, each with
three upper branches, one branch taller than the other two.
Very New Orleans. Or at least like a dream of New Orleans.
A long Southern-mansion-type porch stretched all across the
front of the building. There were overstuffed chairs on the
porch. Hey, what would happen if it rained? But it couldn't
rain. We were under the huge glass roof, smaller buildings
and all. In a nightmare under glass. No human beings on that
long upstairs porch. I looked around at the balconies on the
main building that surrounded us. Nobody on them either. I
made up my mind to try to enjoy dinner, though I'd still
keep an eye out. When Ted came, we'd decide together what
to do next.

Beauregard's was serving dinner on the veranda. In fact,

our table with colorful napkins spouting from the wine-glasses was in earshot of the waterfalls I'd seen when I looked up at this place. But we couldn't see down to the river. A row of snake-plant spikes made a hedge that hid our view. If you were mentally unstable, would the labyrinthine, dreamlike quality of this place confuse you even more?

If that didn't, the weird modern music that suddenly filled the air certainly would. A swell of music, each note shading into another, seemed to fill the whole glass dome around us. And then, as if the music pulled it forth, a great spout of water, colored by spotlights, rose in the center of the place, higher than the building we were in—the building within a building, I mean. Water plumed toward the glass ceiling, changing color from clear to red to blue, then gradually sank away as the music faded, too.

Pop ignored the water spout and ordered gumbo. I'd reached the point where nothing that happened under the glass top could surprise me, or so I thought. I decided to try the jambalaya. Belle said she'd like to have something she could never get back in Monroe County, so she ordered wild duck Napoleon with wild mushrooms. Sandy and Azalea chose the lamb chops. We shared two bottles of white wine.

I had deliberately taken the seat next to Belle. "So what happened after the first grade?" I asked.

"We moved because my father went to teach twelfth-grade math in Monroe County. We lived on a small farm, more a home place, and I had a horse," she said. "That was a good time, except my father expected so much." She was drinking her wine as if it were water. She was quite upset for someone so fearless.

"He needed me to help because my mother was sick a lot,

but she did teach me about wild herbs to cure sickness, herbs her mother had used."

"A family tradition," I remarked.

"I'll drink to that!" she said, and raised her glass.

"You went to the college in Monroe County?" I asked. I kept my eyes busy looking for any sign of *Mad Brad*.

"Of course not. My father wanted me to see more of the state. I went to college at Chapel Hill. I took premed because I wanted to be a vet." She sighed. "I would have liked that. But then I married Ernie, who was from Monroe County. Maybe I hadn't broadened my horizons, but I was happy." She had nearly finished her second glass of wine. Tears came into her eyes.

Pop laughed at something Azalea said. Good. He wouldn't butt in. "Yes, I was happy," Belle said unhappily.

The waiter came by and asked if he could fill her glass. She nodded yes. "Ernie was a CPA. We lived on a farm and raised horses." She let out a sob. Why do I inspire people to cry?

She took another gulp of wine. I had a hunch she wanted to get drunk enough to tell me something.

I asked her if she knew my friend Marietta in Monroe County who used to run an herb nursery. "Slightly," she said, "but I prefer to use wild herbs. Marietta moved to New York, right? To Greenwich Village. Maybe I should move somewhere." She laughed uncomfortably.

Nevertheless, Belle seemed to savor her wild duck Napoleon. She drank steadily.

By the time we were ready to order dessert, she had to talk quite slowly to avoid slurring her words. I could feel the pressure of something inside her that wanted to break free. Every once in a while her body would jerk. Her mouth would work. There was something she was bursting to say.

But each time I was sure she was ready, a wave of terror passed through her eyes, and she shut her mouth.

Pop turned to me. Well, I had been ignoring him, and Pop can't bear that. "Peaches," he said, "you need to put out a revised, updated edition of your book. Why, you don't even have your relatives in it. And they have so many smart ways to remember."

Until recently, Pop hasn't thought much of my book. He says you never admit a flaw—like my bad memory. But Pop is hipped on relatives. I sure didn't want to talk about relatives now—I wanted to give Belle every chance to open up. "Maybe I will do another edition," I said to humor Pop. "Better decide if you want the double chocolate cake or the New Orleans bread pudding."

"Take Cousin Harold," Pop said, totally undiverted. "Harold can't remember a thing without making a list, and he used to be a smart real estate man. Still dresses up in a coat and tie as if he's important." Cousin Harold was eighty-five. Belle reached for the wine bottle and poured herself another glass.

"And furthermore, he loses lists," Pop said. "But you can't keep a good man down. He fastens his list to his necktie with a tie pin," Pop explained. "Takes it off to add something, puts it back till he's ready to go to town. Then he puts it in his coat pocket."

Belle was slowly twirling her glass and staring into it as if it held deep sorrow. I needed to encourage her to tell her troubles quick, before she was too far gone to be coherent.

"The caramel custard sounds good," I told Pop, who ignored me and continued his story:

"One day Cousin Harold went to town to get a loan from the bank." Pop seemed so pleased with himself, he must be getting to the climax of the story. Good. Belle had tears in her eyes again. Good grief.

"Before Cousin Harold could say a word, the loan officer said, 'I can't give you ten thousand dollars, but we could lend you five.'" Pop began to laugh. "You see, it was all written on the list on Harold's tie. He forgot to put it in his pocket." Everybody at the table laughed except for Belle and me.

Tears ran down Belle's cheeks, and she hiccupped. If I didn't hurry and find out what was upsetting her, she would pass out first.

"Pop," I said, "I need you to be quiet and order your dessert." I nudged him. Not too hard.

He glared at me, furious. Then his eyes fell on Belle, and I could see the light dawn. He saw he could be letting part of the plot get away. His frown softened, and he gave me a warm smile. He turned to the hovering waitress. "I'll have the mocha ice cream."

He turned the other way and began talking with Azalea. Good move.

I reached over and patted Belle's hand. "Something is bothering you a lot," I said.

"Something I have to tell you," she said. She gulped down the rest of her wine. I prayed it wouldn't lay her low.

Suddenly she blurted it out. "I was in love with Isaiah Hubbel. Would you believe that? Once I was." She said it quite loudly. All of us stared at her.

"You loved a man you now think killed his wife?" The words were out before I could stop them. How would that feel? Strange.

"I loved a man," she said very slowly, "whose brother

now thinks we are government spies. Whose brother might shoot us."

Amazing, but why did it seem to scare her so? Damn Suzie. She must have known that Belle had some relationship with Isaiah. There had to be all sorts of ins and outs to what was happening now that I wasn't aware of. Why hadn't I found out? It occurred to me that sometimes *not* detecting might be dangerous.

"This trouble is my punishment," Belle said, and burst into such loud sobs that I was glad the people at the next table had left. The diners at the next table over turned and stared. I put my finger to my lips, and she did lower her voice. "That was Brad you saw. He's here. I know it. He'll shoot us. I'm a jinx."

I squeezed her hand. "No. We can't be sure that was him. But we can get out of this place as soon as Ted gets here."

As if on cue, Ted picked that moment to appear, smiling and looking so glad to see us, and yet with a slight frown of confusion as he noticed Belle's red-splotched face. Pop pulled him down to whisper in his ear, but it was a stage whisper. "Peaches is going to do a new edition of her book, and I'm going to help."

Maybe. But first we all had to manage not to drown in tears—or get shot.

CHAPTER
11

SATURDAY EVENING

Belle put her head down on her folded arms and seemed to be asleep. Ted gave me a quick kiss when I stood up to greet him. He felt so solid, so alive. How could he be anything but completely healthy? His high blood pressure didn't show. His color was good, and he carried himself erect. He pulled a chair up to the table on the other side of me from Belle, and put a small suitcase down by his side. He hadn't even been to our room yet. "I've eaten," he said, "but I'll join you for dessert."

He gave Belle a curious look as she rested her head on the table. "What's wrong?"

"Wine," I whispered. "That's Belle Dasher, and she's upset and had too much."

Ted glanced around at the other tables where people

around us were giving her odd glances, too. "But you're be-having," he said and winked.

I was so glad to see Ted that I could have cried, even while I wished he hadn't come. His logical mind would help us solve our problems. Only he was supposed to steer clear of problems. If something happened to Ted—I shivered. I looked over at Belle, who was so angry over losing her husband. I thought, *If she wants to tell me something, it has to do with him.*

Pop spoke up. "Peaches may have seen that crazy man. He could hide in here, and we'd never find him!"

"I'm not sure it was him," I said quickly, trying to quash Ted's start of alarm. "I merely saw a youngish-looking man with white hair. That's unusual, but there could be more than one."

But Ted was immediately serious and pinned me with his eyes. "Did he know you saw him?"

I had to admit he did.

"How did he behave?"

"He hurried off. He did limp, and Belle had said Brad Hubbel does, too, but White Hair didn't limp much. He seemed scared of me."

"So that might be Brad Hubbel, afraid that you want to spy on him," Ted said thoughtfully. "Do you think he could have followed you here?"

If I wanted Ted's help I'd have to be honest with him, wouldn't I? I told him how we might have been followed at first, or not. But then I was sure we weren't.

"Did you make any calls on the car phone about where you were going?" he asked. Oh, boy, I had to admit that at the time I'd forgotten that people can listen in on car phones! I have a hole in my head, and it's between my ears!

But how would someone zero in on a particular phone if they didn't have the number? How would Brad find Pop's car phone number?

I told Ted how Pop had made the hotel reservations on the car phone. "And Brad's a computer nerd," I said. "Suzie said so. He could be into all sorts of electronics stuff. Mentally ill is not the same as dumb."

Ted whistled. He stood back up. "We need to go somewhere else and be sure nobody follows us. We don't need to take a chance."

Ted was so positive, I had to agree. Pop did not. "I intend to stay right here," he said. "That man hasn't got any reason to shoot me or Azalea. I enjoy it here. We have everything." As if to prove him right, the strange music started up again, and the water spout climbed toward the roof, mellowed by changing lights.

"Amazing," Ted said, following it with his eyes, "but I intend to take Peaches somewhere else."

Belle's head jerked up. She was back from the seemingly dead. "I want to go, too." Her face was splotched and damp, but her voice was steadier than it had been, determined as usual.

"This is my husband, Ted," I told Belle, though she'd probably already figured that out.

Pop inclined his head and smiled his gracious arbiter smile. "You can all go stay with the dog."

Ted did a double take, but Belle's face broke into joy. "Yes!" she cried. "I'm for that! And you'll know where we are!"

I explained to Ted about the kennel that rented rooms. Yes. There was such a place. He agreed that might do. Had we talked about it on the telephone? Thank goodness, not that place.

We did finish our elegant desserts before we set forth. I hoped the slight delay would give Pop time to change his mind, though I was just as glad to leave as soon as possible.

Still, I enjoyed my raspberry cheesecake. Ted had the New Orleans bread pudding with bourbon sauce, Azalea split her chocolate cake with Belle, and Pop savored his mocha ice cream. "You need to keep up your strength for the getaway," Pop told Ted and Belle and me with a wise wink, but he still refused to leave with us. "I've paid for my room," he said, "and I may be able to talk my way out of paying for your rooms since your lives have been threatened and you haven't slept in them."

He and Azalea paraded back with us to our rooms, past the artificial river with a boatload of tourists, past all the blooming flowers, real and artificial, past the man for whom no face was too ugly, then the shops, and down a long corridor. No sign of *Mad Brad*, but I was glad we were getting out of that place so full of nooks to hide in. He could appear at any moment. Luckily our rooms were close together. I hugged Pop and Azalea goodbye at the door to theirs. I remembered our room could be climbed into from the balcony, but it was empty. Whew! I still didn't have anything to take with me but the clothes I'd changed out of earlier. Belle didn't even have that. Ted had the small suitcase he'd never unpacked. He'd left the rest of my stuff in the car.

As we set out through corridors and gardens, Ted had his arm through Belle's trying to keep her steady. Unsteady is bad if you might be attacked, and she wanted to hurry. I trailed a little behind, looking in a shop window at an assortment of teapots.

As I passed a hall that branched off to the left, an arm grabbed me. It happened so fast it took the breath out of me. I gasped rather than screamed. Something sharp that must have been a gun was in my back, and a jittery voice said, "Be quiet or I'm going to shoot. Now, walk in front of me down this way. Hurry." At first my mind froze. What do you say to someone who has delusions, especially when you are the delusion? What do you do? You do what they say, if there's a gun in your back.

Shortly the pressure on my back was gone, but the voice said, "The gun is pointed right at your heart. Hurry," he said again and gave me a shove. We were almost running along a path with some kind of exotic lilies on one side, a shop with pictures out to catch my eye on the other. But no person in sight.

Why didn't Scarlett O'Hara or the man who emptied cigarette butts show up? Why didn't someone from some level see us? But then we passed people strolling, who gawked at us but did nothing. The gun must be covered somehow. Only our actions seemed strange. Then I saw someone on a higher path staring at us. It was Jake Hubbel. It couldn't be! I was losing my mind. He disappeared from sight as we came to a curve in the path with a bank of palmettos on each side. Small thickets with dark insides. *Mad Brad* pushed me into a thicket, behind the palmetto fronds. Oh, God help me, out of sight.

"Why are you spying on me?" he whispered. I tried to turn and look at him, but he said, "Keep your head forward."

Palmetto leaves poked into me. I smelled leaf mold and *Mad Brad's* sweat. He smelled out of whack. Sweetish in the wrong way. "Why do you believe I'm spying on you?" I asked.

"My brother told me. My brother never lies." I wondered if that could be true or just another delusion. Suppose his brother really was here. Would he help or egg Brad on? I heard someone walk by. I didn't dare cry out. In the distance the loud, spooky water music started again.

I heard Ted call my name. Belle called my name. They were trying to find me. The gun poked my back again. I didn't dare answer.

Brad went totally tense. "That's her!" he spat.

He meant Belle, I figured. "Why don't you turn us both in to the police?" I asked. Wouldn't that be great!

He began to shake. "I don't trust the police!"

"Why don't you run away so that I can't find you and she can't find you and the police can't find you?" I said.

He began to shake even harder, and the palmetto leaves shook and rustled with him. "You're all spies . . ."

I turned around and looked at him. Yes, he was like the picture. In the half dark, his green eyes glowed catlike, except his face had terror etched in every line. His gun hand was trembling. I assumed the tiger puppet he was holding in such an odd position covered the gun. He was staring out at the walk, not at me. Out where Belle and Ted must be.

I reached and grabbed the tiger in his right hand. Yes, there was a gun inside. I twisted. He pulled against me, trying to aim it at me again. He was amazingly strong. At any moment I expected the gun to go off, which might bring help, but might also kill somebody passing by, maybe Ted or Belle. With his free hand, Brad grabbed my throat. We struggled. I heard a crash, and the palmetto leaves shuddered violently around me. Brad went down, and as I pulled back the palmettos to look, I saw he'd been hit with Ted's suitcase. It lay beside him. Why hadn't he shot one of us? He still held that gun covered with a puppet in his hand. Before he could recover, Ted sat on him and held down that gun hand. Belle pulled his fingers off the gun and grabbed it away. Fear had sobered her fast.

So where were the tourists? Where was the hotel staff? They didn't appear. The water spout and the music had hidden our adventure. Brad was now glassy-eyed and stiff.

I heard footsteps. Brother Jake came running round the curve of the path, the brother who could look as dour as Washington on a quarter or radiate charm and still be country in his jeans and red T-shirt. He was in dour mode. In fact, he was pale, as if he'd had a shock. He looked from one of us to another, eyes frightened.

"Oh, Lord," he said, "who's hurt? Oh, Lord, I'm sorry about this. This is bad." I stood up. Amazingly I wasn't hurt, unless you count palmetto scratches and a tender neck.

Jake took that in. "Lord help me!" he cried. "As soon as I found Brad's note that he'd gone after you all, I started to look. I'll take care of him." Then he smiled that charming smile I didn't trust. "Thank God you're all right." Boy, could he change fast.

"How did you find him?" Ted asked skeptically, still holding Brad immobile. Brad rolled his eyes up at his brother and stayed mute.

"Thank God someone at the car dealership saw him acting a little odd and called me." Jake behaved as if Brad wasn't pinned down near his feet. "He borrowed a car. Someone called me from Shoney's, where he stopped for lunch, and I got there and saw the car just as he took off again. I followed him." I wondered if Jake was lying. He held his hands shut as though he was hiding something.

Belle still held the gun inside the tiger puppet. "He had a

gun!" she accused. I took a handkerchief out of my pocket, held the end of the gun with it, and pulled it out of the puppet. I was holding a toy gun, which must have been harder to find than a real one in Monroe County! I was flabbergasted.

Jake's eyes fell on the toy, and he burst into a big grin. "Why, that's my Elroy's play gun!" he said. He glowed with relief.

Why did that toy gun make me feel like such a fool? Brad had a play gun, but it felt real enough in my back. Belle had a scar on her arm from a real gun he'd fired at her.

Jake relaxed, turned to Brad, and kneeled down beside him. "Don't be scared," he said kindly. "I've persuaded these folks to let you come with me. I've told them you're not who they think you are."

This was all a lie, but it seemed to be working. Ted loosened his hold on Brad, who sat up and looked around with a confused frown, but he was calm.

Jake reached in his jacket pocket and took out a small flask and a bottle of pills. He shook a pill out of the bottle. "You take this pill, and I'll take you home," he said. Brad pulled away from him. He said, "I can't think right when I take those pills."

But Jake insisted, and finally Brad put the pill in his mouth and took a slurp of water. "Now you come with me," Jake said, and took his arm. "Don't worry, no one's going to hurt you." He said that as he would have to a frightened child, and I thought, poor Jake, with two brothers round the bend. He seemed to care for them, to do what he could to help them. Perhaps I'd judged him wrong. Then I could feel that gun in my back again. Jake Hubbel hadn't done enough.

"Don't worry," he said, as calmly as if we hadn't been

scared silly. "I'll get him home and be sure he takes his medication. When he does, he's all right."

I hoped so. Off down the path they went, Jake holding *Mad Brad* by the arm, all but dragging him, but not making me feel safe. I said to Ted, "Why didn't we call the police?"

"They wouldn't understand," Belle said, brushing the dirt off her knees. Whose side was she on?

"I hope Jake knows how to handle his brother," Ted said. "The police wouldn't. And I did hit Brad over the head. This could get murky. I still want us to get out of here. Off where no one but Pop and Azalea know where we are, just in case." So we took our plastic keys to the desk. Neither Brad nor Jake were in sight.

CHAPTER
12

SATURDAY NIGHT

Outside in the real world it was dark, though we were standing in an inner core of light around the red brick hotel entrance. The valet in his snappy uniform got Ted's car from the lot, and we set out with a Nashville map and the address of the Pet Motel in hand. We took a roundabout route, just in case. I realized I was limp from the excitement. Several times I dozed as we drove. But when I jerked awake at a light, I noticed Belle was wide-eyed and tense.

Ted had brought me a suitcase of clothes, which he'd forgotten and left in the car, thank goodness. I'd have a nightgown and toothbrush.

When we got to the Pet Motel, the lights were out on the kennel side, but there was still a light in the Victorian house next door with the wooden lace around its roof. Mrs. Pet Motel had said the rooms were there. We rang the bell, and she greeted us effusively, and pulled us into a Victorian parlor with small red balls on the curtain fringe and a huge flowered rug.

"Oh," she said, "Bailey will be so pleased. I'll go right over and get him. When owners are here, the dogs always prefer to stay with them."

Belle and her dog were shown to one room, and Ted and I to another, with a king-sized bed and frilly pillows, three pretend-leather chairs, and an old-fashioned dresser with three mirrors to show left, right, and forward views. Dog pictures adorned the walls. Champion This and Champion That posed regally with proud owners. Many were autographed to our hostess.

After giving Ted the really thorough hello hug that hadn't been possible in the restaurant, I said, "Well, God willing, that's over with. It really takes it out of me to be threatened like that."

Ted grinned. "So avoid it from now on."

I lost my suitcase and then found it standing right by the door. That's the thing about being really tired. It makes objects misbehave. My toothbrush hid in the bottom of my toiletries case, then suddenly jumped into sight the second time I looked.

I was sitting in one of the leather chairs, unbuckling my shoe when there was a knock on the door.

Belle said, "It's me!" Ted unlocked the door, and she asked, "Can I come in?" She had Bailey under one arm, and he let out a hello yelp and wagged his tail. Belle put him down, and he ran over to me for a pat. He had decided I was family. He gave Ted a friendly sniff. I started to say I was exhausted, that Belle should come back tomorrow.

But Belle seemed so desperate for a listener. She was

shaky, and there were smudges under her eyes. She sat down in one of the other chairs, and Bailey jumped up in her lap. She held onto him as if she needed support, squirming in her chair, seeming unable to find a comfortable position. "I have to tell you something," she said, "I've got to tell somebody." Her piercing eyes said, *Don't stand in my way.*

Good Lord, I thought. What more don't we know?

Ted sat down too, across from Belle. "What is it?" he asked.

"I'm a traitor," she said. She swallowed. She licked her lips. We waited. "I loved my husband, my Ernie." She stared toward the dog pictures on the wall, and looked down at her own hands. Finally she looked back at me. "Ernie was scared of growing old." She clenched her hands together. "He was only fifty. But he'd always been so much fun. People treated him like a kid who knew the best jokes. And when his hair got gray, he could color it. Why not? Then he found some wrinkles."

"Laugh lines," I said.

"He didn't laugh when I said that. This young flibberti-gibbet named Gwen Hallin threw herself at him. Very pretty in a shallow way. Pouty-mouthed. She liked older men. But, damn it, she had no right to go after Ernie."

Where could this be leading, and why was she telling us?

Belle stopped and patted the dog, as if that helped her to stay calm. "I found out he was meeting this Gwen over in Asheville. I was sick. And then I was damn mad. We stopped speaking." She shut her eyes and swallowed. Ted and I both waited. Finally she went on. "We still lived in the same house. He said that proved he intended to spend his old age with me. I said, 'What a thrill.'" Belle's eyes flashed.

She breathed deeply and said, "But, of course, now he never will."

There was a long silence while she fought back tears. "I felt as empty as a winter tree. This was May. I took walks in the woods, and the leaves were spring-green and thin and soft. A very touchy-feely time." Her voice rose. "And Ernie was off touching *her.*"

What could this have to do with the Hubbels, with Brad Hubbel stalking us, or the murder she believed Isaiah Hubbel committed? Why tell me, anyway? I'd told her I don't cover murders, and I certainly don't cover love affairs. And yet I was interested. Who had Belle grown up to be? Why was she so bent on revenge and so angry with herself? Why couldn't she forgive herself? A bloodhound in a gilt-framed photo on her left had a face full of wrinkles, as bloodhounds do. Belle's face had collapsed into sadness lines.

"At least I could collect herbs," she went on. "I had to stay busy or lose my mind. I make some of the potions my grandmother did, because they work."

Perhaps, I thought, an un-love potion. That could be useful.

"I walked up Isaiah Hubbel's mountain picking horsetail first," she said, "down by the brook at the base, then violet leaves." I could see by the faraway look in her eyes that she was back on that mountain. "My heart and all the rest of me ached bad. Trillium was blooming, and a little higher up the mountain, there were yellow hawthorn flowers. It's worse to be alone in the spring."

Get to the point, I wanted to say, but sometimes it's so hard to tell what you've done that you have to sneak up on it. She did say she was a traitor.

"I use hawthorn flowers to make a tincture," Belle said, looking away from me. "I mix it with a tincture from the berries in the fall, and it's good for things to do with the blood and the heart."

Too bad she couldn't take it for her unhappy heart.

"I thought about that man at the top of the mountain," Belle continued. "I'd heard stories. About girls who sneaked up the mountain and met him." She twisted her hands, "And oh, God, I needed to prove I was still attractive. That somebody could desire me. Can you understand that?"

I nodded.

"If Ernie didn't care about me, why did it matter what I did? That's what I thought. I was a damn fool. And I kept on up the mountain, and there Isaiah Hubbel was. Out with his dogs."

Belle stopped talking and looked off into the distance—except there was no distance, so she was actually staring at a picture on the wall of Champion Boris Vlastok, a Russian wolfhound. But plainly that's not what she saw. She was looking into the past.

"Isaiah was good-looking, damn him," Belle's voice grated. "He didn't look dangerous, just standing there in a work shirt and jeans. He had a classic kind of face like you see on statues. With a straight nose and high cheeks. But with sexy, unhappy eyes."

Belle sighed and shook herself as if she wished she could shake off the memory. "He had muscles that bulged. And it was a day when the breeze was like foreplay, and I . . . He seemed so needy. And I was so empty. And so damn angry at Ernie." She looked back at me and then at Ted. "One thing led to another."

"You were in love with Isaiah?" I asked. "Or just lonely and upset and needy yourself?"

"I don't know," Belle admitted. "At the time I could hardly go twelve hours without him. I was carried away. I didn't even care if I got chigger bites in tender places. We met in Isaiah's barn because he was afraid Joan would come back unexpectedly and find us in the house. His wife, that is. God, I was a fool. I knew he was strange, but I thought I helped him. An unexpected noise would make him shake, and I'd hug him tight. Once he heard a helicopter. Probably narcs looking for marijuana. He dived out of sight because that whir reminded him of Vietnam. He was scared of everything. So he had those dogs. They behaved for him, but you should have seen their teeth. They said he had guns hidden around in case he should need one. Why would he need one?"

"You always took risks," I said.

Belle did a double take. "Not always. I woke up one morning and knew I was out of my mind. I looked over at Ernie asleep on his side of the bed. I watched him breathe, so slowly, so evenly. And I thought, suppose he stopped? A man who's asleep looks so—so vulnerable. I knew I cared about Ernie and I felt sick.

"So I told Isaiah that what we were doing was wrong. I had to try to be a better wife. He wasn't even very upset. I guess I was a lark for him. A diversion. A contact with the outside world. Maybe there really were other women who sneaked up the mountain."

In the distance I could hear the faint chorus of dogs over in the kennel section. What had set them off? Bailey let out a few woofs to join in.

Belle didn't notice.

"I told Ernie what I'd done when I was angry," she said. "I asked if we could start over. It turned out that Hot Lips Gwen had left him for another man. A young man. Ernie was upset that I'd left him, too, in a way, even though I'd come back. He was depressed for weeks. I mean *bad* depressed. Some days he wouldn't get dressed. He refused to get help. Finally he went to the doctor, who put him on Prozac, and he began to pull out of it." Belle put the dog down and stood up and began to pace. She stopped in front of a heart-shaped red picture frame. A Pekinese with a red bow in its hair peered out. The Pet Motel owner liked all kinds. Belle frowned at the picture. She was not into foolishness.

"So we tried to put things together like they were before. We both worked extra hard, and we did care about each other and we were happy," Belle said in a surprised voice. Then she began to cry.

"You were happy," I repeated, to encourage her to go on.

"Three months later he was diagnosed with lung cancer. You know, they say you are more likely to get cancer if you're depressed. I'd helped to make him depressed, hadn't I? But radiation seemed to work, and he was all right again. Then last year the cancer came back, too strong to conquer. And I lost him.

"It was Isaiah's fault! As well as my fault! We'd been lovers, and that helped to kill the man I really loved. Then I found out about the DDT. Isaiah helped kill him two ways. Two ways!" She held up two fingers as if we had to see to believe.

"Wait a minute," Ted said. "You're getting carried away now. Depression could have been a contributing factor when your husband died. DDT could have been a contributing factor. I've been looking into the DDT business on the Internet.

Some people believe it can help cause cancer. But the American Cancer Society says that's not proved. And, right now, what matters is that this man's brother intends to kill you when he doesn't take his pills."

"Belle," I said, trying to be gentle but to get through to this volatile woman, "you're going overboard here because you're feeling guilty about what you did." She started when I said that, shut her eyes, and swallowed. Was there even more I didn't know? "You loved Ernie, and he died, and you wish you'd been the best possible wife. I guess that's a natural feeling. But I'm sure he wouldn't want you in danger. He loved you, right?"

"Damned right!" she cried out, eyes opened wide. "He said he loved me even when he went off with that girl."

"O.K.," I said. "He loved you. He'd want you safe. So we need to think about what's going on. The guy who was stalking us is Isaiah's brother. Is there some kind of connection between Brad Hubbel stalking us and Isaiah Hubbel? And how does Jake Hubbel fit in? What haven't you told me about this story?"

"I was so mad at Brad Hubbel," she said, "because he looks just like Isaiah, only younger. I mean, his features do, not his white hair. He looks like the man who made my Ernie depressed—with my help, but he did it."

O.K., she was stuck on that idea.

"It was like looking at my past every day on Main Street," Belle said. "And Brad Hubbel was killing kids. Not right then, but starting them out to be addicted to tobacco. To die of lung cancer or emphysema. To die of cancer like my Ernie."

"So you threw a brick through his window," I said, "and he became more disturbed. He went out of the tobacco business and ended up in Broughton State Hospital. Weren't his brothers angry at you?"

"Damned straight," Belle said. "Jake Hubbel said he'd make me sorry. God knows what Isaiah said—he never came down the mountain, and I never went back up."

I remembered what Brad Hubbel said—how his brother told him we were dangerous.

"So maybe Jake *Make Trouble* Hubbel told Brad that you and I were spies," I said, "in order to get even with you. Maybe he planted the idea. Maybe he isn't through making trouble, and we need to watch out." Good grief, we should have called the police. "Is there anything else about the Hubbels you haven't told us?" I asked.

"No," she said, "and I'm worn out." Abruptly she picked up the dog and left. I wondered if she wanted to avoid more questions. But I was worn out myself and ready for a good night's sleep.

Where Belle was concerned, I was now prepared for absolutely anything. Or so I thought.

CHAPTER
13

THE NEXT WEEK

We deserved a vacation. Ted was able to get away. Suzie was no doubt enjoying my job to the hilt, even if she didn't want to do it forever. Azalea's party would be held the following Saturday. So we moved to the Howard Johnson's, saying goodbye to Belle and Bailey.

That would be the last we'd see of Belle in Tennessee. She said she had decided to rent a car and drop by to see a friend and then go home. I hoped she would stay out of the way of all the Hubbels. I hoped she'd keep that dog out of the way of trouble, too. I'd become too fond of Bailey and I still liked Belle. She was preposterous in a really intriguing way, and oddly brave. I told her to be careful. I told myself to mind my own business.

Ted and I spent a week being tourists with occasional calls to check on Pop and Azalea and Sandy the sitter. No one was shooting at them. "Of course not," Pop said with disdain. "I don't get into these things like you do!" Along about Wednesday, they moved to Azalea's house, next to the house where the spiders had all been zapped. Azalea's house didn't have waterspouts and colored lights and boat rides, but I hoped it would be restful, though not too restful. That brings out the worst in Pop.

Ted and I pulled out all the tourist stops. We even drove over to Memphis for a night and went to Graceland, where I sure was impressed with the homage folks paid to Elvis. Ted said it was worth making the trip just to see the fans who came to revere "the King." Like the bleached blonde with the towering hairdo, or the guy in motorcycle leather. Not your typical museum crowd. For myself, I looked at the pictures of Elvis and thought how fame can be hard—because it seemed to me that the pressures of fame had helped to kill Elvis, just as they'd helped kill Marilyn Monroe. Am I a cynic? Or was I just thinking about pressures that hurt? Some kind of inner pressure was pushing my friend Belle, maybe to destruction. Forget that, I told myself firmly.

There was no sign of a man with white hair and green eyes at the Belle Meade Museum, back in Nashville, or the Hermitage, where there were visitors from all over the world looking at Andrew Jackson's homeplace, no *Mad Brad* at the good restaurants from The Stockyard to a place with Japanese sushi. Thank goodness.

By Friday morning, we were tired of gawking and eating and ready to do something useful. So we decided to go out to Alice and Ed's house to help them get ready for the birthday party.

But first, knowing the paper would be out, I called Suzie. Everything went fine, she said, except they did a story about a new Mexican restaurant called Viva Zapata, and she'd written that it was named for the famous Mexican bandit. "Wouldn't you know a Mexican nationalist happened to be in Monroe County?" she said. "He came by in a rage, yelling, 'Zapata is a great hero!'"

"Perhaps," I said, "it's something in the air in Monroe County. You need a portable brain," I joked, "to keep track of things like who Zapata was." I told her about Professor Bright's suggestion that I get one. Of course it wouldn't tell about Zapata unless Suzie told it first. A portable psychic brain was probably not available yet.

I filled her in on *Mad Brad*. I didn't tell her about Belle's affair. She'd only tell the whole county.

"Jake Hubbel swears he'll see that Brad takes his medication. He swears he'll watch every pill go down his brother's throat. So we didn't press charges. Jake seemed terribly upset at what happened. I hope he'll make a superhuman effort."

There was a long silence. "But keep your door latched," Suzie finally said. "Be ready for anything, Peaches," she cautioned. "You seem to attract trouble."

I hoped she was overreacting. "I'll see you on Tuesday," I told her.

I sat there by the phone, considering. A portable brain would be very handy. I mean, aside from having a place for names and a calendar and an alarm. I could put ideas in it as they came to me, instead of on those little scraps of paper that always insisted on getting lost, and reappearing to thumb their noses at me when I didn't need them anymore. If I wanted to, I could transfer those ideas from the portable brain to my computer. That's what the professor had said. A computer is too big to lose without a real effort!

Ted was standing by the door, suitcase in hand, ready to depart.

"We need to go to a store that sells electronic stuff," I said. "I'm going to get one of those portable memories that Professor Bright told me about. That's just what an absent-minded reporter needs, and I've earned the money." If I was still a sleuth, I told myself, I'd need it even more. Why did some part of me go on thinking like that?

Ted just said, "You mean the thing Professor Bright suggested—the Palm Pilot."

We found ourselves in a store with banks of strange-looking, mostly black devices all around us. The store was empty except for the staff and us. They'd just opened.

The woman behind the counter said, "Oh, yes, we have what you want. I have one myself. I sell Mary Kay® products on the side, and I keep track of everyone and what they like to buy with this." She pulled out a little off-black object that fit in the palm of her hand. "So you call it a portable brain?" She laughed. "Well, why not?"

The small object in her hand was not as big as the notebook I try to carry around in my shoulder bag. It was slightly oval with a lid that she lifted up to reveal what looked like a doll's computer screen. "Now," she said, "would you like to see a list of phone numbers or your pocket calculator or your to-do list or your notepad?"

Hard to believe. All that in an object about three by four inches and no thicker than a very restrained peanut butter and jelly sandwich.

"See," she said, "I punch the little button on the bottom with the tiny phone on it. With the picture on it, you don't even have to remember which button is which." She pressed the button, and a list of names and numbers appeared on the screen.

"But that's not all," she said. She pushed a button with a tiny clock face and a grid on it. Today's date appeared across the top with places to write in what needed to be done each hour. Hers said, "Buy Chinese take-out for supper" and "Party 7:15 at Wallace's." Next to the date was a bar that said SMTWTFS. The days of the week, with today highlighted. "You can go forward or backward by day or month," she said, "and put in future appointments. And if you ask it, it will sound an alarm to remind you of a date." She was as proud as if she'd invented the thing herself.

"That's incredible," I said. "I wish I'd had this gadget when I forgot my dentist appointment."

"But that's not all!" she said, looking terribly pleased with herself. She pushed a button with a tiny picture of a pad and pencil on it. At the top of the screen, the words "To-Do List" appeared. For some reason, that was blank. She pulled a small object like a pencil out of a slot in the back of the little brain. "What shall I write?" she asked.

"Who killed Joan Hubbel?" Now why did I say that?

She looked startled. "But this is for things you have to do."

And she was right—it wasn't up to me to find that out.

She wrote "solve murder" in a marked-off space at the bottom of the screen, and it appeared on the to-do list. "Of course, that's a joke," she said. "Now, you write with a kind of special alphabet," she said. "But it's almost like the regular alphabet, and I've put a sticker with all the letters inside the cover here. I don't need that anymore, but it was useful when I started out."

"Wonderful," I said. "But if I lose this thing then I've lost my mind!"

"Not if you've transferred what you've put in here to your big computer—and there's a way to do that. There's a little booklet that tells you all about that."

This was like black magic. If I transferred the stuff to the big computer I wouldn't need the Palm Pilot in hand at my desk so much, the way I needed my little notebook. It could stay in my shoulder bag.

"Besides," Ted said, "to be safe, you can put your name and address and phone number and "reward" on the top of the cover."

Boy, Ted and the folks who'd made this had thought of everything. Maybe. "But if I put notes about who I suspect and why in here, or if I do a story about some crime and somebody finds this and reads the stuff, I could be in trouble."

Ted frowned. I hadn't meant to say that. It just slipped out.

But the clerk looked so pleased with herself, I thought she might burst. "There's a way to make things you want to keep secret disappear and only reappear with a password."

Wow.

"This booklet tells you how the calculator function works," she went on. "That's handy, too."

"But I don't need that right now," I said. "I'll learn at leisure."

So I bought the thing and got her to take it out of the box. I put the batteries in and put the little "memory" and the booklet on getting started in my shoulder bag, which was hanging over my shoulder as always when I'm out. An object with a place to live is less likely to wander off. When an object's place is hanging off of me—like in my shoulder bag—that makes it even harder to lose. Name of the game. That's why my shoulder bag is almost big enough to hold a horse.

The sales gal beamed. "This will remake your life. It will really remake your life!!"

On to Alice and Ed's. I put the plastic bag with the rest of the portable brain booklets in the glove compartment when we got back to the car. It could live there until we got home.

Azalea met us on the wide front porch of the restored 1795 house. She was wearing an apron that said Good Things Are Cooking. "We're so glad you're here," she chirped. "Pop can't wait to see you."

I went inside and found Pop in the living room, ensconced in his wheelchair near the stone fireplace. This was really some room, with the square-cut log walls and a board ceiling. Azalea had found an antique desk to put on one side and an old steeple clock for the mantelpiece, but the couch and chairs were new and overstuffed and comfortable. Perhaps it was Alice who had put green plants all around. A lovely room, but Pop was not enjoying it. Of course not. He was by himself. Everybody else was working in the kitchen. He beamed as I joined him.

"I have a present for you, Peaches," he said proudly. "Azalea and I got it yesterday because you need to use technology. It will absolutely remake your life!"

Could my life get remade twice in one day?

I was cautious. You have to watch out for Pop when he says things like that.

He wheeled himself over to the table in front of the couch and picked up a box. "This is for you! If you should go back to sleuthing," he said hopefully, "it'll help solve crimes!

But, before you open it, I have to tell you about Cousin Frank who teaches art at the college. He's only an adjunct, but the kids love him." I knew that. Cousin Frank made most of his living doing schmaltzy pictures of old-timey barns to sell to tourists in Asheville. That would hardly help solve crimes. He also did wild surrealist stuff and gave it to relatives. Pop had a canvas in black and purple and red that he hung in his guest room. Azalea usually kept that door shut.

"Frank can't remember the kids' names," Pop said. "The ones in his classes. So he lines them up in groups of five, takes a Polaroid picture, and as soon as it develops itself, he writes the names of the kids in the right order on the back. He can take his time to learn faces. The kids think it's great. He used to call them all Rembrandt and just point at the right one.

"Now open the box," he said grandly. It was a Polaroid camera. I was tempted to laugh. Did Pop consider this brand-new technology? My impatient friend Myrtle had an instant camera twenty years ago.

"I know you have trouble remembering the name of everybody who comes in your newspaper office," Pop proclaimed. "Now you can take a Polaroid of the same people you take a regular news picture of, and immediately write the names on it so there's no chance you'll get the pictures for the paper mixed up later."

He didn't have to remind me how a picture of the man accused of arson, of actually trying to burn down the First Baptist church, was somehow switched with the picture of the head of the Kiwanis Club three weeks ago. Oh, brother! O.K., Pop, you win. This could do the one thing my portable brain couldn't: Remember a face.

I went over and gave Pop a hug and thanked him. I put the

camera in with the portable brain in my shoulder bag. The bag was getting so heavy I might list to one side, but at least I was armed with technology. I wheeled Pop into the kitchen where he'd be part of the preparations even if he was a little bit in the way. He has to be in the thick of things. We all know that. I did not tell him about the "brain." I didn't want to steal his thunder.

At the party the next day, which was Saturday, he had me take a picture of each guest with the birthday present that guest brought, and label it. Everyone thought that was fun.

Too bad I'd given up running down suspects, I told myself. It would have been great to have a labeled picture of each one.

But avoiding suspects and writing warm fuzzy stories was my job now. I could almost do it without a brain, portable as Professor Bright suggested, or otherwise. Still, after we'd helped all Azalea's neighbors from Tennessee wish her a happy birthday, I was more than ready to go home and get back to work. So was Ted.

I called Suzie once more Saturday night.

"Hi," I said. "I'll be on my way tomorrow. Anything new?"

"I'm glad you're coming," she said. "My mother's very sick, and I have to go to South Carolina. I've left you notes at the office on what's in progress. But take care of yourself and be ready for anything, like I said."

I hung up and wondered: Did she know even more about Belle or the Hubbels than what I'd learned? I always thought Suzie told all. She told what suited her, that's what.

CHAPTER
14

MONDAY

I went in to work on Monday with some misgivings, but I couldn't just stop living my life because a man thought I was a spy when he didn't take his pills. Ted didn't try to stop me. After all, if Brad made up his mind to find me, he'd find me, even over in my own Buncombe County.

Martin welcomed me back and gave me a few press releases to rewrite. He was wearing a shirt covered with four-leaf clovers. I think he gets his shirts at tag sales—shirts that people get for birthdays and aren't quite up to wearing. He is. I told his departing back that I liked his shirt. "We could use some four-leaf clovers."

A few minutes and phone rings later, he came back with a hang-dog look. He said, "Jake Hubbel has asked to come by and talk to you and me today."

"Certainly talking with you should be enough," I said briskly. Jake would never be my good luck.

Martin pulled at one earlobe and frowned. "I think he may want to apologize again for letting his brother Brad bother you." *Bother* was putting it mildly. I could still feel that gun in my back. How was I to know it wasn't real?

"I'd like us to stay on Jake's good side," Martin said. "He has pull in this town. He gives to every good cause there is." He did not add what I knew, that Jake was a big advertiser. "He'll be here in about half an hour," Martin said. "I'd appreciate it if you'd come to the meeting."

I started to say no. But what the heck, he wasn't asking me to slant a news story or anything like that. Ted would divorce me for agreeing to do that. But I figured I could go to the meeting and still stay out of trouble. And I was curious. What now?

I stayed busy. A large cheerful woman came in and gave me two birth announcements. Two grandchildren born on the same day. One in Florida, one in Ohio. Human interest. I saw her to the door and thanked her. "I have to hurry," she said. "It's ten-fifteen, and I'm late."

I came back to my desk and sat down. No birth announcements. They'd vanished. That fast! I was searching all over my desk when I heard the door open. I heard Martin say, "Good morning, Jake." Then he leaned in my door and said, "I hope you'll join us."

I wanted to put those announcements in the to-do basket, to be sure they weren't lost forever.

On the bulletin board I noticed that dern flyer that said YOU CAN BE PERFECT. Why hadn't I thrown it out yet? I wanted to pull it down, stamp on it, and put up my own motto: "Use what you can do to get around what you can't do, and to heck with the people who say that's not enough!"

I wrote myself a note: "Find birth announcements," and posted it on my computer. I got up to join Martin and Jake *Make Trouble* Hubbel. And there were the lost announcements in my chair. I'd been sitting on them. I found them! A good omen, I told myself. O.K., so maybe I was grasping at good omens.

Jake and Martin stood in front of Martin's desk. Jake said, "You've been told ugly stuff and lies about my brother Isaiah." He didn't beat around the bush. "Everybody in this county is hearing this ugly stuff. I want you to come meet Isaiah and do a story about his life on that mountain. You do profiles of people like the one about that missionary back from South Africa. The only decent thing is to tell about my brother's life the way it really is, including his service to his country. We have a right to be proud of that."

"We can probably do that," Martin said. I didn't like that *we*.

"I want you to come now," Jake said. "I've prepared him. He's waiting for us." He stood there, feet planted apart, daring us. He eyed me as if I owed him one. For what? Not quite allowing his brother Brad to kill me?

I said, "I'll stay here and be sure everything is O.K. in the office."

"No," Jake Hubbel said. "You heard the rumors. You believed them. I expect you to come."

Martin sent me a pleading look. Well, I asked myself, what harm could it really do, with Martin along? "But Martin will write the story," I said. Jake agreed.

Martin reached for his camera.

"No pictures of the present," Jake said. "I promised Isaiah that. We have pictures of him in his Vietnam War uniform."

So Martin hung his camera back on its hook on the wall, and we set forth.

I admit I was intrigued to see the mountain where so much had happened. Maybe. But crawly feelings in my stomach told me, *Watch out*.

"We'll go in my four-wheel-drive pickup," Jake said. "The road is steep and washed out in one spot. A regular vehicle would have trouble."

It hadn't rained in over a week. I wondered if they left the washout to discourage anyone from going up to visit the King of the Mountain, as Belle called him.

"One minute," I said, and got my shoulder bag that holds everything from Kleenex and a plastic rain hat, to my portable brain and instant camera. For a girl who was not after bear, so to speak, I was loaded for it.

Mountain View Road seemed peaceful in the morning sun. A tow-headed boy was bouncing a ball in the yard of the doublewide with all the whirligigs. At the big old white house, that darn blue Volkswagen was in the driveway just as it was the day I found Belle conked out in the woods. Was Albert Bright, the memory prof, visiting again? The guy whose sister was married to Isaiah Hubbel? A small feist, that spunky mountain-dog breed, barked at us from the yard with the rubber tire swing. There was nobody in sight, not even cars in the drives of the next two houses before the long gravel drive up to Isaiah Hubbel's house. We turned in and began to snake up the so-called mountain. The truck jounced on the rough road. "Hold on tight," Jake warned.

The woods were lovely with wildflowers, something yellow I didn't recognize. I remembered how Belle said the spring flowers helped seduce her. Belle. She would have noticed the dogwood just beginning to show white, and the maples as red as fall but with the color of new life, not the color of leavetaking. The woods smelled fresh and loamy. The long ride up was so lovely and new-green I almost forgot the waffly feeling in my stomach. Then, around a curve, a silver-gray house came into view.

Why had I thought Isaiah Hubbel's house would be dilapidated? Because his life was? This was a square-cut-log house, not with brown logs like mine or Pop's in Tennessee. These logs had weathered to the color of shined pewter. The roof was silvery tin, backed by green pines. Not a small house. You could see the outlines of three rooms along the end of the house. Each room had its own logs mitered into the logs of the next room. Like the Lincoln Log houses I used to build as a kid, except for a long porch on the side that faced down the mountain.

Jake said, "This was the family homeplace." There was awe or affection in his voice. The family homeplace mattered. "I lived here as a kid," he said. "There've been Hubbels in this house since my great-grandfather built it over a hundred years ago." We all got out of the pickup, and he led the way toward the house.

I sensed that something was missing, though I couldn't think what it was. Something that ought to be here. I was nearly to the top of the steps to the porch, steps made of half-rounds of log, when it came to me. No dogs. Not that I longed for Dobermans to accost me. "Where are the dogs?" I whispered to Martin. In a pen, perhaps. But why weren't they barking? As if to warn us that the porch, with its slat rockers set out, was not a place of peace and quiet, a gust of wind hit us and made all the chairs rock.

"There's a storm coming," Martin said.

The view down the mountain from the porch was delicate as lace—dark tree outlines and young green leaves, still again as if the gust had been a feint.

Jake knocked on the front door. Martin stood poised to go inside with him, but nobody came. Another gust hit us and diminished. An unpredictable wind.

Still no answer to Jake's knock. I noticed that all but one of the potted begonias along the half-round log rail of the porch were wilted, were begging for water. I could hear some insect buzzing. A crow cawed on some tree out of sight. Otherwise dead silence. Jake tried the door, opened it, and stuck his head in. Strange. If Isaiah was so paranoid, I would have expected him to lock the door. I had the impression Jake thought the front door would be locked.

"Wait here a minute," he said. "Let me be sure he's O.K. with this." He shut the door and left us on the porch. It must be hard to deal with a brother so full of fears, I realized. Meanwhile the wind continued to come in waves. In a short while, Jake came back. "I don't see Isaiah," he said, "but come on in out of the cold. I haven't finished looking."

I stepped inside out of the wind, which was sure of itself now and whipping at my shirt. A gust came in with us and rattled gold-rimmed china plates that hung on the wall.

"Shut the door tight," Jake said. "Sometimes it doesn't catch." He sounded distracted and was hurrying forward.

We'd stepped into family history, and into eerie silence. "Isaiah," his brother called, as if the man might suddenly decide to break his silence. Was Isaiah prone to hide? No answer. I was so startled by the room, I almost forgot to be unnerved by the silence. I had the impression everything that had ever happened in this family had left a trace. On one side of a big stone fireplace just to our left was a primitive armchair made of logs and holding huge dark green cushions. On the other side were two small straight chairs, mahogany perhaps, with intricately carved backs. We walked past a fairly modern couch that faced the fireplace.

Jake was frowning. "Isaiah?" he called again, more urgently. I was so distracted, I bumped a set of shelves that held small figurines, china vases, and candlesticks. They teetered.

Jake was headed toward a doorway that led to a small hall, with Martin right at his heels. I held back.

My eye was drawn to the couch. On one end was a thin red leash. Was it Bailey's leash? How odd. Was Belle here? Not judging by the silence. The leash scared me. Had Belle come up here to confront Isaiah Hubbel with her suspicions that he'd killed his wife? Had something gone wrong? But Jake Hubbel said he'd just been here to see Isaiah. He'd told his brother we were coming, asked him to be ready to talk to us. Maybe Isaiah had lost his nerve. He could even be crouched behind that Victorian-looking loveseat with the red velvet cushions on the other side of the room. I looked. Not there.

I made myself follow Jake and Martin into a small room with a high-backed recliner chair and a TV set. "He'd certainly hear us if he was here," Jake said. Isaiah was nowhere in sight. The chair faced away from us, toward the TV, toward a wall with pictures of various relatives in clothes from the 1920's, the 1990's, and more. One picture was vintage, about 1900. I bet it was the one that Great-Grandpa Hubbel had used to electioneer. He wore a formal dark suit and had a belligerent square jaw like Jake's.

This was definitely not a redneck house. It belonged to a

family with pretensions to live up to. Jake probably wore that John Deere cap to look rural, to sell more cars in this rural county.

There was a desk with a computer near the door. Suzie said Isaiah Hubbel surfed the Internet. Amazing. He never left his mountain but he could chat with Addis Ababa or Finland or Sierra Leone.

Nothing ominous here that I could see, but the silence was still unnerving. No sound but the house creaking in the wind. Out a window to my right, I saw trees writhing in the wind.

Jake Hubbel went around to the front of the high-backed chair. He let out a choked cry. Then he managed words: "Isaiah! Can you hear me?" Jake's voice came out high-pitched with fright. He leaned over and ministered to his brother in some way, hidden from me by the back of the chair. He stood up and looked me straight in the eye, amazed. "My God, he's dead."

CHAPTER
15

IMMEDIATELY AFTERWARD

Martin took a tissue out of a box on the table by the chair, picked up the phone with it, and dialed 911. He reported Isaiah Hubbel shot. He explained where we were.

In the distance, a door slammed. Jake had been staring at his brother, frozen. The sudden, loud noise shocked him back to action. He ran out of the room with alarm on his face as if he was afraid whoever had slammed that door would get away. Martin followed him.

I went around to the front of the recliner, took the Polaroid camera out of my bag, and photographed Isaiah Hubbel, plainly dead. Pop would approve. Isaiah could no longer care. The undeveloped picture popped out of the camera, milky gray. I held it by the edge, waiting for the image to come clear, and studied Isaiah.

I'd heard so much about him and had never seen him

alive. He wasn't young, but even at a glance I could see he was strikingly good-looking, with classic features and curly gray hair. He was wearing a red flannel shirt and was appropriately pale as death, but no wounds showed except for a small, round, dark hole in the front of his shirt. I realized that the color of his shirt largely masked the blood. There was only a part of the red that looked wet. The small table by his side held a jar of pencils, a box of tissues, and all sorts of other useful stuff. I couldn't stop to contemplate. I heard steps coming. I shut the camera and put it in my shoulder bag. I put the half-developed picture in my shirt pocket.

Jake ran back in the room, looking distraught, not angry and self-assured as I'd seen him before. "It was the damn door," he said. "It blew open. Then it slammed and blew open again." He gave me a dirty look. "I thought it was . . ." He stopped, pulled off his John Deere cap, and crushed it in his hands. "I thought it might be whoever did this, getting out of here. We couldn't find anyone."

I looked at the body with its staring eyes. "I'm going to be sick," I said.

"Then go to the damn bathroom right down the hall," Jake said with disdain.

Actually, I wasn't going to be sick. I wanted to know what else was in this house. Were there any significant objects around besides that red leash? I wouldn't touch anything, just take a quick look. A part of me knew I shouldn't, but another part of me knew this would be my only chance. I wanted some evidence to prove that Belle wasn't the only visitor who might have been in this house around the time that Isaiah Hubbel was shot. I wanted that a lot. On the way out the door, I passed Martin coming in. I reached in my pocket and handed him the picture of Isaiah's body.

In the hallway a long shelf held a collection of handmade brown and white baskets. I hurried by so fast the weaving seemed to undulate. Nothing was solid. My old chum Belle said Isaiah killed his wife, but someone had killed Isaiah. And Belle may have been here.

The bathroom, with an old-fashioned, white enamel, claw-foot tub, was on my left, the door half open. I went inside and shut the door. I took a tissue from a box on the toilet top for opening the cabinet under the sink to see if there really was a gun even in the bathroom as Maureen had said. I was going to be good, but I figured I could just check that one thing, so I opened the cabinet. It smelled musty and held extra rolls of toilet paper, a plastic bottle of bleach, and an ancient-looking rag. No gun. But wait! Maureen had said the gun was taped inside the top of the toilet tank. Now I remembered. I took the top off and looked at the underside. No gun. But a bit of tape was stuck to the top as if something had been fastened there. Had someone taken a gun from there? Who knew it was there besides Maureen? I put the top back the way I found it.

Out in the hall again, I noticed an open door on my right. I looked into a room with frilly curtains. Joan's room? An open closet door revealed some of her clothes. A lot of black and white. A white terry bathrobe hung over a small chair as if she was still living here. The bed was single, and covered with a quilt in many shades of blue, in the shape of a large star. So where had Isaiah slept? Evidently not here. Had he kept a gun in this room? I mustn't push my luck and search, but I noticed an open laundry hamper with the dirty clothes half tossed in. Odd in this neat room. I peered into the hamper but I didn't move the clothes.

At any moment I expected Jake Hubbel to call me to find

out why it was taking me so long to be sick. He was evidently too upset to notice. Good. I came back out to the hall and found a stairway up. Quite steep. That was because the ceilings were so high. I ran up quick and found that upstairs the rooms were cluttered and less formal. On one side of the stairwell was a bed with a hand-pieced crazy quilt and the covers pulled back in a triangle. Several shirts hung on a coat tree, and an old dresser stood along the back wall. One drawer of the dresser hung open. I glanced into it. Underwear and socks. There was no wall separating this nook from the stairs, only a rustic railing. Isaiah's nook perhaps? Isaiah who left his wife's larger, more comfortable room untouched when she vanished, as if it was off limits. Because he'd killed her? And had someone found revenge?

On the other side of the stairwell was an attic room with a door. Inside were suitcases, odd chairs, a kitchen cabinet. Boxes of papers and books were all over the floor. One suitcase was thrown open, but there was nothing in it. Papers were strewn everywhere. The stone chimney from downstairs thrust its way through this upstairs room and out through the ceiling. A jacket had been left at the foot of a cot in one corner of the room. The same kind of jacket that *Mad Brad* had worn in Tennessee. I felt a jolt of hope. Had he come to this house and killed Isaiah? Better him than Belle. He had a medical excuse. I felt a jolt of fear. Of course, *Mad Brad* was the one most likely to be hiding in this house. But there was no sign of Brad in the flesh. I ran down the stairs so fast it's amazing I didn't fall.

I heard the sound of a car coming up the road.

I could hear Jake and Martin hurrying toward the front door to investigate. I thought this was fast for the sheriff's folks to have arrived. They must have been in the neighborhood.

I hurried down the hall to the door of the room where Isaiah lay dead. I heard a car door slam. One person arriving? I heard the front door opening. Isaiah and Martin gone out to meet the law? I don't know what possessed me, but I hurried around and took another picture of the body. With all important things, it's good to have two records. We paper losers have that creed. But Martin had the other picture in safekeeping. Maybe that two-record thing was simply habit. Or maybe I had some kind of hunch that this could be important. I snapped the picture and held it in my hand as it began to develop. I heard voices getting closer. I put the camera in my bag, the picture in my pocket. I left the murder scene and joined Jake and Martin as they came back in the front door.

The law did not come with them, and, in fact, had not arrived. Instead, there stood Maureen in a pretty blue velvety dress that matched her eyes, and carrying a bunch of jonquils.

"Hi," she said. "I came to see Uncle Isaiah."

Jake adjusted the John Deere cap on his head and seemed too choked to speak.

Maureen frowned. "Is something wrong?" She looked from one of us to the other.

Jake glared at her and said, "Yes! You're damn right something is wrong! Somebody shot Isaiah. And don't you dare say 'I told you so.'"

CHAPTER
16

A FEW MOMENTS LATER

What on earth did Jake mean? *Don't say 'I told you so.'*
Why would Maureen have told him that Isaiah Hubbel was
going to get shot? Just because of the guns? I didn't have too
much time to think about that because the sheriff's men arrived, and there I was, being grilled. I'd been one of those
who found the body, right?

My friend the red-haired deputy took me in the kitchen
and questioned me while Martin and Jake and Maureen
were interviewed in other rooms. He laughed when I said I
was only on the scene as a reporter.

He was the one who did the news for the firefighters, the
one who had acted so pleased when he said he'd heard that
I was murder-prone, just naturally drawn to murders the way
some aunt of his was accident prone. Thanks a lot! Well, this

dead man would certainly convince him I was. I should have stood my ground and stayed back at the office.

"Have a seat," the deputy said, indicating the straight-backed kitchen chairs. I sat down across from him at the small table. "Now, what made you come here?" he said. "Did you just get a feeling?" Not your conventional deputy. I hoped it wouldn't get him in trouble. I liked his eyes. I noticed a birthmark on his cheek in the shape of a star. How appropriate.

"My only feeling," I said, "was that I should stay away from this place." I told him about Maureen Hubbel saying her uncle Isaiah kept a gun in each room, and about Belle believing Isaiah had murdered his wife. That was no secret.

I wondered if there was a gun in the pine cupboard behind the deputy, or in the cupboard under the sink, or what. "This place sounded as if it was just waiting for a disaster," I said. "I only came today as a favor to Martin because Jake Hubbel wanted us to know the good side of his brother, because of all the rumors we'd heard. I wasn't even going to write a feature about him. Martin was going to do that." And probably I was persuaded to come because I was so curious, I admitted to myself. Was I murder prone?

Out the window over the sink, the sky was now dazzling blue, and the trees were still. The storm had blown itself out. I had a feeling the storm inside this house would get more dangerous.

"You're friends with Belle Dasher," he said. "You found her in the woods hit over the head." Belle was a dangerous subject.

"I was afraid I'd found her dead," I said.

"Me, too," he said, "because you were there."

Good grief, was he stuck on that?

"Do you know where Belle Dasher was this morning?" he asked. That caught me off guard. I didn't really know, but the leash on the couch made me think she'd been there with Bailey. I didn't have to speculate. They could do that.

"I haven't seen her today," I said.

He looked skeptical. He pressed me to tell when I'd last seen her. So I told him everything except about her affair with Isaiah Hubbel. He didn't ask me about it, so I figured I could keep that to myself. At least for now. One woman owes a certain degree of privacy to another. I'd let her keep the cupboard doors of her life shut.

"But you saw things around here that made you think, right? That made you get goose bumps. My granny says that can happen when a person is on the right track."

"Not exactly goose bumps," I said. "But I knew something was wrong when the dogs didn't bark."

"You didn't have 'feelings' about anything here?"

I figured it couldn't hurt to tell my feelings. "I felt the house was full of clues to what kind of man Isaiah Hubbel was. But I haven't sorted them out yet, except this house makes me feel weird. Like the people in it were so separated. Each one into a fear of his or her own. And nobody watered the flowerpots on the front porch, except for one."

To my surprise, he actually wrote that down.

Then he had me trace my steps from the moment I entered the house. I admitted looking under the toilet tank top. He whistled at the piece of tape.

I admitted having photographed poor Isaiah. "You better keep that picture," he said after he looked at the Polaroid shot I had in hand. "We take our own, and that may tune you into something. Now, if you have any more 'feelings,' just call me. And be sure to ask for me. Not all our folks believe in this kind of thing, but I figure any way we can catch a killer is a good way." Too bad I wasn't sleuthing. Too bad I couldn't use his help.

"I do have a feeling right now," I said. "I have a feeling that these cupboards hold a clue." Was that true, or was I just still incurably curious? A closed cupboard is such a challenge. But he didn't open them for me.

"I'll look in those cupboards extra careful," he said. Then he let me go and gave me a ride back to the office. I had a "feeling" as we passed the Ford dealership. Whatever was going wrong involved the kind of people all the Hubbels were, not just Isaiah: proud and looking out for their own. Nothing wrong with that unless you carried it too far. Well, I thought as I walked into the newspaper office, Martin was the one who would look into that. He and the sheriff and Deputy—Oh, my gosh, I didn't know the deputy's name. He must have told me, but I'd been too upset to pay attention. So, O.K., I may be murder prone and I may seem calm. But I'm outraged that one human being feels he has a right to kill another.

I hoped Martin would know who my deputy was, or Suzie would know which deputy had red hair and a birthmark. Of course. If you know who knows, it's almost as good as knowing a name to begin with. It takes longer, but on the other hand, you learn more in the process. Too bad Martin was out, probably still at Isaiah's house. Suzie wasn't home. Pat in Advertising came back from visiting clients and asked if anything was up. I said, "Boy, was there ever," and filled her in.

"Jake Hubbel is one of our biggest advertisers," she said. "Thank goodness *he* wasn't murdered." Well, everybody has his own slant.

I ate a late lunch at my desk and tried not to dwell on the Hubbels, dead or alive. I did the story about the Monroe Players and marked a picture of a man with a deliberately silly grin to go with it. I looked at Suzie's story about the high school fundraiser. She'd done a good job.

I checked for anything else on my desk that needed doing and found a small package with some new mail, addressed to "Peaches Dann, Author." A fan must have found out about my new job. The package contained an artificial red geranium, along with a note on flowered paper. *"How to Survive Without a Memory* is the book I've always needed," my fan wrote. I needed that lift! "As a token of my appreciation, this flower goes with your Rule No. 3—*never hesitate to do something that some folks think looks silly, if that thing really works for you.* Fasten this flower to the tip of your car radio antenna. I haven't lost my car in a parking lot since I did this."

Well, this geranium might not look professional, but I made a note to follow my own rule.

While I was reading the note, something gnawed at the back of my mind. Something to do with my pictures of Isaiah Hubbel. The one I took first and gave to Martin, and the one I took afterwards and had in my bag. I took it out and stared at it. Since the first picture was taken, someone had closed Isaiah Hubbel's eyes. It was easier to look at him with his eyes closed. But something else was different. I couldn't think what. Never mind. Not my worry. Still, I couldn't quite turn the worry off.

Isaiah's death was beginning to get to me. When I first see death I feel numb. Angry but numb. Which is actually useful. My mind stays clear. But gradually the realization grows that this living, breathing person who had needs and wants just as I do, has been mowed down without pity. And the person who did that is lurking somewhere. Talk about goose bumps.

I thought of Isaiah Hubbel with his nerve screwed up to tell us about his experiences in the war, experiences so terrible that he lost his ability to relate to outsiders, even to leave his mountain. Someone then went into his house, into the room where he must have felt safe sitting in his favorite chair, and shot him.

What was gnawing at my mind about Isaiah Hubbel in that chair? Something was wrong—I mean aside from the obvious fact that he was dead. Something was wrong, but I couldn't think what.

Martin didn't come back. That wasn't unusual. News happened where it happened, and he covered it wherever it was.

I said goodbye to Pat in Advertising, who said she'd lock up. I went home to my safe and comfortable house to share my day with Ted and hear about his. With any luck, his day would have been less violent. I told myself he was not murder prone.

CHAPTER
17

LATE MONDAY AFTERNOON

How lucky I am to have a warm family to go home to. Not that we're a large family in residence. Just Ted and me and the cat. Pop can be another story, ready to stir things up at any cost, but he's at his own house, thank goodness, and Azalea knows how to handle him.

I live in a cul-de-sac with lots of trees. Talk about murder prone, maybe I'm square-cut-log prone. My house is not as old as the 1795 one Pop and Azalea restored in Tennessee. It's probably not as old as the one where Isaiah Hubbel died, either. That one is silver-gray with age. But mine is a chocolate stack-cake. The logs were creosoted to make them last, which also makes them dark brown. The chinking between is creamy white. My welcoming home. Alongside the house is a large stone terrace where we can sit and relax in warm weather, but today I wanted to be enclosed by walls. Not that walls had helped Isaiah Hubbel, but I'd feel protected inside mine, among my favorite things, such as the antique log-cabin-pattern quilt that hangs in the dining area. I'm always pleased by the wonderful greens and browns and the red dots that symbolized the fireplace to warm every house.

Rain and wind made it hard to drive. The weatherman had said we might even have tornadoes, but I got home safely. There was a brown Honda in my driveway. Suzie had said be ready for anything. She'd been right.

But somehow I was not ready for the young man who was banging on our door. He wore a citified brown business suit, wet from the rain, and city shoes and he carried a large rifle. At least he didn't have white hair. I could rule out *Mad Brad* even from a distance.

I don't know guns, but the one this man held was certainly large enough to kill a deer, and possibly a rhinoceros, except there aren't any rhinoceroses in Buncombe County. He saw me and started running full tilt toward the car, getting even wetter. My heart beat hard, but I rolled my window down two inches. The car windows are not bulletproof anyway. The young man came right to the window, out of breath, and gasped, "I'm worried sick about my mother."

"I'll bet you're Belle Dasher's son," I blurted. "You're George." That figured. But why the gun?

He looked startled, as if I were psychic. "Yes. But where is she?" he demanded.

"Come in the house," I said as I got out of the car, holding my umbrella over both of us. The gun looked dangerous, but he didn't. He looked scared. He also looked a little like Belle. Same square jaw, same direct eyes. I unlocked the door, opened it wide, and he came inside, dripping.

"Is that gun loaded?" I asked.

He stared at it in horror. "I assumed it wasn't," he said. "But I don't know. I don't know guns. How do you tell?" Not your typical resident of Monroe County.

"Just don't point it at anybody," I said firmly. I didn't want him to shoot me by mistake while he found out if it was loaded. So, if he didn't know guns, why was he carrying one?

"Sit down," I said, pointing to a wooden rocker that wouldn't mind if he was wet. I sat down on the couch. "Now, what's wrong?"

"This morning," he said, "I called the number my mother gave me in Tennessee, and she's not there." He began to rock in an agitated way.

So where was Belle? I'd have loved to think she'd spent the day saving a hurt cat or socking the one that hurt it, or some such. But why was Bailey's leash on Isaiah Hubbel's couch? I didn't ask George that. I waited to hear his story. His and the gun's.

"Ted and I saw your mother Sunday before last," I said. "Then she went her way, and we went ours. I had the impression she was coming back to Monroe County."

"You're her friend," he said urgently in a please-say-it's-true tone. "I need your help. I need to talk to somebody who knows about things, but isn't"—he groped for a word—"official."

What did he mean about *things?* Did he know Isaiah was dead?

He put the gun on the table next to the chair. He pointed at it and said, "I went to my mother's place early this morning. She wasn't there. I called her at the number I had for her at a motel in Tennessee. They said she checked out several days ago and didn't say a word about where she was going next. I thought I saw her car drive right by her house without stopping and go in the direction of Isaiah Hubbel's house. She'd said so much angry stuff about him, I panicked. I drove up his mountain, but her car wasn't there. Thank God it wasn't there. So I drove back down and looked several other places." He hardly stopped for breath.

"Then I heard on the radio . . ." His voice began to shake. "I heard on the radio that Isaiah Hubbel had been shot. I was so scared! I know my mother wouldn't shoot anybody. I know it. But still I was scared." He began to shake all over.

"You're wet and cold," I said. "Put this throw around you." I handed him the one with sunflowers all over it, an odd contrast to his fear.

"I went back to her house to look more carefully for any clue to where she could be. I walked through her house and checked every room, even the wastebaskets, and in her bedroom her bed looked a little lopsided." There were frown lines between his eyes, and he balled his hands into fists. "She has a big puffy quilt she uses instead of a bedspread. I pulled it back to see what could be under it."

For a horrible moment I thought he was going to say a body.

He turned to me with amazement. "This gun was under her quilt."

Whew!

I heard the front door open. I started. It was Ted, thank goodness.

"This is George Dasher, Belle's son," I told Ted as he took off his raincoat and hung it up on the coat tree. I stood up, and he gave me a hug.

He said, "I just heard the news on the radio on the way home."

"You mean about Isaiah Hubbel?" I asked. He nodded.

"George is upset about that, too," I said, and I asked George to tell his story again.

"Why would my mother hide a gun?" he ended. "Why?"

"You never saw this gun before that?" Ted asked. He was sitting in the overstuffed chair next to George's rocker.

"Never," George said intently. "I was afraid . . ." He paused as if he had to explore what he was afraid of before he could just say it. "She's been acting so strange since my father died. I don't know whether she's just still so upset that she behaves in ways that don't make sense to me. Or what. I don't know what to do. Maybe she had this gun to make her feel safe." A look of terror flashed through his eyes. "But what kind of gun was Isaiah Hubbel killed with?"

"I think it was a handgun," I said. I didn't explain that only a handgun could have been taped to the toilet tank top, and then vanish. If that was really what happened.

Interesting. I did not tell George about the leash. There could be more than one red leash in the world. The less said the better.

He smiled, and some of the tension went out of him. "I hope to God you're right," he said. He stood up. "I guess I'll put this gun right back where I found it." That sounded like a bad idea to me, but I wasn't sure what he should do.

"I think you need a drink," Ted said.

George said no, but coffee would be wonderful. Turned out he'd been so upset he never ate lunch.

We all went into our nice lemon-yellow kitchen, and Ted made coffee while I made curried tuna fish sandwiches with chutney, checking first that he liked spice. That was quick, and he needed something special. We sat down at the kitchen table, and he bit into his sandwich as intensely as a starving man.

"My mother has always been emotional," he said between bites. He said it as if he was still trying to sort things out. "She cries at the movies." He smiled, amused. "Once a man next to her got up and moved because he couldn't stand it. When she gets mad, she gets super-mad. She tells people off." He frowned, bothered by that. "But she's a great friend. When Alice Hooper, her best friend, was getting ready to move to Canada, Ma went over and helped her pack all her stuff. She stayed until it was all in the moving van, and then she took Alice out to dinner at the Western Steer."

"When did her friend leave?" I asked.

"About six months ago. Ma took it hard. Then her dog died. The little dachshund is new. From the Friends of Animals breed-saver folks."

How typical of Belle to get an orphan dog.

Poor Belle, she'd had a year of loss, big and small. And she was impulsive and emotional to begin with. I again remembered the time she walked right up and socked the school bully because he was going after a sensitive fat kid who didn't know how to fight back. Then there was the brick last year. She'd cracked up a little when she threw that, I figured. Also, Suzie said she'd been drinking. Now George was obviously scared she'd absolutely cracked and killed Isaiah with the rhinoceros gun.

What would it take beyond believing that Isaiah caused her cancer, helped kill her husband, and killed his own wife? It would take some special cruelty to trigger action. Something he did that enraged her. I couldn't imagine what. But I was sure Belle hadn't told me everything. I prayed she hadn't killed Isaiah with the handgun from the toilet top.

"I've tried to help Mother," George said. He fingered his coffee cup. "But I don't really know what to do. I don't know how to help and still have a life. I wanted to marry a wonderful girl who would have upset my mother something awful. I even gave that up, at least for now." He sighed.

"Maureen Hubbel?" I asked. I have my impulsive blurts, too.

But he didn't seem to mind. In fact, he smiled. "Yes. Maureen's great. She's so enthusiastic about life. She . . ." He shrugged.

So he hadn't told Maureen the real reason he couldn't marry her. Out of loyalty to his mother, perhaps.

"If I hear anything, I'll get in touch," I said. "Leave me your telephone number."

"Be very careful with that gun," Ted added. "Lock it up somewhere. Have you got a closet that locks?"

George said "Yes, and I'd better put it there."

"It looks as if Isaiah Hubbel may have been killed with his own gun," I said. "You don't want that to happen to your mother."

So why hadn't I told him what I suspected? About the leash. Was it because I'd promised Ted not to get mixed up in solving any murders? Or was it because I wanted to protect Belle? But this was her own son. I guess I figured she had a right to tell him herself, whatever happened.

CHAPTER
18

George felt a little better when he left, I think. Perhaps he should have felt worse. I sure did. I rinsed off his plate and put it in the dishwasher. I wished I could rinse off my worries.

"Let's go sit in the soft," Ted said. That means the living room, where the chairs are more comfortable long-term. I followed him in. My eyes went to the cross-stitch sampler I did as a kid, hanging on the wall near the front door. The stitches weren't perfect, but you don't throw those things out. It said "Welcome to this house."

Isaiah had been waiting for us, ready to welcome us, when someone shot him.

I shivered. I took comfort from my favorite things such as the lamp with the carved face emerging from the wood. The wooden face always seemed about to wink, as if to say, It'll be all right. Silk, the cat I acquired from Pop, ran over and rubbed against my leg. I needed that.

Ted stood next to me. I could feel his warmth. "I hope that finding Isaiah's body wasn't too gruesome," he said.

I told him with my head against his shoulder. "Not a lot of blood or anything. But it did upset me." I tried to make light of finding the body. "The deputy who took my statement says I'm murder prone." I burst into tears. Not like me. I don't cry; I decide what to do next. Ted put his arms around me, and I wept.

"Somehow," I sobbed, "when there's been a murder that touches my life and I can *do* something, I feel better. When I can't, I feel helpless, as if evil is winning. I don't want to be murder prone and also no use at all." As soon as I blurted that out, I was ashamed of myself. I'd make Ted feel bad on top of everything else.

He pointed to the overstuffed chair and said, "You need to sit down." He handed me a glass of white wine I hadn't even seen him pour and gave me a kind where-else-does-it-hurt glance. He said, "Tell me what happened."

"Yes, that will help," I said, firmly pulling myself together. I told him all the details. It took a while. "Don't worry," I said, holding myself rigid. "I am not going to get mixed up in this."

At that moment the doorbell rang. "Don't answer it," I said. "It's going to be something else to do with the murder. I'm jinxed! And I'll feel even more helpless." I realized that was foolish. We had to answer.

We both went to the door, and there stood Belle. Belle! Found again. Rain blew in around her on sharp gusts. She was holding Bailey and struggling with an umbrella that had blown inside out. Bailey had on a green leash, not the familiar red one. A clap of thunder. How appropriate for the weather to get worse.

"Come in," I said. "Your son, George, is looking for you," I added. "He's worried to death. Where have you been?"

I knew one place she'd been. The red leash on the couch at Isaiah Hubbel's house evidently really had been Bailey's. I wanted to groan.

Ted shut the door behind Belle, pointed to the couch, and said, "Come sit down and tell us."

"I didn't kill Isaiah Hubbel," she announced, standing stock-still and dripping on the floor. She said it angrily, as if we'd accused her. She took off her raincoat, hung it on the coat tree, and plunked herself on the couch. She took off Bailey's incriminating leash. He ran over to greet me. The dog that might get his much-loved mistress the death sentence.

"What *did* you do?" I asked. I sounded angry. No point in that. I knew she wouldn't get right to the point. She'd meander up to it.

"This morning, early, I saw Maureen Hubbel in the grocery store," Belle said. "She was telling some woman with odd-looking blond hair that she was on the way to take Isaiah Hubbel's dogs to the vet. I meant to leave before Maureen saw me. I tried to hide behind a canned ham display. But she came around that way and tried to butter me up. She's sweet on my son, but I'm damned if I want him to go out with a Hubbel." Her eyes flashed so that I expected smoke to come out of her ears. Another clap of thunder.

"I followed Maureen's car at a distance," Belle continued, "and as soon as she came back down Hubbel Mountain with the dogs in her car, I meant to go up. I'd made up my mind I ought to go confront Isaiah, not skulk around and search his place at night. The nighttime thing was a dumb idea. But I didn't want to go when he could sic the dogs on me. The last time I talked to him, he said that's what he'd do if I ever darkened his door again."

Bailey jumped back up on the couch next to Belle. "And you took Bailey with you," I said.

"I followed straight after Maureen," Belle said. "This was my chance. When I saw her bring the dogs down the mountain, I waited for her to drive out of sight." Lightning flashed through the window, followed by a double rumble.

"But they say Isaiah had a gun hidden in every room," I said. "Not just dogs."

She shrugged. "So I take chances," she said angrily. "Why not? But I made a mistake. I was so busy thinking about what I'd say to Isaiah that I hit a cat that ran out in the road." She stopped and hugged Bailey as if she could make up to one animal what she'd done to another. "I didn't hurt the poor cat bad, but I had to find the owner and I went to several houses before I finally did. It's lucky Bailey likes cats. I promised to pay the vet bill and all that. Then I went up." This time the thunder sounded close. A funny little click in the distance said the lightning had hit something.

I did wish she'd get to the point.

"I stopped in a woods-road out of sight of the house and walked up. I guess I wanted to surprise that skunk. Isaiah was out on the porch about to water the flowers. He was just as damn good-looking, just as I-need-you-looking as I remembered. Damn it. He made my stomach roll over. My insides quivered. But when he saw it was me, he froze. He stopped watering the plant by the steps and he said, "You weren't invited here.""

"I kept coming and, yes, Bailey was with me. I felt safer

with a dog. Isaiah went inside, but I grabbed the door before he could shut it tight and I followed him in. That fancy living room made me angry. I'd never been in the house, only the barn." Belle clenched her fists in her lap. "That's where he thought I belonged: the barn. He kept me out of that fine house. I was his roll in the hay. Except hay itches. He had an old blanket. I looked at his fancy living room and I thought: Well, damn him! He could at least have had a better blanket."

And did that little hurt help fuel murder?

"Which was stupid," Belle added. "That's not what I cared about. I cared because we hurt Ernie, and Isaiah helped to kill him. That made me so angry I couldn't think straight. I just blurted out what I thought.

"I said to him: 'There's an old well on this place, and you threw DDT in that well, and it made your neighbors sick and my husband died and you don't care.' He went red in the face and he said, 'You're crazy. Why would I do that?'

"And I knew by the way he said it I'd guessed right. So why couldn't anyone find the well?"

"How could you know that?" Ted asked.

"I knew Isaiah Hubbel," she said. "I may never have been in his house, but I knew how he fidgeted when he lied. Because he'd lied to me when I asked him if he loved me. God knows why I asked him, but I did. Back when I felt so unloved. I knew by the way he wiggled when he said 'Of course,' that he didn't love me. I never let myself know at the time. Later I remembered."

That was so roundabout that my head swam. I fastened my eyes on the face-lamp. The comfort had gone out of it. The face, half carved out of the wood, was like Belle, always half hidden. Every time she told me more, I felt there was even more that she wasn't telling.

"So what did you do then?" I asked.

"I said to him: 'You killed your wife.' " Belle's eyes became angry slits as she told us that. "And just as I said it, the clock on the mantel struck ten. Like a bell tolling." She clenched her fists. "As if the clock was saying, Yes, she's dead."

"And what did he do?" I asked.

Belle shrugged. "He lied. He said, 'Come sit down and let me tell you about my wife,' and I sat on the couch near that huge old fireplace and I said, again, 'You killed her.' He laughed. He still had those laugh lines by his eyes. He was so darned handsome. Which annoyed me even more.

"He stayed calm. He said, 'My wife would never give anyone the pleasure of being dead. She wants to be in charge, no matter what. You're not in charge when you're dead.' He began to turn red. 'And you want to push me around. You want me to say I killed her, when I never would. Damn it, I miss her! I don't know where she's gone!' Oh, he was a clever liar!"

Now the thunder was not quite as loud. Good. I don't like thunderstorms. Belle seemed not to notice. "Isaiah began to act so angry," she went on, "with frown lines, and neck cords sticking out, that I figured I'd better get out while the getting was good. I figured he wasn't going to tell me anything else."

"Why do you think you're the prime suspect?" Ted asked.

"Miranda Snow at the bottom of the hill saw me go up there," Belle said, "but she doesn't remember exactly what time. But I know the time and I know Isaiah was alive. She told the sheriff she saw me. He questioned all the neighbors, or his men did. I could tell when he questioned me he figured I had the opportunity and the motive."

I groaned inside again. And the leash. Of course he thought that. Small thunder crash. The storm was moving away.

"Why did you take off Bailey's leash?" I asked sadly.

She flushed. "That was dumb! When we went in, he ran around the leg of a chair and got caught. It was easier to get him loose by taking the leash off. When we left, it was faster to carry him. I forgot the leash."

I know firsthand that forgetful moments can cause havoc. Alas.

"And what were you doing after you left us in Nashville and before this morning?" I asked. Because I suddenly remembered how odd it had seemed that she wanted to go to Nashville with me and Pop and Azalea. That could be important.

"I was working at a homeless shelter in Nashville," she said.

I could believe that.

"But why now?" Ted asked.

"They were short-handed," Belle said, "and I knew the guy who runs it, back when he was a kid. I took his picture for his mother to give his grandma for her birthday. His place helps homeless men, women, and children."

"And that man was Isaiah's friend!" I cried. The dernedest things come back to me. Me, who sometimes can't remember where I put my shoes. "Suzie said Isaiah had an E-mail friend he was in touch with every day, somebody he'd known for years!"

"Yes," she said, startled. "They were in Vietnam together. If Isaiah confided in anybody, I figured he'd tell Lee."

"So what did you learn?" Ted asked.

"Nothing," she said dourly. "He's a Baptist minister. Though he doesn't have a church. All I could get him to say, even when I hung around for several days, was that anything Isaiah ever told him would be confidential."

Belle looked at the floor as she said that. Then she looked up and smiled broadly. "If I get through this, I'm going to go work in that shelter! I hope you'll help me."

I prayed that ambition would make her less reckless.

"Your son, George, was just here, and he found a gun in your bed. Why was that?" Ted asked. I'd been so upset about her timing on the mountain that I almost forgot about the gun.

"Oh, that!" she said. "When I went to leave Isaiah's house, I saw that gun leaning on the wall by the front door. He kept it there to shoot anyone who threatened him. That's what I figured. He was worse, more paranoid than he used to be. His eyes did strange things. I didn't think he'd hesitate to shoot me. So I grabbed the gun as I ran out. Which was dumb, because he had other guns. But I ran down the mountain fast, to the wood-road where I'd hidden my car, and he didn't shoot at me."

"He expected company," I said. "Me and Martin and his brother."

"Did you tell the sheriff about the gun?" Ted asked.

"Yes," she said, "but when he sent someone there to my house to get the gun, it was gone! My own son took it, and I didn't know that until now." She began to laugh hysterically.

Ted picked up the phone on the table by the couch and took it to her. "Call the sheriff," he said. "You want to give him all the evidence you can that you are telling him the whole truth."

So she called and left a message on his voice mail since he was out. "This is Belle Dasher. I know who took the gun I told you was at my house. I'll call back."

Belle looked thoughtful after she hung up. "When we prove Isaiah killed Joan," she said, "all Joan's relatives will have a motive at least as good as mine."

Joan. When I saw Isaiah Hubbel dead, the fact that his wife might be dead, too, had slipped out of my mind. If Isaiah and his wife were both dead, that could give a whole different slant to who did it. The old saying is "Who gains?" Stop! This was not my puzzle to unravel.

But Ted said, "Has it occurred to you, Belle, that there might be someone who killed both Isaiah and his wife, and maybe that person is the one who hit you over the head?"

Belle stared at him as if he'd lost his mind. "A tree branch hit me on the head," she said angrily. Then she said she had work to do. She got up off the couch with a bounce, put her rain things back on, and left, dog and all.

She was not much help. As soon as she was gone, Ted went out to the kitchen and got the wine bottle to refill our glasses. He poured some into mine and said: "We have to have a serious talk."

He said it in that portentous tone people use when they are about to announce that you have an incurable disease or that they want a divorce. I braced myself. Was being murder prone grounds? No, I told myself—no, no!

Ted smiled. Whew! "You do have a talent for getting mixed up in catastrophes," he said. He raised an eyebrow and shook his head. "It's unbelievable. And you do have a talent for sorting them out. That's why your friends and relatives drag you in. You scare me to death because you take chances. So I agreed when you said you wouldn't let yourself get drawn into trying to help anybody mixed up in murder ever again."

"Because you don't need the shock," I said, "and you're the most valuable person to me."

"Because of my health," he said. Suddenly he looked extremely sheepish. He didn't meet my eyes. "I wasn't being entirely honest," he said. Ted, who is Mr. Straight Facts himself?

"You mean you don't have high blood pressure?" I said. I was of two minds. Angry and pleased to death.

"I have high blood pressure," he said, "but it's not so serious that it can't be controlled with beta blockers. I talked to my doctor today to be sure I understood all the ins and outs. He said most people believe a shock or a worry will be dangerous if you have high blood pressure. But what's dangerous, at least in a situation like mine, is not taking your medication. Not taking care of yourself in the long run. The doc said, 'You can't stop living your life.' Of course that's right. He'd already told me that earlier, but I wanted to be absolutely sure."

"So this catastrophe I'm mixed up in isn't dangerous for you?"

He squirmed. "The truth is that when you said you'd stay out of danger to help protect my health, I agreed because of *your* health. So you wouldn't get yourself in perilous situations. I take the medication that keeps my blood pressure down—excitement isn't going to kill me."

Ted, of all people, had lied to me. Well, no, he really hadn't. He just let me believe a mistake.

"And what we're doing isn't working," he said. "You're in danger, just the same, and you feel rotten on top of that."

"You're right," I said. "*Mad Brad* could appear at any moment. Whoever has killed one or two Hubbels may think I'm onto them because everybody comes and tells me things." *And—whoever—could even try to get rid of me!* I didn't say that out loud.

"So what should we do?" I asked Ted. "It didn't even help to try to escape to Tennessee."

"Let's sit down together and try to figure this mess out. You're a reporter. You can ask questions. You do better when you're *doing* something. You're right about that."

"The deputy whose name I have to find out asked me to let him know if I have any hunches," I said. "That gives us a great way to pass on anything we find out."

Ted began to laugh. "Job One for Great Detective: Find out name of helpful friendly law contact!"

CHAPTER

19

MONDAY, 7:30 P.M.

"Actually, the first thing we need to do," Ted said, "is to sit down and make a chart of everything we already know. You've picked up a lot of information without even trying."

That was putting it mildly. I seem to be a magnet for murder information even when I try to avoid it.

We sat down at the kitchen table, and while a chicken casserole from the freezer heated up, we brainstormed and made a suspect chart. Everyone was a suspect, because that's the most fruitful way to explore.

I had been practicing writing in my portable brain. I pulled up the cover and made notes, writing with the little stylus. Later, I could put the resulting notes into my computer and print them out for Ted. Amazing.

"All right," Ted said, "Belle showed up first and claimed

Isaiah Hubbel had killed his wife. So what do we know about Belle?"

"She may be holding back and lying to us still. But my hunch is that she wouldn't kill," I said. "She had a possible motive because she had long-standing and more recent anger at Isaiah Hubbel. She could have lost her head and shot him. She was there at about the right time. She could have used the gun that Maureen said was in the bathroom, which wasn't there right after we found Isaiah's body. She could have used the gun she says she took when she left. She's impulsive and she has nerve. But she loves life, so I hope she didn't kill." I had to write fast on the little screen to keep up with my thoughts. So a few letters came out as typos. Never mind.

"Suzie knew Belle had been to visit you and knew she had accused Isaiah of murder. She knew it almost too fast, even for her," Ted said. "Could Suzie be mixed up in this somehow?"

Now there was an odd thought. "We have to include Suzie," I said. "But so far we don't know a motive, or where she was this morning, or whether she knew, or discovered by chance, there was a gun in the bathroom. Suzie doesn't strike me as the type to own a gun, and it did seem as though she tried to help us escape danger by going to Tennessee. But maybe Suzie was one of the women who went up the mountain to see Isaiah Hubbel!" I said, half joking. "But after all, why not?" I wrote her in.

"Jake Hubbel would have been hard pressed to zip up the mountain as soon as Belle left and shoot his brother, and immediately come get us," I said, "and he certainly seemed totally cracked up by his brother's death. If he had a reason to kill Isaiah, we don't know it."

"Put him on the list," Ted said, "with a question mark under opportunity, a question mark under motive, and 'bathroom gun?' under 'means.'" It took me a minute to figure how to write question marks in my little portable brain, but I consulted the punctuation instructions inside the cover.

"Jake had guns of his own," I said, thinking of the gun rack handy in his truck. "But if he was smart he wouldn't have used his own gun given a choice."

"Even Martin should be on this list," Ted said. "How long before Jake Hubbel showed up did he get to the office?"

"About fifteen minutes," I said. "But unless Jake lied about the fact he'd just left his brother alive, Martin could not have killed Isaiah and been back at the office when Jake got there. Martin didn't have a chance to go into the house ahead of Jake and me and maybe kill Isaiah with a silencer. Besides, what possible motive could he have?" We couldn't think of one.

"Brad could have done it!" I said. "Jake says he's taking his medication, and Suzie says he's a lamb when he does. But maybe Brad pretended to take it and didn't. We have no way of knowing. We need to find out where Brad was this morning." I added him to the list.

"We also need to know exactly how Brad traced you to the Opryland Hotel," Ted said. "It may not be related to Isaiah's death, but it suggests either he had help, or unusual electronic know-how."

"I can't believe Maureen is a killer," I said. "She was fond of her uncle, at least so she claimed. But she's a member of a family that's pretty darn dysfunctional. Maybe she has some secret rage we don't know about. Or maybe her uncle was doing something to alienate George Dasher. Maybe she lost her temper over that and killed him. Also she inherits the mountain. But does she want the mountain?" I put her on the list to be thorough. Hey, I was getting good at writing fast in this gadget.

"Who else?" I asked.

"There's always Isaiah's wife, Joan," Ted said. "Until her body is found, she's a possible suspect."

"And there's George Dasher," I added. "Maybe he wanted to avenge his mother somehow. I was drawn to him, but he did seem emotional like Belle."

"Belle said Isaiah had that E-mail friend named Lee in Nashville," Ted offered.

"Somebody he wrote every day and confided in," I said. "Belle says it's the same man who was his good friend in Vietnam. But would his good friend kill him?"

"Belle thought it was important to go see this man and try to find out if anything Isaiah told him might be a clue to whether Isaiah killed Joan," Ted pointed out.

"Some friend *that* would be, if he even suggested Isaiah committed murder! But he told Belle that everything Isaiah said was confidential. Even when she hung around, he didn't let a thing drop. But he might know something that would help us figure out who killed Isaiah. Belle will know where to reach him."

I picked up the phone that always sits on the end of the kitchen table, and called Belle. She wasn't home yet.

I sighed. "There's so much we don't know. Something is gnawing at the back of my mind—something I've seen and can't quite remember."

"So don't try too hard," Ted said. "Relax and see what comes. Consult your intuition."

I shut my eyes and made my mind blank. "Something

about the scene of Isaiah Hubbel's death," I said. "Something didn't fit."

"Could you tell from the Polaroid pictures you took?" he asked.

The answer came to me in a rush and surprised me. "I need to compare the first picture I took of Isaiah Hubbel, the one I gave Martin, with the one I have here. Yes. That's it! Something was different the second time I saw Isaiah, the second time I took a picture. And not just that his eyes were closed. The pictures will tell! God bless Pop for giving me the camera. God bless you for thinking· of that."

The timer went off. The chicken was ready. I was ravenous. This had been a long day. "Tomorrow morning," I said, "I'll find out."

I felt a rush of happiness. Tomorrow morning I could begin to look into this ugly death in fruitful ways. I could try to find out what went wrong, not just at the moment the crime was committed, but in a larger sense. Find out what brought the killer and the victim to the tragic point of no return, which is what is fascinating about a murder. And I didn't have to feel guilty at all!

CHAPTER
20

MONDAY NIGHT AND
TUESDAY MORNING

We watched the late-night TV news that showed Isaiah's body being loaded into the coroner's van. There were shots of his isolated house.

Murder. The picture of Isaiah dead winked in and out of my mind, complete with bullet hole. From one of the guns he kept around the house? From one that Belle stole? I wondered if I could sleep.

But there's nothing like the warm body of a loving spouse to chase away the horror of a cold dead body. I hadn't actually touched that dead body, but I had seen the pale face. Thank God for Ted. I fell asleep exhausted and so glad to be alive.

In the morning I reached for the phone to call Martin, to

be sure he'd be at the office or at least that the picture would be there. The phone rang in my hand.

"Hey," Pop said, "I see you're at it again. You won't be able to stay out of this Hubbel murder now!" he crowed. "I bet you're glad I introduced you to a good suspect."

Introduced us? And then, good grief—we'd forgotten to put Professor Albert Bright on the list. He was Joan Hubbel's brother, the brother who said he was worried because she'd disappeared.

"Yes," I said, "your Memory-Professor Bright acted very strange, didn't he? First saying no when you asked him to lunch to meet me, then calling back to say yes after Belle Dasher got hit over the head near his sister's house. And why wasn't he willing to ask the sheriff for the details about what was wrong when he saw all the blue lights flashing at the bottom of Isaiah Hubbel's mountain?" I tried to act on top of the Professor Bright connection. "He came to lunch with you in order to ask me instead of the sheriff," I said. "Very fishy."

Not only had I forgotten to put Mr. Memory Prof on the list, but even Ted forgot. If I let Pop know that, he'd never let us live it down.

I changed the subject. After all, I ought to tell Pop the camera had been useful. "I took a couple of pictures of the crime scene with the camera you gave me," I said. "It's amazing to see them pop out and develop themselves. I think those pictures are going to be a big help."

"Absolutely," Pop agreed. "When can you get here for us to examine them?"

Well, I'd gotten myself into that, hadn't I?

"A little pipsqueak newspaper like the *Word* won't care if you're late," he announced. "I want to see those pictures now!" Did he expect the *New York Times* in Monroe County?

"I'll describe the picture I have with me," I said. "I gave the other one to Martin, since he's writing the story."

I told him how Isaiah must have been sitting in his favorite chair in front of the TV when someone evidently came in and shot him right in the chest. Pop whistled. "I wonder if Albert Bright is a good shot."

"He wouldn't have to be," I said. "Whoever pulled the trigger must have been close. It's a small room."

"Without windows?" Pop asked.

I hadn't thought of a shooting through the window. Not possible unless Isaiah Hubbel's chair had been turned around. Could that be? Before the wind came up, the morning had been mild. Could the window have been open?

"Well," Pop said, "go on to work and hurry up. Bring Martin's picture, too."

"Pop," I said, "please don't do anything that could make trouble. Just keep this to yourself and wait till I get there and show you the pictures. Or else I won't share."

I puzzled about Albert Bright on my way to work. But I did notice the white clouds were doing beautiful things in the blue sky, and the maples were beyond the cloud-of-red stage, with seed pods like tiny wings—in fact, every tree now had tiny leaves. The world was one of those paintings made with little dots of color. Pointillist, I think they're called. I thought of Belle and made myself enjoy it. Belle with her great gift for appreciating the world around her. I wished I didn't feel she was holding back on the whole truth.

I found Martin just hanging up the phone at his desk. He had on an almost normal shirt with all kinds of dogs on it. A picture of a hunting dog on the scent was on his pocket. In honor of tracking whodunit?

"Could I look at the picture I took of Isaiah Hubbel?" I asked. On the wall behind Martin, the caption on the poster of a mountain vista seen through rhododendron blossoms read *Find peace and tranquillity in a mountain vacation.* Across the bottom, it said *Monroe County, North Carolina.* Something from the Chamber of Commerce. Peace and tranquillity. Ha!

The picture I'd given Martin was on the top of his to-do basket. He held it out to me.

I put the two pictures on his desk side by side. "I took this other picture maybe fifteen minutes later," I said. "I have a hunch they're not alike."

He came around and stood next to me to examine them. At a glance they looked the same. Isaiah Hubbel dead. I examined the earlier one more closely, the picture on the right. The dead eyes in that classic face, well aged as it was, gave me goose pimples. I thought of the stories of demon lovers. Even dead he was sexy. The bullet hole was near the middle of his chest. His shirt was blood-red, above faded blue jeans. A small square table to the right of the chair held a box of tissues, the TV remote, an ashtray with cigarette butts in it, a pack of Camels, a folder of matches, a tin of nuts, and a jar of hard candies. A pint canning jar with a screw-on top, the kind my mother put tomatoes in, was next to the matches. It looked empty at first glance, but no, actually it contained some kind of clear liquid. How odd. And a small drinking glass was near that. The lettering on the jar was large, but at an angle where it was hard to make out.

I examined the other picture, to see what it showed, the one I'd taken just a short while later, after I looked around the house. I'd put that picture on the left. I'd already noticed that someone had closed Isaiah Hubbel's eyes. That was such an improvement, I almost said thank you out loud. Now he looked dead-pale but asleep. I examined the table by his side. The pint jar was gone. The glass was gone.

Martin seemed electrified. "Jake Hubbel moved that jar and that glass! He must have! But why on earth? He made me come with him to look out in the back yard, then check that the back door was locked. He stopped and he drank a glass of water in the kitchen. From that glass, I bet. To wash it out."

"Unless there was someone else hiding in the front of the house," I said, "who took that glass and the jar when you went in the back. He could have let himself out the front door. Nobody searched the living room. Which is odd. Someone could have been behind the couch. And Jake never searched the upstairs. So why was he worried about the back door?"

People act in bizarre ways when they are in shock, but Jake sure had been illogical—or else very clever. "But why get rid of a jar and a glass?" I asked. "Isaiah wasn't poisoned. Or if he was, then why was he shot? What was in the jar?"

Martin said, "Wait, I'll find the magnifying glass." Then we both stared at the enlarged label on the jar through the round glass. Now we could make out the words. "That jar reads Pure Corn," I said. "How odd."

Martin said, "I think it means pure corn whiskey. White lightning. The old-timers put that up in big canning jars or sometimes in barrels, not usually in pint jars. This could be the product of our small-time local moonshiner."

"But Isaiah wouldn't go out to get whiskey," I said.

"Would the bootlegger bring it to him?" Then I did a mental double-take. "You mean there's still a bootlegger making whiskey here in Monroe County?"

Martin laughed. "The bootlegger was the middleman. He didn't make the stuff. He got it to the customer. We used to have serious bootleggers here. But more moonshiners. They made it. That's how people sold their corn crops in the Great Depression, and even back before that. But our local moonshiner is a tourist attraction. The gift shop down the street more or less sells the stuff."

"More or less?" I said, amazed.

"They can't legally sell it," he explained. "But the tourists think it's a lark to buy some old-fashioned moonshine whiskey. So he gives them the whiskey and sells them a tour of his still and a little demonstration and a booklet his granddaughter helped him write about the good old days of running white lightning. When he started, he would otherwise have been on welfare, and since the tourists love it, the sheriff looks the other way. I think he's the sheriff's wife's cousin, or some such. And you know, I think he's related to the Hubbels, too."

I was coming to realize that most people were related in Monroe County, except a few professors at the college and the new people who came in the sixties with the romantic idea that they could avoid evil if they got back to the land. They came to the paper with letters to the editor about the environment or notices of vegetarian cooking classes, or poetry readings or craft exhibits. All sorts of craftsmen moved to the county because it was cheap to live here and because crafts have a long tradition in Monroe County, maybe older than moonshine.

"I'll show these pictures to the red-haired deputy who's

so helpful," I said. "Perhaps the sheriff's folks have already found the jar and the glass, but they may not know they could be related to Isaiah Hubbel's death in some strange way."

Martin looked surprised. "I thought you wanted to stay out of this." He went back around and sat down at his desk.

I squirmed. "I did," I said, "because I was worried about Ted and his high blood pressure. But he says he's O.K. as long as he takes his medication, and I seem to get in more trouble if I try to ignore murder than I do if I try to help figure it out. I seem to get hunches about what to look into that work out." I realized I was grinning like a fool. As my cousin Angela says, I was grinning like a mule eating briars. It was so nice to let my natural proclivities do just as they pleased.

Martin tilted back in his desk chair and cocked his head to one side. "Well, O.K., follow your hunches, as long as the other news gets covered, too," he said. "This seems to be a big enough story so two of us can work on it. I'll go talk to the sheriff about the progress of the case so far. What will you do next after you give those pictures to Willie Wynatt? We don't want to overlap."

Ah! If you just wait and listen, a name will usually volunteer itself. Willie Wynatt. Will he help me out? *Why Not!* I liked that!

"After I take the pictures to Deputy Willie Wynatt," I said, "I think I'll go and buy a tour of a moonshine whiskey still and get some white lightning."

CHAPTER
21

LATER ON TUESDAY

By the time I got back to my own desk, I saw rain out the window. Before I could find my umbrella, which plays hide and seek, and go over to the sheriff's office, Deputy Willie Wynatt walked in. *Why not!*

"Hi," I said. "Sit down." He inspired me to be informal with his relaxed grin.

I pulled out the pictures, held up the later one, and said, "You were right that this picture might inspire some thought. Because, you see, I gave Martin a picture I took right after we found the body and I assumed it was exactly the same as this one that I took about fifteen minutes later. But they aren't alike!"

"Martin didn't mention any picture," Willie said, sober now. He remained standing. "I guess he saw us taking our own. But the one he got from you is different from the one you kept?"

I put the two pictures down on my desk, and he examined them, nodding thoughtfully. "The first one you took is the one with the jar and glass?"

"That's right."

"Hey, that explains it," he said, bouncing on his toes and grinning. "Hey, we searched pretty thoroughly. We were afraid we'd miss something. And a couple of books were sticking out a little more than the others on the bookshelf. That jar was behind those books. We had a laugh about who was hiding corn whiskey. We smelled it, and it sure was corn whiskey. Had that poor man's wife hid the whiskey before she left? But it worried me. It didn't seem to make sense."

"But it must mean something." I was sure of that.

He rubbed his chin and began to pace. A very physical thinker. "If somebody hid it yesterday, they hid it quick," he said, "but they wiped off their fingerprints good. We did look into that. Now tell me again exactly who was where and when."

I explained that Jake Hubbel and Martin and I all went into the TV room. Jake went around Isaiah's chair, which was facing away from me so that I couldn't see anything but Jake's head over the top of the chair. Then Jake cried out that Isaiah was dead, the front door slammed, and Martin and Jake rushed off to try to catch whoever slammed it. I went around the chair and took a picture of Isaiah. Then Jake came back and said the wind slammed the door, and Martin called 911. Or did he call before they went? Yes. That was it." So where was he when Jake came back? Looking around, I guessed.

"I went down the hall to the bathroom and left both of them in the TV room." I'd talked so fast I was out of breath.

"Because you wanted to see the rest of the house," Willie Wynatt said, with a wink.

"I looked in the bathroom and even in the top of the toilet tank where Maureen said a gun was taped. No gun. I looked in what must have been Joan's room," I said. Joan, who plainly had occupied that room alone. "But I only looked at surfaces, I didn't open drawers or cupboard doors in her room. I knew I shouldn't. But somebody had. Her laundry was spilling out of a hamper. Then I went upstairs, and a drawer was hanging open up there."

I explained that Martin had told me that while I must have been upstairs, he and Jake went to check on the back door and the back yard. Jake went into the kitchen and drank a glass of water. Willie nodded. Martin must have told him that. "Then," I said, "I came back down the stairs. I heard a car in the drive—in fact, someone honked a horn, and I heard Jake and Martin walking toward the front door. That's when I took the second picture."

Willie stopped pacing and scratched his head. "So Jake could have hidden that jar when Martin was looking at something else, and taken the glass to the kitchen. But there was time for somebody else to sneak in quick. Still, I bet it was Jake."

"But why?" I asked.

Willie shook his head. "We don't know, do we? We still have to cut a way into that rhododendron hell, near the house," he said, sitting down and drumming his fingers. "I don't think a body could be in there, but we might find something."

A rhododendron hell is a thicket you can hardly see or force your way into. A good place to throw a gun, maybe.

"I'll need these," he said, taking the two pictures. He wrote me a receipt for them. "Let me know if you find anything out."

"Who do you suspect?" I asked.

Willie grinned again. "Everybody, including you!" That seemed to amuse him.

"Maureen says Isaiah had a house full of guns," I said, "so anybody could have found a weapon on the spot."

He whistled. "You wouldn't have believed those guns."

"What kinds?" I asked. I felt I ought to know, this being Monroe County and all.

"Well, believe it or not, he had a machine gun under the pillow of that bed of his upstairs. I hope he put it on the table by his bed when he went to sleep." My deputy was wide-eyed. "He had a double-barreled shotgun on a cupboard shelf in the kitchen, not too far from the door—a real antique, maybe a gun his father hunted with. It still works, but if it didn't work, it would have made a great club to hit someone over the head with." Willie chuckled at that, then became more serious again. "He had an ancient Army-issue .45-caliber pistol in a drawer in the room where he was found dead, but that seems to be out of commission. His niece Maureen says that recently he kept a gun near the front door. That's probably the shotgun that Belle Dasher made off with. She brought it to us, and it's not the gun that killed Isaiah."

I thanked God for that. "I can hardly believe his relatives weren't scared to visit him," I said. "How could his wife live in the same house?"

Why Not shrugged. "They grew up with guns. They did

have a code of honking three times when they drove up," he said, "so he'd know it was family."

"So maybe the killer knew that and honked three times," I said.

"We just don't know."

"But none of those guns sound like they'd fit in the top of the toilet tank." I said.

"No," he agreed. "We haven't found that gun. That's likely the gun that killed Isaiah Hubbel. But we can guess what it was. It would take a special gun to fit in that tank and not rust."

I'm not a gun person, but I was fascinated. "What?"

"A small revolver," he said, "a snubby, a two-inch, and because of the moisture it couldn't be blue steel. He'd have needed stainless or alloy with synthetic grips instead of wood. I hear he was patriotic, so he'd pick American made. Maybe a Smith revolver."

"You'd recognize that if you found it!"

He sighed. "But we haven't found that gun, and this is a mighty big county to hide a gun in."

"But how strange," I said, "that whoever shot Isaiah used the gun that would have been hardest to find. Except, of course, if they knew all along where it was."

He nodded. "Or if he had it with him. It would fit in a pocket. If you hear anything, or get any hunches . . ."

I said I'd certainly let him know, and he departed.

In my mind, I saw Isaiah's handsome face again. Asleep next to a machine gun. And he was shot in spite of that. I felt cold.

I was glad the next story I had to write was about a wedding, a double wedding for twins. I was glad to think of love instead of death.

Perhaps that's why I noticed that the redbud out my window now had heart-shaped leaves. The rain had stopped, and a drop of water glistened on the downward point of each tiny leaf. A few tired pink blossoms still clung among the leaves, but Belle's two kinds of bees had moved on to fresher blooms. Yes, Belle. She pulled my mind back to death and moonshine. I needed to find out something about that jar of moonshine that proved someone else killed Isaiah. Someone besides Belle.

I grabbed my shoulder bag and took off for the Mountain Bounty gift shop. That was the place where Martin said a tourist could find out how to see a still and taste white lightning.

As I walked down Main Street past the funeral parlor, the drugstore, and Ellie's Cafe, I had the feeling someone was watching me. I looked around and saw only a man putting out a reserved-for-a-funeral sign in front of the funeral home, and someone coming out of the drugstore. I reminded myself to be alert.

CHAPTER
22

The gift shop stood on Main Street, just one among many one-story shops, not too far from the Travelers Rest Bed and Breakfast, which was at the end of the street where shops gave way to nice old houses. The gift shop was a pleasant walk down the rain-washed street, now shined by sun. In spite of blooming spring flowers, including red and yellow tulips in a window box, tiny Christmas lights outlined the door of the shop. Inside, several kinds of sachet clashed, but not unpleasantly. "Can I help you?" asked a musical voice. I said I'd just look around.

I figured I'd see how they alerted a tourist to the possibility of acquiring genuine moonshine. The musical voice resolved itself into a pleasant, dark-haired woman with large hands and feet, I couldn't remember having met. Her family must be short on births, deaths, graduations, and club meet-

ings, so she stayed out of my office. She asked if I was looking for any particular kind of thing, and I allowed as how I
was interested in anything that had to do with the history of
the area. That should be a way to sashay into moonshine.

She pointed to a patchwork quilt with large and small
squares in many colors, which she said was in an old-
fashioned pattern, and showed me a traditional mountain
toy—a loose-jointed wooden man—and she showed me
how he'd dance on a wooden paddle when you shook him.
Interesting, but not a murder-solver. She picked up a pottery
pitcher, and said, "Many of our potters use traditional
styles." This was getting me nowhere.

"Do you have any books?" I asked, and the woman took
me over to a stand with booklets face out. She picked up a
booklet with patchwork gals in sunbonnets on a quilt on the
cover. *Mountain Quilting,* was the title. One on rug-hooking
had a small rug covered with flowers. There was a booklet
on wood-carving and—hooray!—one on moonshiners, with
an old man on the cover in overalls and a black felt hat. I
picked that up and leafed through it.

"I guess when times were hard you had a lot of moonshiners around here?" I asked.

"The Scots-Irish settled these mountains," she said, suddenly a little prim about the mouth. "Whiskey-making was
a tradition. In the old days, most families had a still. If any
family abused the whiskey, the community pressure made
them stop."

I wondered if she wasn't romanticizing human nature,
and there weren't some bad apples, but it was a nice thought.

"Then, when Prohibition came, whiskey would bring a
good price. Besides, people around here felt that it was none
of the government's business whether they made whiskey."

She picked up what looked like a handcrafted whiskbroom, and ran the twig end against her fingers. She seemed to have a great need to finger the merchandise.

"Well, I can see how they felt the government was trying to change their tradition," I said, to get across the idea that I wasn't opposed to strong drink. Actually, I am only opposed to folks who abuse strong drink, like my cousin Robbie who plowed into his neighbor's brand new car, rammed that car through the man's picture window, killed his neighbor's canary, and then tried to pick a fight with his neighbor's wife.

"I understand," I said, "that there was a real art to making good whiskey."

"Oh, yes," she said. "Old-timers claim that store-bought whiskey can't hold a candle to moonshine. The best stuff was smooth and clear as spring water." Now she was beaming at me as if I were a long-lost cousin.

"I wish I could have tasted it," I said.

She explained that might be possible. There was an old-timer who loved the art, had held on to his still, and would be glad to let me have a little demonstration, answer some questions, and give me one of the books about moonshine. All for twenty-five dollars. Of course, he couldn't sell me the whiskey, but he'd let me sample it, and if he liked me he might give me a jar.

I tried not to blink at the price and said I'd enjoy that. "He must be a great age if he made moonshine during Prohibition," I said. "But his memory is still sharp?"

"He's sharp about making whiskey," she said, "because he keeps telling the story and keeps making the whiskey. Some days he gets a little vague on other things. Of course, he never could remember faces." She picked up a hand mirror decorated with ceramic flowers and looked at herself in it as if to be sure her face was still there.

"Can't remember faces at all?" I asked.

"That's why he could never keep a regular job. My niece is a special-education teacher, and she says they know now that there are some people with this particular learning disability. They can't remember faces. Even if they can remember almost anything else."

I'm not good at faces till I've seen them a few times, but I could see that not being able to remember them at all would be a bummer. And not very helpful to me if I asked Mr. Moonshine who'd come and watched his demonstration lately.

I hoped this was not one of his vague days. I wondered out loud how many people had the chance to watch him make moonshine.

"Two or three, some days," she said. "Tourists have told their friends how interesting this was. But some days there are none at all. More come on weekends, especially in the summer."

I hoped only a few had come this week. That might make it easier to figure who might have bought whiskey here and taken it to Isaiah, and why. But if the old man couldn't recognize faces, that was going to make this whole thing harder.

"When can I watch the demonstration?" I asked.

She said I was in luck: some other people were coming back to watch in half an hour. "But it's better not to talk about this with local people," she said. "Some of them believe that any liquor is a deadly sin. We try not to wave this still in front of their noses." Obviously she didn't mean that literally.

I said I'd keep quiet, and I'd keep looking around the shop till it was time to go. Actually, I sat down on a small bench and read the moonshine book. Might as well be prepared.

Half an hour later, a young Alabama-sounding couple came in, and the blond woman, adorned with numerous rings, told me, "My great-granddaddy was a bootlegger." She pointed at the book I was reading. "That's where the family money came from." Her husband looked rather annoyed. He wore a seersucker jacket and took himself seriously.

The shopkeeper collected $25 from me and $35 from the couple. Evidently there was a special rate for two together. She put a Back Shortly sign on the door and took us off in a Ford Mustang up a back road, and then a dirt road. I watched carefully for landmarks, like a sagging barn with two bearskins nailed to it, where we turned right, and a huge old gnarled tree cleft in the middle like lightning had hit it, where we turned left. I entered them in my portable brain. Boy, this was easier than the BB days—Before Brain, when if I forgot my notebook, I had to make the landmarks into a poem to remember. Such as *go right where bears bite,* and *go left by tree's cleft*. It didn't have to be a good poem. But the PB was sure easier! Hooray for progress. I should have been warier of progress.

We came to a stop by a white farmhouse where a man was sitting in a rocking chair on the front porch. He wore the same kind of black felt hat I'd seen on the book cover, overalls, and high-topped shoes. He looked so old and wrinkled, I was amazed at how spryly he got up from his chair. He shook hands with us as if we were about to embark on some very serious mutual endeavor. He thanked Mrs. Gift Shop for bringing us.

"I'll be back in an hour," she said, and disappeared down the road.

First the old man waved his arm at an old car in a shed with an open front, an old black Ford. "Transporters used these cars," he said. "They was daring boys. They went round these mountain roads so fast the cars whined. My daughter found this car jacked up in a barn. It still runs," he said with pride. "You can see the back seat's out. Now a car like this would carry a right smart amount of moonshine. And those transporter boys had tricks to help 'em in a chase. They threw nails out the back to make a flat tire." He grinned at this wonderful joke. "They spilled oil on the road in back to make those revenuers skid."

Then he added: "Now, if any of you are descended from revenuers, I apologize for those transporter boys—but, if you make whiskey, you have to find a way to get it to the ones who want to drink it."

Next he led us down a path to an unpainted shed in back of the house. This one had a closed door with a big padlock on it. Suddenly I had that feeling of being watched again. I looked around carefully but no one was in sight.

Mr. Moonshine Expert was related to the Hubbels, Suzie had said. I should have asked her how closely.

The old man opened the padlock and led us in. Inside was rough wood like the outside, with a dirt floor, packed smooth and shiny. Many-paned windows on one side looked old and recycled from some other building. The frames were painted white and peeling. The light from the windows fell on a large copper object about the shape of a turnip sitting on a rock base. Pipes came out of it, leading to a barrel.

Nearby were several other barrels, and I could smell fermentation.

But the old man ignored what must be his still and took us over to a wall of pictures. They were all in glassine envelopes and tacked to the wall. A few were photos, a lot were newspaper clippings. A name was written large on each one. So he could recognize words, if not faces.

"This is my pa," he said as he pointed to the first one. "Now, he was the one who made whiskey the Asheville folks really favored. I helped him. But I was born late. He died when I was sixteen year old. Pa made his whiskey of pure corn and made his own malt from sprouted corn. The best did that." He turned and smiled proudly. He had no teeth. "Some folks made it cheap and fast with sugar. Pa made sugar-whiskey now and then if we needed money bad. But mostly he made a fine whiskey. He was allus proud of it even when the revenuers caught him and he had to do a year in prison."

Mr. Moonshine was like his relatives the Hubbels, I thought. Loyal and proud, no matter what. Was he somehow mixed up in whatever was wrong?

I noticed that behind him, on the wall opposite the windows, was a rough wood cabinet with a padlock on the doors. Was that where he put the finished moonshine?

He was talking about the old days. He pointed to a newspaper clipping that said simply *Bees.*

"Now the folks who kept bees hated the moonshiners," he said. "Because a bee will love that fermenting mash. Will come and get drunk and die of it. They say a revenuer will follow a swarm of bees when he's looking for a still. I think that's how they found Pa's. He had it hidden in a cave. But they found it and they took their moonshine picks, that's what they called them things, and knocked big square holes in it, and hauled it off. But when Pa got out of prison he went right back to making whiskey. He was good at it. Why, people wanted his whiskey for medicine: For colds and flu, there's nothing better than corn whiskey mixed with honey. Calms a cough. And whiskey'll keep a man alive after he's bit by a snake. They used it all sorts of ways."

I listened but I also looked around. I looked for any sign one of my suspects had been here. But what did I expect to find? There wasn't much in this shed, a few big bags of corn, some miscellaneous objects on top of the padlocked cabinet.

"Now here's the revenuers with fifty gallons of moon-shine," he said. "About to pour it all out." A yellowed news-paper clipping showed several men standing proudly surrounded by gallon canning jars. The old man's pint jars—if the pint jar by Isaiah was his, and it must be—were a small token of that past.

I wished I could photograph the objects on top of the pad-locked cabinet. If anything in this room showed who had been here, that collection might. But I'd wait to ask until we were about to leave.

I tried to memorize the objects: two caps, one with the ubiquitous John Deere logo. Maybe the black felt hat our host wore was part of a bootlegger costume. When his audi-ence wasn't there, perhaps he didn't bother. A big box of kitchen matches on the cupboard might be there to light the fire under his still. A monkey wrench. Good grief, what was that for? There was a pack of spearmint gum, several sticks missing, an open pack of menthol cigarettes, a box of tis-sues. Funny, Mr. Moonshiner struck me as the type who would blow his nose on an old-fashioned red-printed farmer's handkerchief. Was that a clue? I needed a way to remember that list in case I couldn't take a picture. Let's see, I could make them all into a sentence. *Two caps match* (for matches) *and wrench my heart, by gum. That's kool.*

I added a picture in my mind of the old man wearing two caps, one arm raised to bean me with the wrench. Shocking action helps the memory. His other hand was holding a lighted match. He was chewing gum, and a cigarette hung between his lips. But wait, I hadn't included the tissue in my remember image. I made Mr. Moonshiner's nose running so he needed a tissue. Running to a shocking degree.

If something could turn out to be important, it's good to remember it more than one way.

Hey! I forgot I had my portable brain. I took it out and wrote the objects in that, too.

Meanwhile, the old man turned to the barrels in the shed.

"Now, this is the beer," he said. "The corn mash working with the malt. I make the malt myself. I put that corn in a sack and wet it good and it sprouts, I grind it and mix it in with my meal. Listen. You can hear it working now, like meat frying."

Yes, I could! And I could smell it working. Who else had sniffed that smell this week?

I turned my head slightly toward the window and thought I saw a face vanishing. My heart beat hard. But whatever I saw disappeared so fast it was a blur. What I saw was probably the motion of my own head turning, I told myself.

"We take that beer and put it in this still," the old man was saying, pointing to the copper turnip, "and we build a fire, not too hot. It has to run slow, about one hundred seventy degrees, or else the beer will stick to the still."

Heck, he wasn't actually going to make white lightning,

just tell us about it and let us smell the beer. I was disappointed.

Perhaps he sensed that. He stopped, dug in the pocket of his overalls, and pulled out a pack of Camels. He reached for the kitchen matches on the padlocked cupboard, took one out of the box, struck it, and lit the cigarette.

"We have to wait till the beer is ready," he said. "Then we make that whiskey right away. When the liquor comes out," he went on, "we strain it through coals. In the old days some folks used these here hats to strain the whiskey." He took off his black hat and gave us a big smile. I tried to imagine whether they'd strain the whiskey, then wear the hat again.

When he finished his spiel, he said, "Now I reckon you'd like to taste some pure corn whiskey." He took a key out of his pocket and unlocked the cupboard. Inside were three pint jars of white liquid with the familiar label. That label could have been the last thing Isaiah Hubbel saw: *Pure corn*. Yes. Mr. Moonshiner's whiskey was exactly what someone took Isaiah! I was right.

CHAPTER
23

IMMEDIATELY AFTERWARD

The old man opened a jar and poured a small amount of moonshine into three little glasses. He handed one to each of us. The husband who took himself so seriously took a sip and blinked. The wife tasted it, grinned, and said, "You make the good stuff."

The old man swelled up with pride. "Now sip on that slow," he said. "You ain't used to it."

I tasted and I blinked, too, but I was not surprised. This fire on my tongue was what I'd expected. I kept sipping and told the old man that, yes, this was special. I'm not a whiskey drinker myself, but I needed him to give me a jar for reasons of detection.

He made no move to give us the three sealed jars of corn whiskey that sat in plain sight with the cupboard door open. I was annoyed.

Three little jars in a great big empty cupboard. The master supply was somewhere else. Then I heard a car approaching. Mrs. Gift Shop, no doubt. The Alabama couple put down their glasses amid the junk on top of the cupboard, said "Thank you," and went outside.

I thanked the old man and asked if I could take some pictures of the still and barrels. "No," he said, "but you can take a picture of me outside." Well, I'd do that, but not yet.

"Do you remember who bought whiskey this week?" I asked.

"I never sell whiskey," he said, shocked.

Good automatic reflex.

"But did you present anyone with a jar of whiskey?" I asked.

He eyed me suspiciously.

"I need to find out who gave some to a friend of mine. He has no way to thank them." Well, that was technically true if you count Isaiah as a friend of mine.

"Did you give it to anyone this week?" I repeated.

He frowned and seemed to be casting back. "One of them is kin," he said. "She brings me chocolate cakes. I give her whiskey." His whole face lit up when he mentioned chocolate cake. "Once in a while, she comes. Maybe it was this week." Was that his Hubbel kin?

"If I could find her, would she make me a chocolate cake?" I asked.

He still smiled. "I don't think so. She works."

I heard a car horn. That must be Mrs. Gift Shop again. "What kind of work does your relative do?" I asked quickly.

Now he looked confused. "She just works."

I thanked him for showing me how whiskey was made in a still, and for telling me about the daredevil tricks of the transporter boys. I said goodbye. I wasn't going to get more information now, and Mrs. Gift Shop would be coming in to haul me off.

"This has been so interesting," I said.

My eye fell on a jar labeled Tips. I took ten dollars out of my pocket and put it in the jar.

He reached in the cupboard and took out a pint jar of whiskey. "I want you to have this," he said, "as a present."

Then he came outside and graciously stood by the old Ford while I snapped a picture of him wearing his black felt hat and big grin.

As we rode back toward the gift shop, I checked my notes of our route. I would probably want to come back and bring him a chocolate cake. That seemed to be the way to his heart. Then I realized what I didn't know.

"I didn't get his name," I told Mrs. Gift Shop.

"We just call him Jeeter," she said. She gave me a stern glance that said, *That's all you need to know.* Never mind, I knew where he lived.

Back at the shop, I lingered and bought a jar of apple jelly. I showed Mrs. Gift Shop a graduation picture of Maureen Hubbel, a real-estate-ad picture of Joan Hubbel, and an appointed-head-of-the-department picture of Albert Bright. Just what I'd been able to find in our files. I also had a Polaroid picture I took of Belle Dasher. I asked Mrs. Gift Shop if any of them had come in her shop recently. She asked me why I wanted to know. I admitted I was a reporter checking out some things about the murder of Isaiah Hubbel. She went blue-white, but I promised not to mention the gift shop in any murder story, unless it was involved in the crime.

"Never!" she cried. Then she got interested. She examined the pictures. "No," she said. "I'm new here, and there are lots of folks I don't know. I'm from Jackson County. But I haven't seen any of these folks. I'm sure of that. I wish I could help."

Was she putting me on?

CHAPTER
24

TUESDAY, AFTER 5 P.M.

Back at the office, I tried to call Belle to get the Nashville man's number. No luck. I had no name for the shelter, so Information couldn't help. I saw a note to myself to go visit Pop after work. I'd try the Nashville man again later. I punched Ted's number into the phone on my desk. I doodled a maze on the bottom edge of a press release about a new national TV show, something we'd never use unless they shot a scene in Monroe County. I wished it were as easy in regular life to know what could be useful.

As if he'd read my mind, Ted said, "I've found out something useful. I'll tell you about it when you get here."

I wanted to hurry to see Pop and get on home, so I didn't ask for details. "I won't have the pictures I promised to show Pop," I said, "because I gave them to Deputy *Why Not*. But I'll have a genuine jar of white lightning."

"Pop may prefer that." Ted laughed. "Shall I pull something out of the freezer for supper?"

"How about lasagna? And there's lettuce all washed in the fridge, so we can have a salad."

"If you sample the white lightning," he warned, "let me know if you need a ride back from Pop's."

From what I'd tasted of the stuff, he had a point.

I called Pop to say I was on my way. "Well, hurry up," he said gaily. "Albert Bright will be here shortly, and he'll have to tell us more than he ever meant to tell! I have his number!" Albert Bright, memory prof and Pop's favorite suspect.

"How come?" I asked with my heart sinking. This sounded as if it was going to be one of Pop's crazy machinations. I mean, I know he works to keep his life full of action and excitement, and that's a neat trick when you're in your eighties and wheelchair bound. But, after all, he'd married Azalea, the eternal optimist, when he was already antique, which was also a neat trick. That should spice his life up, shouldn't it?

"Albert Bright is going to tell us his secret," Pop explained portentously. Inadvertently I glanced up at the big wall calendar by my desk with all the dates written in. The murder was Monday, just yesterday. No solid suspects yet.

"What secret?" I asked.

"That's what we're going to find out," Pop said, plainly annoyed. "I told him you wanted to give him the chance to talk to you about his secret before you told that deputy Suzie said was your friend."

"Pop, I don't know any secret, and I bet you don't either, so what are you up to?" I was too tired after a long day to want to play games.

Peeved silence. How can I tell Pop is peeved over the phone without hearing a word? Years of practice.

"You're a champion bluffer, Peaches," Pop said in his but-tering-up voice. "You'll make the most of this encounter." His voice sharpened. "So don't whine. It doesn't suit you."

I had *not* been whining. But there's no point in getting mad at Pop. He's like a natural force, a tornado or a light-ning bolt. The best thing is to protect yourself and work around the voltage. And there was one point in Pop's favor. Mr. Professor had agreed to come to Pop's to meet me when he heard I knew a "secret." Why did he do that? Could Albert Bright really know some hidden fact related to Isaiah Hubbel's death? Isaiah, who was, after all, his brother-in-law? Was he afraid I'd discovered that fact?

When I pulled into Pop's drive, Albert Bright's blue Volkswagen Bug was already there.

O.K., I thought, *play it by ear.*

Albert *Halibut* Bright was sitting at the round table with Pop, as fidgety as the first time I met him. Fingering that odd red macramé-chain for his glasses. He jumped up politely, and I said, "Please sit down." I sat down on the other side of Pop.

"I am so sorry about your sister's husband," I said.

He sighed. "That's a tragedy, and we still don't know where she is or what's happened to her. We can't even let her know." He washed his dry hands together.

Be cool and let him bring up what he's come about, I told myself. *So talk about memory. That's what you have in com-mon.*

"Today I met an interesting old man who is totally unable to remember faces," I said. "That's a most unusual memory glitch. I bet you know about that kind of thing."

I noticed he went pale. He stuttered. "Who—who was that?"

"Monroe County's resident moonshiner," I said, and pulled out the bag with the jar of moonshine and the book. He blinked and went even paler. I felt I was onto something.

"I couldn't bring you the pictures I told you about," I said to Pop. "But here's a jar of white lightning. The very kind that was in the first picture I took of poor Isaiah Hubbel. The jar disappeared from the table next to Isaiah after I left the room for a few minutes and then took another picture a little later."

"On the day he died?" Albert asked in a choked voice. "You mean you took pictures after he was dead?"

"Yes," I said. "I'm sorry to upset you. But why would a jar of moonshine disappear? Who could have removed it so fast?"

Albert Bright did not answer. I could wait.

Pop beamed. "We should sample this stuff to be sure it's real."

"Mr. Moonshine says it's good medicine that will cure practically anything that ails you, and even lengthen your life," I said. My cousin Dora, who believed Prohibition was a high point in American history, would not agree.

Pop called, "Sandy, could you bring us some little glasses?"

Sandy, Pop's sitter-on-duty, was in the kitchen, perhaps fixing Pop's supper, and she came out with four small juice glasses. She'd forgotten Azalea was out. Never mind, Azalea would be back.

"I'll pour," I said firmly. I unscrewed the top from the small jar and poured us each a small amount. I sniffed mine. The smell was too mild to warn you. "Be careful," I said. "This stuff tastes gentle at first sip and then kicks like a mule."

"Wowee!" Pop cried out. "That's something!"

The professor's hand actually shook as he accepted his, and he took a generous swallow as if he needed the medicine. Then he took a gulp of air and then another. My whole face, not just my tongue, was on fire after my sip. I felt beet-red, but he stayed pale.

Was it something about moonshine that scared him hollow?

"I understand that people who can't remember faces may otherwise have excellent memories," I remarked. "They can remember people they meet by voice or by smell, or any other sense, just not visually." I wanted him to think that if he had visited the moonshiner I could find out, face or no.

"Yes," he said. "We don't have one memory. We have many kinds of memory. If one kind doesn't work, we can get around that with the other kinds." He sounded dry and professorial, maybe trying to get me off the moonshine track. He took another sip, as if to get his nerve up, and he said, "I understand there is something you want to talk to me about."

So, O.K., I'd have to admit I knew nothing or play my hunch.

"I hear you went to see the moonshine man," I said. Why else was he acting so strange?

Pop beamed. "Pour me a little more of that stuff, Peaches. That's good!" He turned to the professor. "And of course that man gave you a jar of hooch."

"Yes," he blurted. "I don't know how you found out. I took that jar for a present to Isaiah. But I did that on Saturday. I was never there on Monday at all. Never on the day he was killed." His hands writhed. Boy, was he tense, but trying to be calm and reasoned. Was he on the level or lying?

"Isaiah loved old-fashioned corn whiskey, and he couldn't go get it for himself so he rarely got any," he explained. "It was his favorite present. So I went to ask what he'd heard about Joan, if anything, and I took him a jar." The professor gave me a defiant glance, as if to say, Want to make something of it?

"Where were you on Monday morning?" Pop asked, really relishing his success at ferreting out secrets. His cheeks were moonshine-pink.

"I was teaching a class!" the professor said defensively. "A seminar from nine to twelve."

"I saw a car just like yours on Mountain Road the day of the murder," I said.

"But not mine," he said quickly.

Check the class, I told myself. But I figured he'd be too smart to lie about something that simple to prove or disprove.

"Did you see anything when you visited Isaiah Saturday," I asked, "that seemed out of the ordinary or suspicious in any way?"

He said no.

"Did anybody see you go there on Saturday?" I asked.

Pop said, "You always need a witness!" His voice was somewhat slurred.

That witness question bothered the professor. He washed his hands harder. "No, not that I know of," he said. "But I wasn't really noticing. The neighbors might have seen me come."

He took another sip of white lightning. So did Pop. Azalea, who'd been out doing errands, came in just then and joined us. Pop gave her a glass, and one sip made her whistle. Pop grinned at her and said, "Hot diggity dog!"

"Did Isaiah tell you anything useful about Joan and where she might be?" I asked the professor, trying to keep on track. It was very odd she'd totally vanished. Lucky for her, perhaps, that she vanished well before Isaiah was killed.

"Isaiah said she left a note saying she needed some space to think, and then took off. Nobody knew where she'd gone. He was upset about that. And you know, come to think of it, when he talked about how she'd vanished he seemed scared." Albert frowned as if he'd made a discovery and needed to think more about it.

"Life is scary," Pop announced sadly. Dern him, he was getting drunk!

"You mean Isaiah seemed scared for her or for himself?" I asked.

"I don't know," the professor said. "Of course he'd be scared for her, scared that something bad happened to her. He said he'd talked to that good friend he has on the Internet about it." Oh, yes, the friend who made Joan jealous. The man in Nashville who'd been with Isaiah in Vietnam.

The professor's frown deepened. "But it may have been more than just worrying because he hadn't heard from her. She'd taken off before and not called home for as much as a week."

Now, why hadn't anyone told me she'd done that before? They'd said she kept in touch. Of course this was longer.

"I think Isaiah acted more strangely, much jumpier, than I ever saw him before. But it's hard to be sure what you really remember," Albert said, "and how other, later knowledge could have distorted your memory." He began to sound like a college lecturer again. "You know that memory can change over time. Memory can be influenced by what we hear or see later." I poured him a little bit more moonshine. But he didn't tell us anything else useful.

I said I had to meet Ted for supper and I hugged Pop and Azalea and whispered to be sure to put Albert in the guest room if he was not in good driving condition. Azalea winked, so I could see she already had it in mind. I wouldn't put it past Pop in his tipsy state to deliberately get Albert as high as possible to see if his tongue would wag. God knows what Pop would blurt out.

Turned out Albert was too smart to let Pop ply him with strong drink. He stood up right after I did. His color was back. He smiled. "I want to thank you," he said, "for letting me know the white lightning I took Isaiah may turn out somehow to be related to his death. I will call the sheriff right away and explain how the whiskey got to his house. I hope that will be helpful." He shook all our hands enthusiastically as he went out.

There was a spring in his step as he left, as if we'd done him a favor. So maybe the "secret" he admitted to was a diversion. Damn. After all, he had an alibi. So what was the real secret? Maybe we'd blown it. Or maybe not. I had a sudden strong hunch that everything the professor said was not just a diversion but a lie. That he was using us somehow. That he was busy muddying up the waters. Why?

"I don't believe that man," Pop said, and then hiccuped. "He's too pleased with himself!" For once, we agreed. I went in the kitchen, said hello to Sandy, and called Ted to alert him I was on my way.

I heard great laughter from Pop and Azalea in the other room. What was that saying about how whiskey makes the heart glad?

I was glad to remember that the old moonshiner said that real old-fashioned corn whiskey never gave you a hangover. I wondered how much he exaggerated. Maybe, like the snakebite cure, it wasn't true. Whiskey makes snakebites worse. A first-aid teacher told me that.

CHAPTER
25

DINNERTIME

Ted had taken the lasagna out of the freezer and made a salad so we could sit at the kitchen table and share what we'd learned. What is it about a kitchen table that lends itself to creative back-and-forth? Maybe it's the good smells of dinner in the oven that makes all sorts of juices flow. Or the informality of a kitchen table that suggests anything goes. So all sorts of thoughts, wild and otherwise, feel free to pop up.

The darkness outside the window by the table seemed to cut us off from the rest of the world. Two wineglasses marked our places, and a bottle of red wine stood before us. Nice gentle red wine that wouldn't kick.

"It's strange," I said. "When I was trying not to get mixed up in murder, everybody seemed to conspire to see that I learned as much as possible, first about the supposed-murder of Joan Hubbel and then this in-your-face murder of poor Isaiah. But now that we're trying to find facts, I think everybody I talk to is giving me the runaround."

"You're probably just more alert to that," Ted said cheerfully. "Did that college professor tell you lies?" He poured us each a glass of wine.

"Perhaps," I said. "But you tell me what you found out first. Maybe that's solid."

"I bumped into that nice deputy who thinks you're psychic about murder," Ted said, raising one eyebrow in a fey salute. "He says you look a lot like his grandmother who had the Sight. But just in case you didn't see it in a vision, he told me they've found out that Isaiah Hubbel changed his will shortly after his wife disappeared. The old will left everything to Joan. The new one leaves everything including his so-called mountain to Maureen. She told the sheriff that and said she was amazed."

"Perhaps she was," I said hopefully.

Ted shrugged. "Of course, the sheriff could have found out anyway with an order to Isaiah's attorney. She may have known that."

I whistled. "She doesn't seem to be a gold digger." Then something began to come back to me. A news release in her hand. "Wait a minute," I said. "She's an actress. With the Monroe Players. They're not professional, but they're good. I think she was somebody or other in *The Mouse Trap*. So maybe she fooled me. But I don't want that to be true," I said. "I like Maureen." I sipped my wine and sighed.

"What else?" I asked, and Ted said wasn't that enough for a day when he'd had to teach, too? But I knew by the twinkle in his eye there was something else.

"I tried to fill in holes," he said. "What we didn't know

that we should be curious about. For instance, exactly how did Brad Hubbel learn you were going to the Opryland Hotel? Maybe it doesn't matter now, but maybe it does."

I said, "I don't think he could have followed us, not all the way without being spotted, though he might have done it in the beginning of the trip when we were on those winding roads."

Ted fingered his glass. "So he must have been able to hear Pop telling Alice where you were going, or Pop making reservations on the car phone."

"How can you do that?"

"I went by an electronics store and asked a nice young woman how someone manages to eavesdrop. I should have thought to do that in Nashville, but I didn't. You won't believe how easy it is," Ted said, putting his glass down and leaning forward. "All you need is a police scanner and disrespect for the law."

"And where do you get a police scanner?" I asked. "I assume the police don't give them away."

"That type of scanner," he explained, "is available at any electronic equipment shop. The disrespect for the law comes in because the scanner has to be illegally modified if you want to listen in on car phone conversations."

"How do you learn to do that?" I asked. "I sure wouldn't know how."

"You can get directions for doing it on the Internet if you are the handy type. Also, you can buy secondhand scanners already modified. But Brad was an electronics whiz, right? And he thought he was being spied on so he needed to protect himself."

Out the kitchen window I saw a shooting star. "Protect himself from Martians," I said dryly. "And then what? If

Mad Brad had a modified scanner, how would he know Pop's car phone number? It's not listed in the phone book. Almost nobody has it but you and me and Azalea and Alice."

"There's no need to know the phone number."

Now that really confused me. "How else would you zero in?"

"Let's say you're driving along in back of a car. You don't have to be close, just within about a quarter of a mile. You direct your scanner to pick up all numbers within range. If you get several, you zero in on the one where you recognize the voice or the subject of the conversation. But if there's not much traffic, you may only get your target. That's it!"

I whistled. "Boy, the person listening in wouldn't even need to be in sight on our winding roads."

"So here's the word from your technical expert," he said. "Do not tell secrets on your car telephone. Do not tell where you're going if you don't want to be followed from afar, or possibly met."

I shivered. "I'll use phone booths and friends," I said. "Why does progress always have to have a flip side? What else did you learn?"

"Your turn," he said. "I've talked enough."

I told about the moonshiner who couldn't remember faces.

"Amazing," Ted said. "How did he spot the revenuers? How did he know when to run and hide?"

I couldn't answer that, but I told Ted I was surprised that the old man seemed to regard the art of whiskey-making with such reverence. But then, at $25 a visitor, plus tips, he could afford to.

"And why did Albert Bright seem so pleased after he told

on himself for visiting Mr. Moonshine?" I asked. "Pleased about taking that jar of corn liquor to Isaiah Hubbel, who was murdered with it right by his side?"

"Very strange," Ted agreed. "If the jar got there in such an innocent way, why did someone steal it and remove every trace of it, right after Isaiah Hubbel was killed?"

We both shook our heads, confused.

"But never mind," said Ted. "It helps to list what you know and what you don't know, even when the second list seems longer."

A bell went off. That meant the lasagna was ready. Thank you, kitchen timer. With my new portable brain, my life could be full of bells. Like back in high school. I jumped up, pulled the lasagna out of the oven, bubbling with cheese and tomato, and put it on a hot-mat on the table. I set our places. Meanwhile Ted got the salad and dressing. I realized I was starving.

"What will you do next?" Ted asked, as we munched happily away.

"I want to know more about the Hubbel family," I said. "There's something about the way each one relates to the others that's causing all this. That's my hunch. Suzie would know some and know where to find out more. But I keep calling Suzie at her mother's, and she isn't there. Tomorrow, I'll track her down. Remind me when we finish supper to put that in my portable brain."

CHAPTER
26

WEDNESDAY, 9 A.M.

On Wednesday morning I arrived at the paper and found Martin worried about not having enough copy to fill up the available space. I'd been spending my time on the murder story that wasn't ready to be reported in detail yet, except for what the sheriff told us officially, and Martin was going to write that. Of course, Martin had gone back and taken pictures of the Hubbel house on the mountain, and he had a picture of Isaiah in his Vietnam War uniform. He said he felt the picture of the dead body in the chair was a little too much for a community newspaper. Besides, I'd given that picture to Deputy *Why Not*.

Martin showed me the Vietnam picture: Isaiah as a dark young man almost as handsome as a movie star. Slightly weak chin. Vulnerable, somehow. Was there something strange about the eyes? Or was that hindsight? Much younger, of course, than the dead Isaiah. He held his head proudly. This must have been early on in the war. I felt sad that the war ravaged him. Left him imprisoned on his mountain. Could there be some connection between the war and his death? No clue to that so far. The picture would make Martin's story more poignant.

"But a newspaper has to have more than one story," Martin said with a laugh. "The old saying is that a community weekly has to mention everybody in town at least once a year."

I told him what I had: one golden wedding, a fire, and a water board meeting. But we were thin on regular news. I'd have to get on the phone and gather some.

Maybe my luck was still holding. A woman came in the door carrying a briefcase. She was about forty-five, I figured, wearing no-nonsense pants and a jacket, comfortable flat shoes, with a nurturing face. I'd met her somewhere or other before. I pegged her for a schoolteacher.

"You remember our conversation," she said confidently. I could probably have bluffed it, but she looked so kindly I didn't bother.

"I will if you remind me," I said. "I know we've met, but to tell the truth I'm not good at remembering faces or names, but I remember plots. What was the plot of our conversation?"

"A contest," she said. "For high school students. I'm Amanda Black. I teach twelfth-grade English."

I almost jumped up and hugged her. "Oh, yes," I rejoiced, "I remember. The kids were going to write papers related to local history, were going to interview older folks and get stuff from the library, too, and the best three papers would be printed in the *Word*." Great! Our readers loved local history.

"The papers were all so good, we had trouble choosing. I have the top three, but you might want to publish some of the others, too," she said.

I looked quickly through the ten she brought, and could hardly believe my luck. One was an interview with the writer's uncle about the men who went from Monroe County to the Vietnam War, including the uncle himself.

"That's recent history," she said, "but I thought that considering what happened to poor Isaiah Hubbel, you might want to include it. He's mentioned in it briefly."

"That's wonderful!" I told her. Remembering all that empty space, I said, "I think we may want to use at least two this week, one about the men who went to the Vietnam War as a sidebar to the murder story, and this other one about Civil War veterans buried in the Random Hill cemetery, including the great-grandfather of the girl who wrote it. What a great project this must have been!"

She said the kids had learned a lot, and then she went off, leaving me with those precious ten stories about the county. I looked at them again. There was even a story about a murder right after the Civil War. Revenge for the fact that someone fighting on the Northern side had killed someone in the Southern ranks after the war was actually over. This county had been badly split during the war, and after—and this was a place where people held grudges. Even now, apparently. Who had such a grudge against Isaiah Hubbel that they killed him?

All right, I'd filled some space, or had the wherewithal! And my luck held. Here came the Methodist minister with a story about a fundraising drive to enlarge the church hall. The story was already written. Two pages. God bless him.

He noticed a file folder I'd marked "Isaiah Hubbel" in large red letters so I wouldn't misplace it. I'd had it out of the file to see what back stories we had about him. There wasn't much.

"I used to go up and visit Isaiah Hubbel," the minister told me. "He was afraid of everything."

"What do you remember about him?" I asked.

"Just that he was a sad man," he said in an I-don't-talk-about-my-visits voice.

He walked over to my bulletin board and studied the YOU CAN BE PERFECT flyer. It sure stirred comment, maybe because it was shocking. "That was a sad young man," he said, "the one who gave these out. Two unhappy men, both dead."

He read the words aloud, " 'You can be perfect.' " He shook his head. "I don't interpret what the Bible says about being perfect quite the way he did. To me it means that each person should be his own best self as much as he can." He came back over to my desk and looked me in the eye. "Perfectionism is not the same as being perfect," he said in a passionate tone of voice.

I could see perfectionism pinched him somehow. And I was grateful for the story he brought. Maybe my listening ear could even help the clergy.

"I had a young cousin down East," he said, "who had to do everything exactly right from the time she was a little kid. She became a champion runner. She won a race that might have been a step to the Olympics, and she kept right on running to a bridge and jumped off it. Tried to kill herself."

I must have looked shocked. "But why? She won."

"She said she couldn't stand the pressure any longer. The pressure was that she had to make herself win every single time."

I tried to imagine that. Personally I'm pleased as pie if I get through the day with no goofs I can't make right.

"Thank goodness," he said, "she got help."

Somehow his earlier words came back to me: *Two unhappy men. Both dead.*

"You don't think perfectionism had anything to do with the murder of the young man who gave out the flyers? Or Isaiah Hubbel being killed?" As I said it, it sounded so unlikely, I felt stupid.

"No," he said, "but maybe it had to do with their being unhappy. The boy must have been unhappy to yell at the people who wouldn't take his flyers. It's sadder, don't you think, when an unhappy person dies?"

He smiled. "I've bent your ear," he said, "and now my Sunday sermon is half written! Thank you."

I could put a sign on my desk: *In return for written stories, at least three hundred words, feel free to try your sermons out here.* But I wouldn't.

Anyway, now I had enough copy for the paper and I could track down Suzie, my Hubbel expert. She'd be useful, even on the phone.

That's what I thought. But this was really my lucky day. Before I could begin the search, she arrived, suitcase in hand. She came rushing in, out of breath, plunked herself in the chair across from my desk, and said, "What a time for Ma to get sick! Turned out to be a false alarm, too. I mean, I've heard part of what's gone on, but not from you, and you're the eyewitness to the body of that poor man." She paused, caught her breath, and said, "I tried to call you a couple of times, but you were out, so I figured I'd wait to hear in person."

That meant she'd managed to get most of the details from somebody else, but she wasn't sure they were right. So I began to tell her from the beginning about how Jake Hubbel and Martin and I found Isaiah Hubbel dead. How I looked through the rest of Isaiah Hubbel's house, only superficially, though I did discover that the gun Maureen Hubbel said was kept in the bathroom wasn't there.

"And somebody had been searching for something," I said. "They'd turned over a laundry hamper, for example."

"Probably Isaiah's jar of money," she said.

"A jar of money?"

"He kept it in case he ever had to escape from the mountain." She smiled at me. "Peaches, you expect people to be logical. People are not logical."

I knew she was right, but this got stranger and stranger. I told Suzie how I took two pictures of the body and the jar of moonshine disappeared between the two.

"Jake took it," she said. "He's the family clean-up man. He tries to fix what goes wrong, and smooth over what he can't fix. His mother would have wanted that. She wanted everything just right. Her children's shoes were always shined. She believed in putting up a front."

"Is his mother still alive?" I asked.

"No," Suzie said, "but she molded him that way, and he's stuck. Almost any family could use a clean-up man, but it makes it harder to find out who killed who and why."

"So you think a member of the family killed Isaiah?"

"That's always possible," she said with a shrug. "Who knows?"

I explained I wanted to find out more about each member of the family.

"You have to understand," she said, "they're all very loyal to each other. They carry a good thing too far. That's why Jake goes to great lengths to protect Brad. Their uncle was a Baptist preacher, a Bible-thumping type during Prohibition who called whiskey devil-water, but he hid his brother's still in his attic when the revenuers were close to finding it."

"Blood," I said, "was not only thicker than water, but thicker than whiskey!"

"Herbert, who runs the nursery, is the nicest of the lot." That was Maureen's father. "But when Jake was accused of reckless driving when they were younger, Herbert said he was in the car with Jake and saw the other car pull out in front of him. Another witness said that wasn't so. I believe the other witness because . . ." Suzie stopped in midsentence and cocked an ear. She must have heard the outside door open. Suzie has super-ears.

"You need to talk to Jake Hubbel's aunt Sharon," she said quickly. "She's in the Monroe Estate nursing home. They don't visit her enough, and that woman just loves to talk. She knows more than I do. And then, after I unpack and call to be sure how Ma is, let's have lunch. We haven't had much chance to talk. You can come to my house. That'll be private."

She raised an eyebrow, and I could see she was indicating a woman with two small children who came right in and asked where to leave a wedding announcement. I said I'd take care of it, and to please give me a number to call if I had any questions. She wrote the number down but looked quite wary, as if I might ask if the bride was pregnant or the groom had a good enough job. I am certainly more tactful than that.

"Visiting hours," Suzie said after the woman departed, "are all day long. You can go to the nursing home right now." Her eyes said, *So, do it!* She picked up her suitcase and walked out of my office, calling, "See you for lunch whenever you get there. I'll wait."

Before I left, I glanced through the story about Monroe boys who served in Vietnam. The mention of Isaiah Hubbel was unfortunately very brief: "Isaiah Hubbel and his good friend Lee Fortune Roberts were in Vietnam at the same time, and managed to get together in Saigon more than once, my grandpa says. After the war, Lee Fortune Roberts had some troubles, but he was called to be a preacher and moved to Nashville. Isaiah Hubbel stayed here." Stayed here was putting it mildly. No mention of Isaiah's breakdown. I pulled out my portable brain and wrote in: *Lee Fortune Roberts, Nashville. E-mail friend? Will he know about Isaiah's last weeks and his fears and hopes, and how he might have been in danger? Call Belle to see if she knows how to reach him.*

Then I set out for the nursing home.

CHAPTER
27

I left a note for Martin and went out to my car which was parked in front of the office. I started to get in and realized something was wrong. The front tire was flat. How could that happen with the car just sitting there? I walked around the car. The other front tire was flat, too. Somebody had punctured my tires. I was mad. In a rural county such as Monroe, there's no way to function without a car. Someone wanted me powerless.

Somebody who knew my car! But that wasn't hard. There's a geranium on the end of my radio antenna. The only one of its kind in Monroe County. But what skunk used my find-it trick to do me in?

Mad Brad! I thought. I was furious. I should have turned him over to the police when he threatened me in Nashville!

Then the on-the-other-hand side of me kicked in. The person who killed Isaiah Hubbel could have slashed my tires. Nobody in sight on the street. Main Street in Monroetown was not your standard busy thoroughfare. Flat tires were a warning for me to mind my own business and not go nosing around. Without a car I couldn't go nosing around. Damn.

I kicked one of the flat tires and only managed to hurt my toe. I looked up and down the street for someone I knew to appear. Maybe I could get a ride to the service station. Maybe someone could fix my tires.

There was a familiar-looking car in front of the pharmacy. I couldn't think whose it was. I walked down toward the store, where fake antique apothecary jars were displayed in the front window. The car was reflected in the window. Whose was it? I went over to the car and then noticed that all the windows were rolled down about an inch. Bailey jumped up, front paws against the passenger-side window, and welcomed me with excited yips. Aha. I told him hi, then went into the pharmacy to find Belle. Just the one I wanted to see! I hurried past bandages and other first-aid supplies with a sign that said Be Prepared. With no car, I definitely wasn't prepared. Past a rack of greeting cards including one with a cartoon policeman and the words "Trust Nobody." What could the occasion for that be? Trust nobody—including Belle? But certainly Belle would have no reason to puncture my tires, would she?

She was at the counter just getting her change. She put a small bag in her pocketbook and turned to me with a welcoming smile. "Good morning."

"It would be wonderful if you could give me a ride to get my tires fixed," I said. "Somebody punctured them. And I also need an address."

"Punctured your tires!" She seemed shocked. "But you

mustn't fix them till you let the sheriff look at them," she told me firmly. Of course she was right.

"But I've got to go over to Monroe Estate Nursing Home right now," I said. I was all psyched up to go. If I spent the morning with the sheriff I might never get there. Tomorrow was Thursday. Deadline day for everything.

"Oh, giving you a ride is no problem," Belle said, almost as if she'd been waiting to do just that. "I want to drop by there myself. I understand they have a visiting-pets program for the residents. I could take Bailey in once a week. He's so silky and warm that one hug is worth two operations. Did you know that people with pets live longer?"

Random thought: Isaiah Hubbel would almost certainly have lived longer if his dogs hadn't been off at the vet! Maureen Hubbel took them. They liked Maureen. Did that give her an alibi or an opportunity?

"I'll take you to the nursing home and then ask them about Bailey," Belle said. "How long will you be there?"

"A while," I said. "I want to talk to one of the patients for background for a story. But then I have to go over to Suzie's for lunch."

"No problem," she said. "I go by Suzie's on my way home. If you're going to be long, I'll take Bailey for a walk. That's a lovely part of the county."

Belle was being super-helpful. On the other hand, she was worried the sheriff thought she killed Isaiah Hubbel. She wanted me to prove she didn't. So she would be nice to me. Or, if she feared I might find out she did do it, she might want to watch me closely. But as mad as she was at fate, she still loved life and enjoyed good company. I told myself I was good company.

Bailey went mad with joy as we got in the car, jumping

from back seat to front seat and back again in an explosion of energy. The minute I was settled, he jumped in my lap and soon lay down as quiet as a rug.

"Belle," I said, "this Lee Fortune Roberts that Isaiah knew as a kid and went to Vietnam with, the one who's a Baptist minister now—he's the one who works at the homeless shelter in Nashville? The one who's a friend of yours—right? How do I get in touch with him?"

Long silence. Finally she said, "He won't tell you anything. He says it's all confidential."

"But since someone shot Isaiah, he may change his mind," I said. Besides, Belle had wanted to hurt Isaiah. Now he was beyond being hurt. Death had changed everything.

"Lee is at the Reynolds Shelter," Belle said. She pulled out a small notebook and gave me his number, almost defiantly. "I imagine he'll come to the funeral," she said. "If he can get away. He lived just down the mountain from Isaiah when they were kids. They kept in touch. But he sure knows how to keep his mouth shut."

There were long views on the way to the nursing home. Our mountains are like that. While you are between two wrinkles in the earth, you can see the wildflowers clearly on both sides of the road, and then you can come out into a wide space and see range after range of mountains blue and green against the distance.

"We're not so big, are we?" Belle remarked, staring out at the mountains. "Not in the total scheme of things."

"Does that make you feel better about Isaiah being shot?" I asked. "Does that make murder seem less fearful? Because the victim is not so important in the total scheme of things?"

I blurted that out and then felt it was almost an accusation.

Belle turned and stared at me so long that I wanted to yell, *Hey! Keep your eyes on the road.*

"No matter how small we are," Belle said, "we're important to ourselves. Whoever murdered Isaiah Hubbel did it to help himself."

"And who do you think it was?"

She thought for a long time. "Isaiah had a way of making people feel trapped. Of making them feel that they had to do things his way because he lived in his own hell. After a while you were angry at him for making you feel that way. And angrier as time went on. That helped me break it off. But it was hard because he did live in his own hell, complete with nightmares. I think someone who felt trapped killed him. He might even have had a new girlfriend we don't know about."

I thought of that handsome dead face, not young but still handsome. Maybe Suzie had heard some gossip about a girlfriend. Wouldn't she have told me?

We stopped in front of a red brick building, big and low, with a sign that said Monroe Estate. Institutional, but the trees planted near it, and just leafing out, softened the boxy lines. Time for me to concentrate on what I could learn here. We went up the front steps into a hall that smelled of air freshener and antiseptic. Three residents in wheelchairs sat in the hall, staring at us with blank eyes. One jerked with some kind of palsy, one seemed almost comatose, and the third, who looked to be about eighty, said, "Where is my mother? I want Mama."

"That's pitiful," Belle said. She walked over and patted the woman's long bony hand, saying, "You will go home to your mother, but you have to be patient." That actually seemed to satisfy the old woman for about one minute. Then we heard her calling out behind us, asking for her mama again.

Belle made an unhappy face. "How awful," she said, "to want the impossible every minute. If anything will bring her to her mother, it will be death. And they'll do everything they can to keep her from death."

We heard the woman still calling in the distance as we followed signs to the office and found a plump, cheerful woman behind a desk with a picture of three laughing little girls in a gold frame on it. Strange contrast. Cheerful Woman didn't let the patients get her down. At least not so it showed. We explained that I wanted to visit Sharon Hubbel, and Belle wanted to talk to the person in charge of recreation for the patients.

Cheerful Woman said Sharon would be so pleased. She got lonely. "And don't mind her roommate. Some days she's a little off the wall." She gave me directions and said she could talk to Belle about the pet program.

Fortunately, after one wrong turn in the halls, which all looked and smelled alike, I met a man in a wheelchair who set me on the right path to Sharon Hubbel's room. His body might be giving out, but his mind was sharp.

I needed to be sharp. Why had Suzie referred to this Sharon as Jake Hubbel's aunt and not the aunt of all the Hubbel brothers? That suddenly struck me as strange. If they were brothers, they had the same aunt, right? But then, we'd been talking specifically about Jake.

There was a card with Sharon's name on the door to her room, and next to it a spray of artificial yellow flowers. Plastic forsythia likely to outlast the patient.

Inside, a bright-eyed woman sat in a chair with a small

pink blanket over her knees and a TV remote in one claw-like hand.

"It's about time you came," she said, and clicked the TV off. But she hadn't known I was coming. She didn't know who I was. She sat in a chair next to the second bed in the small room.

"Are you the Navy?" asked a frail, wrinkled woman in the nearer bed. "I've just reported the pirate, and they didn't seem upset at all." She must be the sometimes-off-the-wall one.

Bright-eyes said, "Be quiet, Mandy. This woman wants to talk to me." Now how did she know that?

"I'm looking for Sharon Hubbel," I said.

"Of course," she replied. "Nobody comes to see Mandy, and damn few people come to see me."

"I'm a friend of Suzie Scott," I said, walking closer to her chair, "and I work for the newspaper."

"So I bet you're the one who found Isaiah Hubbel dead." She sat up straight, eyes even brighter. "You and that editor and Jake. I heard it on the TV and then I heard the nurses talking. They talk as if we're not here. I could have told them a thing or two, but I didn't." She laughed, as though that was a great accomplishment and served them right.

"Pirates can kill you," said the woman in the other bed.

"I understand you're the Hubbel boys' aunt," I said to Sharon. "I want to learn about Isaiah, even what he was like when he was a kid."

She beamed and indicated I should sit in a greenish over-stuffed chair. "Now," she said, "I can see you have sense enough to know what to ask! Isaiah was the nicest one in the whole highfalutin' family. That's what he was like as a child. His father was the stubbornnest man in the county, and proud because *his* father had been a state senator. Which he could afford to be with moonshine money from *his* father. It doesn't matter how you got your money. Once you've got it you can put on airs. Too bad he died young. I married Isaiah's uncle Mike. They were all so damn good-looking. They tried to make me put on airs. But I'm a plain woman. I act like I feel and say what I think. Isaiah was too nice for his own good. Too sensitive. He was sickly as a child, and his mother protected him. Well, in a way she protected him, and in a way she kept at him to do everything right. She wanted all of us to do everything just right, even in-laws like me. She used to say, 'There's only one right way to do what you intend to do,' and all the time she looked like she was sniffing a load in your pants."

"Why?" I asked. "Why was she so picky?"

"We had a lot of folks who made moonshine," Sharon said, "who felt it was their right. A way to have enough in hard county in a hard time. People were proud of making good whiskey as their ancestors did back in Scotland. It was a tradition. The Hubbels were like that. They told family stories all about it. Like the one about the great-uncle who was caught by a revenuer and brought before a judge. And the judge asked him 'What kind of liquor do you make?' and he said, 'Only the very best.'"

"But why did that make Isaiah's mother into a perfectionist?"

"There were some who thought that drinking was a sin, and some of the churches were down on it. She came from one of those families. She was ashamed of what her husband came from. She shouldn't have married him, I say. But those Hubbel men, they always got the women—one of 'em got me. So she married him. She couldn't change him. But she wanted her children, Jake and Brad and Isaiah and Herbert and Mabel, to be downright shining stars. There's not a one talks like the family came from a back cove.

"Isaiah wasn't ready for a war. The war destroyed him, and nobody made him get help. I tried and I failed. I was healthy in those days."

"So you don't believe the story that's been going around about him polluting his neighbors' wells, or the story that he killed his wife?"

"No," she said firmly. "Probably hogwash."

"Belle Dasher . . ." I began.

"Interesting woman," Sharon said. "Good imagination! I never knew her to lie on purpose. She does get carried away."

"So you think Joan Hubbel may not be dead?"

"Strange woman," she said. "Joan likes crazy people." She spoke as if Joan was still alive. "She was always fond of Brad Hubbel, even at his worst. Could calm him down some. And she's stuck by Isaiah on his mountain, hasn't she? She can sell to anybody. Good at real estate. She's a great convincer."

"What else?" I asked Sharon.

"A very controlling woman. Wants to be in charge. That puts some people off. But not Jake Hubbel. He was used to his mama. Anybody used to his mama was used to being told."

"What do you mean about Jake and Joan?" I asked Sharon. "You mean . . . ?"

"I think he's always been sweet on Joan. Hated to see her marry his brother. That was back before the Vietnam War. Long time ago. To some of the aides here, that could be the Civil War. But Jake Hubbel married a very attractive woman. The sheriff's niece. She died last year. Tragic accident. Her car hit a tree."

"Jake Hubbel come to see us," said Off-The-Wall. I had forgotten she was there.

"Did he?" I asked Sharon.

"At Christmas," Sharon said. "Jake Hubbel and Maureen came by, but that was a while back."

"He was looking for the pirate," Mandy remarked.

I was on my way out and chuckling over Sharon's roommate and her delusions when I passed a man with a patch over one eye.

If I was a little bit off kilter, I could think he was a pirate.

I stopped at the office. Cheerful behind the desk said Belle was waiting for me outside.

"Who is the nice-looking young man with the patch over one eye?" I asked her.

"Oh, that's Dr. James Jackard," she said. "Just making rounds. He's our doctor on call."

So it was easy for a frail mind to interpret what she saw wrong. I felt sorry for these folks in the twilight of life.

Let that be a lesson to you, I said to myself. *What you think you see and what you really see are not always the same thing.* I knew that. But some part of me felt I needed to be reminded.

CHAPTER
28

WEDNESDAY, 12:30 P.M.

Belle had allowed Bailey to pee on a nursing home tree, which seemed disrespectful, but I figured the tree was large enough to take it without damage. The tree was as tall as the nursing home, with leaves exactly the light green of Belle's shirt. We all got in her car, Bailey in my lap again, quivering with life as small dogs do.

"I've been out of my mind," Belle said. She gripped the steering wheel and started the car with a lurch.

"Should you drive?" I asked.

"Not the serious kind of out of my mind," she said scornfully. "I've been afraid of dying, scared by my fifty-fifty chance, acting like there's no tomorrow. Now I see that's dumb. It will do me good to visit this place every Friday." She nodded back at Monroe Estates. "That I-want-Mama woman, poor thing, will remind me that dying is not as bad as living too long."

I shuddered to think this new realization could make her even more reckless. But then I realized that with Isaiah Hubbel dead, there was no longer a chance she'd go up the mountain and he'd shoot her. She'd been up the mountain, been up in the daytime, thank God, and—if I could believe her—he hadn't been violent at all, just acted as though he *might* become violent if she didn't get out.

"You went to see Isaiah Hubbel the day he died," I remarked.

"I was angry at him," she said. "I'm glad he's out of his misery. Even him." She maneuvered a sharp curve. "But *I* didn't put him out of his misery, no matter what the sheriff thinks."

"He was still alive when you left at a little after ten o'clock? After you heard the clock strike? You're sure the clock struck ten?"

"Yes," she said, "I heard the clock and I saw it, too."

"You still think he killed his wife?"

"Yes, I do," she snapped. "And I told the sheriff he should look in that rhododendron hell near Isaiah's house. A thicket like that could have important clues hidden inside. A desperate man might manage to get a body in there. Fear gives us super strength."

I knew she told the sheriff.

Willie *Why Not* had mentioned it. Said they hadn't looked yet, but that was yesterday.

"The sheriff didn't take what I said seriously," she snorted, "but he swore he'd look."

I made a note in my portable brain to go see Willie Wynatt after lunch. When life gets exciting, it is possible to forget absolutely anything, even where the body might be found and who might have found it.

Belle let me off at Suzie's restored Victorian house, not too far from my office.

Suzie liked fresh paint, and the white house with dark green gingerbread trim positively glowed. I banged the brass knocker on the bright white front door, and Suzie answered in nothing flat.

"You must be hungry," she said after she gave me a hello hug. Since she got me my job, she treated me like family. "It's nearly one o'clock."

She led me into a small dining room where all sorts of goodies were laid out on the table: sliced chicken, cheeses, sliced tomatoes, pickles, mayonnaise, carrot sticks, whole wheat and white bread.

She stuck a glass of milk in front of me. Luckily I like milk. "We can eat while we talk," she announced, as if that was a privilege.

I began to make myself a sandwich with everything on it. At the same time I told her the details about talking to Sharon. Otherwise she might have exploded with curiosity.

"Sharon said Isaiah was too sensitive," I remarked. "That doesn't fit with killing his wife." The picture of him came back strong. "Dead with his eyes open," I said. "That got to me. Partly because he was still so handsome. If women really did sneak up that mountain to see him, maybe one of their husbands found out and killed him. Except the moonshine factor doesn't fit with that."

Was it my imagination or did Suzie get a kind of moony look on her face? She was only a little older than Isaiah and well put together.

"Were you ever attracted to Isaiah?" I came right out with it.

She laughed. "I do have better sense than that. Here, have some pickles."

She was in a hurry to change the subject. "I heard you went off to visit Jeeter to try to find out more about moonshine and what it had to do with this."

I bit into my sandwich. It was good.

"I didn't find out much," I said. " Jake had the best chance to make the moonshine disappear. But someone else, hidden in the living room, could have done it while Jake and Martin were in the kitchen and I was upstairs, and that person could have cleared out quick."

"Or Martin could have done it," Suzie said. She was so intense, she forgot to eat. "But I can't think why. Of course, he does have a very pretty wife. People say they fight a lot. Her parents spoiled her. But I can't believe she'd sneak off to see Isaiah Hubbel." She frowned at the thought. A jealous frown?

"But Martin was at the office with me," I said.

She winked. "Then you have an alibi."

"Maybe the killer knew the dogs would be gone," I said. "The dogs would have . . ." Then it hit me right between the eyes. "Good grief, I didn't ask Maureen why she came back to Isaiah's house just as we were expecting the sheriff, with a bunch of jonquils and no dogs! Belle had told me that Maureen took Isaiah's dogs to the vet the very morning he was killed. How come she came back without them? With no dogs, he was unprotected. How could I forget about the dogs!"

"You can still ask Maureen," Suzie said with a shrug, "but

Isaiah wasn't unprotected. He had a bunch of guns. Everybody knew that."

"Dogs warn," I said. "Guns don't. How could I forget the dogs!"

"Peaches," Suzie said, "nobody can predict what you'll forget, but nobody can be sure what you'll suddenly remember, or what strange fact you'll notice. If I were the killer, you'd make me very nervous."

"Maybe nervous enough to puncture my tires?" I asked. Then I told her about my tires and more about the nursing home. About Sharon Hubbel saying that Jake had been sweet on Isaiah's Joan. "So maybe Jake was enraged if he thought Isaiah killed Joan, and so Jake killed his brother." I said it, but somehow it didn't ring true.

"When they were in high school," Suzie said, "Jake went out with Joan. But that was a long time ago."

"The woman in the room with Sharon seems to be talking nonsense," I said, and stopped for a swig of milk. "But people who are a little out of it sometimes mix bits of truth with the rest. She said that Jake Hubbel came to visit Sharon and was looking for 'the pirate.' Now, there's a doctor at the nursing home with a patch over one eye . . ."

Suzie patted my arm, and I almost spilled the milk. "That's Dr. Jackard. I've known him all my life. He is the kindest person I've ever known. You are beginning to clutch at straws. Here, have a piece of chocolate cake. I'll get you some coffee."

Yes. My brain was overheating, partly with frustration. I made myself stop and enjoy the first bite of cake, rich and dark and tender. Suzy had cut herself a slice, too.

"Suzie," I said with a sigh, "you make superb cake." I

tried to pause as if there was no connection. "Somebody," I said, "trades Jeeter chocolate cake for whiskey."

"It isn't me," Suzie protested. She savored a bite. "I prefer chocolate cake. I don't mind if you suspect me, but the real killer will be very nervous. Watch out."

Of course she minded.

CHAPTER
29

WEDNESDAY, 2 P.M.

The Sheriff's Department is right down the street from our office, just past Allison's Dress Shop and the library. Suzie dropped me off at the paper, and I called Deputy Wynatt and told him about my tires. Then I went out and looked at them more closely.

An older man from the funeral home down the street was setting out Reserved for Funeral signs in all the empty parking spots. He eyed my car sadly.

"Sorry," I said, "someone punctured my tires. I can't move my car till the tires are fixed, and that may take a while." Hey, he worked down the street. I said, "Earlier today, did you see anyone suspicious around my car?"

He looked pointedly at my red geranium antenna and said, "No," in an injured tone. He obviously thought I would hurt the dignity of his funeral. Well, at least the deceased wouldn't mind.

Willie Wynatt appeared at the curb in his Sheriff's Department car, jumped out and went over to my car, squatted down and examined each tire. He examined the street around each tire. He walked around the car and examined every bit of the nearby street and the sidewalk. He picked up a gum wrapper, made a wry face, and said, "This seems to be the only clue." He took a photograph of each tire. Hey, the law needs a technological memory the same as I do!

"So, what more have you learned about Isaiah Hubbel's death?" I asked Deputy Wynatt. No point in wasting the opportunity.

"We cut our way into that rhododendron hell," he told me. "But all we found was an old dug well that had evidently gone dry which somebody then used for a dump. Must have been years ago. There was an overgrown path cut in already but only wide enough for one thin man to edge in sideways."

"And what was in the dump?"

"Rusted tin cans, broken dishes, old bottles and containers, that kind of thing. Boxes and bags rotted and fallen apart. No bodies," he added. "Your friend Belle was sure there was a body there." He laughed. "Be a mighty strong man could force his way in there with a body before we hacked a wider path in."

"Can I go look at it?" I asked.

"Sure," he said, "if you feel that would help. Call Norman's Garage to fix your tires. Tell him I said he should come get them. Tell him your car is the only one in front of your office with the red geranium on it, and you'll be out on a story." He gave me a lopsided grin. "Norman's my first cousin, and he owes me one. I'll give you a ride over to Hubbel's place."

That probably meant it was still a crime scene where I couldn't go alone. I went back in my office and called Norman's Garage as directed.

"So you went to see Jeeter," Willie remarked when I came back out. He was still standing near my car. "He's my mother's first cousin. Did he give you some moonshine?"

"Everybody in town knows everything that happens," I said. "Why do they need a newspaper, for heaven's sake!"

"We know more than really happens," he said. "You help us figure out what really didn't. Come get in my car," he added.

"If you know about the moonshine operation, why don't you have to arrest Jeeter?" I asked as I settled into the passenger seat.

He laughed. "He doesn't exactly sell it." He winked at me from the driver's seat. "And he's always been too proud to go on welfare. We admire that." He started up the car and headed toward Hubbel Mountain.

"Do you have any new suspects for the Hubbel murder?" I asked.

"Yes," he said. "Everybody at this end of the county who hasn't got an alibi for the time of the murder, but specially Belle Dasher. Who do you think it was?"

"Not Belle," I said quickly. "No person I know who had the opportunity seems like the right one. Not so far. But I may change my mind." I hoped he would too.

It struck me that the houses around the foot of Hubbel Mountain looked dejected. Maybe that was because the sun was behind a cloud. Nobody was out in a yard, not even a car in a driveway, and so the houses seemed deserted. We drove up the Hubbel driveway, knowing that house would, or at least should, be deserted. Husband dead. Wife vanished. Dogs God knows where. I still needed to find that out. We parked near the house and walked a little uphill to the rhododendron thicket, passing a fenced dog pen—thoroughly empty. I felt bad to see the rhododendron bushes hacked, but now a path went right to the center of the thicket. Inside there was an empty space where flat rocks surrounded what had evidently once been a well. A corroded tin cover with holes eaten through in places, which must once have been a roof over the well, lay near it. Somebody had dug trash out of the well and piled it up to one side. It was half disintegrated, as if it had been there a long time: broken glass, cans nearly rusted away, an old piece of cloth, and oddly some heavy paper sacks. On one I realized the faded lettering said DDT. Yes! DDT! Belle would want to know that.

"The tin cover was over this stuff," Willie said, "protecting it some, at least for a long time."

I looked down into the well. There was more trash.

"The trash down there is packed so tight we could tell it hadn't been recently disturbed," Willie explained. "If someone could have gotten a body in here and buried it under trash, we could tell the trash had been moved. Just like you can tell new-turned earth, even if it's been tamped down."

I could see what he meant. The trash still in the well seemed bonded together by time.

I was disappointed. I wanted the well to hold some wonderful revelation. All it seemed to show was that the DDT, which so upset Belle, could have been here for a long time, protected under the tin roof. When the roof disintegrated, rain could have washed it down into the well, down through the old veins in the earth where water had bubbled up when the well was dug, and then down the mountain. But how could there have been enough DDT to make anyone sick? Was that possible?

I remembered what Sharon Hubbel had said, that Isaiah's mother bought enough insecticide to keep the feed and seed store going. Strange that trying too hard to see that things went right could cause destruction down the road. Whatever else the DDT in the water did, it was a symptom of trying too hard. Of overkill. If I could believe Sharon.

We came back out of the rhododendron thicket and heard frantic barking.

"Run!" Willie yelled, and I saw two big black dogs hurtling up the mountain. I ran so fast I almost pitched forward over a stick on the ground, but I caught myself and grabbed the handle of the car door. I wrenched it open and jumped inside just as one of the dogs came abreast. I pulled that door shut fast. Thank God we both managed to get inside and shut the doors before the two black dogs sprang against the car, leaping against the windows and snarling. Amazingly, I could now see they wore leather leashes, which whipped against the window, and the metal snappers banged against the car windows till I was afraid the windows would break.

Had Isaiah's dogs come back? Had someone seen us come up the mountain and set them loose on purpose to scare us? But why did the dogs have leashes?

Willie looked rather pleased with himself. "I could have shot those dogs," he said, "but I hate to shoot a dog that's doing what it's trained to do. To protect its homeplace. I'm glad we didn't have to do that."

The dogs kept barking and lunging at the windows.

"I'd better get you back to the paper," he said. "Then I'll get someone to help me catch those dogs."

I did not volunteer to help. Personally, I like small friendly dogs, not the kind who look like they might bite your arm off.

Willie started up his car, and at the same time I became aware of a woman running up the hill. She had on high heels and a long skirt. She almost fell several times but managed to keep herself upright. She wore a flapping bandanna and strange-looking dark glasses with rhinestones across the top. And her hands had knots at the finger joints. I could tell because she held up one hand in the stop-that-car position.

Willie obliged.

The dogs left off attacking the car and ran over to her, and she grabbed their leashes. Whereupon they sat down and became well behaved. Amazing.

She walked over to the car, and Willie rolled the window down.

"They ran away from me," the woman said between labored breaths. "I'll put them in their pen"—she nodded at the dogs—"and then I'd like to talk to you."

So we got out of Willie's car as soon as we'd watched her put the dogs in the metal link enclosure and latch the gate. Thank God for strong latches. She came over to me and said, "You're from the newspaper, aren't you? I saw you when I brought in ads." She turned to Willie. "Please, both of you, come inside."

Immediately it hit me. Almost knocked the breath out of me! This was Joan Hubbel. She wasn't dead in the well or anywhere else; she was right here in the flesh. And calm and in command. That blue bandanna and the rhinestone-trimmed dark glasses certainly changed her, made her look like a flaky tourist. But now I saw how her nose and mouth resembled her picture in the real estate ads. Yes, This was Joan. Who else would the dogs obey?

She knew Willie. She was inviting us into her house. Suppose she was just back from God knows where, and didn't even know her husband was dead? I felt possibilities swirling around us. Suppose she had been in town all along in disguise? Suppose she'd lost her mind living on the hill with Isaiah, who never went down the hill?

We followed her up onto the porch where all the plants now needed water so badly that it pained me, and into the living room. Willie Wynatt let her lead the way, waiting, like me, to see what would happen next. I had a feeling that as a deputy he should be doing something official instead. But I couldn't think what, and besides, Willie followed his hunches even more than I did.

I did hope that in case she *had* gone crazy, he had his hand on his gun, but he seemed quite relaxed.

"We've not felt safe about you, Cousin Joan," he said as she paused to open the door. "Nobody knew where you were or if you were all right. I'm glad to see you looking so fine."

Cousin Joan? Was there anybody in this county who wasn't related? Well, yes, there were the new people, but they didn't seem to be mixed up in this murder case, except for Belle.

"Cousin Joan" turned around to face us, took off her dark glasses, and peeled off the bandanna. She was a fine-looking woman with short, curly blond hair and a well-defined face—definite chin, high cheekbones, Roman nose. Now she matched her picture. Except didn't she used to have brown hair? And her picture had looked happy. Now she had circles under her eyes and desperation lines around her mouth.

"So you recognized me," she said to Willie, standing there in front of the door. "And of course you want to know where I've been." She slanted her brilliant blue eyes first to Willie and then to me. "Since I heard that my poor Isaiah was murdered," she said angrily, "I've even been scared for myself. Because what possible reason could there be to kill a man who never goes anywhere?" She waved a hand down the hill. Her voice was well defined but somehow desperate, like her expression.

"What could he do?" she demanded. "Make somebody mad at him on the Internet? Tell them where he lived? Discover gold under our mountain?" She threw both hands wide as if to embrace the mountain. "What could he do?" Those eyes defied us.

She turned and opened the door and led us into the Hubbel living room with its log walls and mementos from the past.

She fell into the big chair. "Dear God, this is where it happened. Here at home." She squared her shoulders and said, "Maybe somehow I can help you find out who did this, because it's not right to kill a man who never hurt anybody. Sit down," she commanded, indicating the other chairs and the couch in front of the big stone fireplace.

I sat on the couch. Willie picked a straight chair.

"This was a terrible thing," she said, "I heard about it on TV. And it's my fault. I shouldn't have left him. If I'd been here I could have sensed that something was wrong."

Willie nodded.

She clutched the seat of her chair, one hand on each side.

"He relied on me, and I failed him." She bit her lips together and didn't cry.

"Where have you been?" Willie asked again, direct but in a kind voice.

"I couldn't take it any longer," she said. She turned her eyes away from us and stared toward the front door, at the wall where the antique china dishes were hung. I noticed one showed a picture of wolves chasing an old-fashioned sleigh. What wolves chased the Hubbels?

"But I couldn't make up my mind to leave him, either," she said. "I had to have time by myself to think. By myself, without people calling me up. So I just took off and drove. I went to Chattanooga and I went to the aquarium. I probably still have the map they gave me, if you want proof I was there." There was challenge in her voice. "Watching fish swim can clear my mind," she said, "but it didn't help this time. I went to the Hermitage in Nashville and wandered around, wondering what problems the other tourists had in their lives. They all seemed so calm."

Good grief, we might have bumped into her there.

"I drove from one town to the next but I couldn't think what to do. I was so upset I looked the wrong way, and a car hit me broadside. Luckily it was his fault, and I wasn't hurt. But that's why I'm driving a rental.

"Then I had the feeling it would help me to stand by a waterfall." She brought her eyes back to us. "I drove all the way back to Linville Falls and watched the water spurting down, and that's where I heard on TV that my poor Isaiah had been murdered. I was in shock."

I shivered. I'd known a man who was murdered at Linville Falls. I assumed the bad-news TV was not at the Falls, but someplace she was staying nearby.

"I'll always feel guilty," she said, "but at least I don't have to make up my mind whether to leave him, do I?" The irony of that turned her voice harsh.

"Did you feel anything Monday morning?" Willie asked eagerly. "Did you have vibes that something bad was happening to your husband?" Of course, Willie would want to know that.

"I'd had a nightmare the night before," she said. "I dreamed that a monster was trying to swallow me and Isaiah." I noticed a dragon was carved on the part of the chair that showed over Willie's shoulder. An odd chair to find in a log house in the mountains.

"We were on an island, somewhere with no place to hide, and we couldn't run fast. So I was depressed Monday morning," she said. "And then things got worse.

"Monday morning, when Isaiah must've been killed, I did feel uneasy. As if something was wrong. Like I might be getting the flu." Willie nodded encouragement. "I stayed at the bed-and-breakfast until noon. And on the noon news . . ." She began to cry.

"Exactly why did you stay at the B and B till noon?" I asked. If she'd been talking to the owner, that would be an alibi.

"You won't believe this," she said. "I had this hunch I ought to go home."

Willie nodded again.

"I was packing up my stuff, and Mrs. Jackson, the woman who runs Falling Waters, told me that she was going out to do errands and take her five-year-old to the doctor. The kid was a menace." Now Joan spit her words angrily. That woman said when I was ready to leave I should just latch the outside door behind me. That was about eight o'clock. But her darned five-year-old locked the door to my room from the outside. I didn't find that out till they were gone. I was mad enough to chew nails. But I didn't know I should do anything—yes, anything—to get out and go home."

"You couldn't climb out the window?" I asked. I figured that's what I would have done.

"I couldn't climb out the window because I was on the second floor, and it was an old house with high floors. Oh! I was mad. I could actually see a ladder out the window but I couldn't get to it. You don't like to break down somebody's antique Victorian door. So I cooled my heels and watched the TV travel channel and then I watched the news." She cried some more.

"I'm so sorry," I said, remembering the dead man's open eyes.

Willie was more practical. "Do you have the name and number of the place where you stayed?" he asked her.

She stopped in mid-sob. Her eyes shot fire. "Certainly you don't think I'm a suspect! You don't look after a man for years and then kill him!"

"Everybody has to be a suspect," Willie told her, "whether we like it or not."

Of course. And the most believable thing about her story was that it was so improbable. If she was going to make a story up, I figured she'd do better than that. Besides, it could be checked.

She stalked over to the other side of the room, to a table flanked by chairs with red velvet seats. Red as the shirt Isaiah Hubbel died in, which was as red as his blood. Her black pocketbook lay on the table, and she grabbed it and brought it back. She looked through a kind of a mini-file place on one side of her pocketbook. A little portable brain just like mine fell out on the table. She had one, too! She searched the pocketbook a little further and pulled out a receipt.

"This is from the Falling Waters Bed and Breakfast. The number's on there," she said angrily.

Willie said "Thank you," and put it in his pocket. "I know this is hard for you."

"When I came here with Jake and Martin and found Isaiah, there were no dogs on the property," I said.

"Everything went wrong at once!" Joan cried. "Almost as if someone planned it! Maureen Hubbel sucked up to my husband. She did him favors. He doted on those dogs. On Monday morning, Maureen took the dogs to the vet to get their teeth cleaned, to get the tartar build-up removed."

Amazed silence. A man had died because of tartar build-up? Then, "Why did she come back without them?" I asked.

"Well, a Doberman has to have anesthesia for work on his teeth," Joan said. "So it takes a while. She left them at the vet's about quarter of nine, the vet told me, and she couldn't pick them up till four. It was Isaiah's birthday. That may be why she came back." She paused. "Then I realized that since I was supposed to have vanished, maybe dead, I could slip back and try to figure out what happened. Somebody had to pay for killing Isaiah!"

"You should've let the sheriff know," Willie said firmly.

First I thought that was silly of Joan to think she could do better than the sheriff just because nobody expected her to be around, and then I had to laugh at myself. Because I have done better than a sheriff, through sheer good luck and not giving up, and one time by losing my pocketbook. But hey, why didn't she tell about the dogs!

"I bought this bandanna and the dark glasses at a thrift shop," Joan said, picking up the outrageous glasses. "I remembered reading an Agatha Christie story once where someone got away by just dyeing their hair and wearing dark glasses," she said. "Eyes and hair color are the first things we notice. I nosed around town Monday afternoon late and stayed with my brother Albert that night. I couldn't give in to grief. I had to find out what happened first."

Albert. That was Albert Bright. Pop's favorite suspect! So that was his hidden secret? He knew Joan was alive and in town! Had he found out we didn't know that?"

"On Tuesday," she said, "I went to see Isaiah's brother Jake and found out all I could, staying out of sight as much as possible. Poor Jake. The loss was terrible for him, too."

Outside I heard the dogs begin to bark again. Was someone coming up the hill? Or was it another animal passing by? I blurted, "But what about the dogs?"

Joan shrugged. "Jake knew Maureen took the dogs to the veterinary hospital, and he'd called and asked them to hold the dogs a day because of the murder. He picked them up for me this morning. I thought Isaiah's dogs might nose out something that humans missed. I mean, they are my dogs, too. But Isaiah was the one they really cared about." She choked on a sob. "So I brought them here and drove my car into a wood road in a low place, where you couldn't see it except from that road, and started up the mountain. Then the dogs got excited and broke loose. But all they found was you two!"

She turned to me and said, "Now tell me exactly what you saw when you came in this house."

I looked at Willie, and he nodded almost imperceptibly.

I told her everything I'd seen that was in the public record. She'd find that out anyway. Also I told her about the two pictures and the moonshine that vanished between picture number one and picture number two. Albert Bright knew that, so she probably did, too.

"It was Izzy's birthday!" she said sadly. "Albert brought that moonshine early for his birthday. But why on earth would anyone steal his birthday present?"

Then she asked Willie some questions about what had happened. So far she had seemed in control of herself, even when she was upset.

Finally she let go and sobbed violently. She blurted out, "I didn't want Isaiah's life to end this way." Her voice had the ring of truth in it. I could see Willie thought so, too.

CHAPTER
30

WEDNESDAY, 5 P.M.

It was late, so when Deputy *Why Not* dropped me off to get my car, with the tires fixed, I headed for home, emotionally worn out. Almost immediately my car phone rang. It was Pop.

"I need to know what you've found out, Peaches," he said. "How else can I be helpful?"

I paused. This had been a long day. I wasn't sure I was up to Pop being "helpful."

"And I have made an important discovery," he said.

I jumped in then. "Remember, we're talking on a cell phone," I said. "Don't tell me anything you don't want known all over. Remember what happened in Tennessee."

"Then you have to come here right now!" he announced triumphantly. "This is important!"

I could have stopped and talked to him on a pay phone but

I knew he'd keep at me till I arrived in person. I called home and left Ted a message on the answering machine. Told him I had to stop by Pop's and said I'd pick up Chinese or pizza on the way home.

It takes a while to get to Pop's from Monroe County. All the way, I mulled over what Joan Hubbel had to say. I didn't feel she was telling the whole truth. But I felt she'd meant it with her whole heart when she said, "I didn't want Isaiah's life to end this way!"

So what else did I know about Joan? I wished I could get my portable brain out and review. But I couldn't do that and drive at the same time.

Could she be the woman who took Mr. Jeeter-Moonshine-Man cakes in exchange for whiskey? More likely that was Suzie or Maureen, or some woman unknown.

But if Joan was locked in at Falling Waters, she couldn't have taken Isaiah moonshine the day he died. Besides, Albert Bright said he'd given Jeeter the moonshine. Why would he lie? Of course, my Polaroid picture was no proof the moonshine arrived the day Isaiah died. Just proof it disappeared that day. Isaiah could have had it on his library shelf for a week and got it out the day he died. He could have had it for a year. But its disappearance made that seem unlikely.

I wouldn't want to be a close relative of someone as do-it-my-way as Joan, but basically I liked her. I didn't think she was mean.

There were no cars except Pop and Azalea's Cadillac and the sitter's Ford in the drive when I arrived at Pop's house on Town Mountain Road. Good. So his important discovery probably didn't involve sounding out a suspect. Not like the

Albert Bright setup. I'd had enough of talking to a suspect for one day.

I noticed the daffodils near the front door were beginning to fade, just like me. Except they wouldn't revive till next year. I hurried up the front steps, knocked, and tried the door. It wasn't locked. I went in and found Pop sitting at his favorite table all by himself.

"Azalea has joined a history club," he said in a self-pitying voice. "They're going out to dinner tonight. I'm here all by myself. Why don't you stay for supper? Cousin Olive brought me one of her super chocolate cakes, and I thought we'd have a little moonshine."

Chocolate cake! And Cousin Olive wasn't even a suspect! I noticed Pop had a kind of twinkle in his eye. Was he putting me on about the moonshine?

"If you're having enough real food for dinner," I said, "I'll call and suggest that Ted should come, too. I don't want to desert him with no notice if I don't have to."

Whereupon Max, the evening sitter, came in from the kitchen and said that a big pot of homemade chicken soup and cornbread were on the menu. With chocolate cake, that should do it. So I picked up the phone that Pop keeps at his elbow, called Ted, and caught him just as he got home. He agreed to come to Pop's. It's not too far from our house if you come by Webb Cove Road.

"I found out something that will interest Pop," Ted said. "Albert's class was not officially canceled on the morning that Isaiah was killed. But I found out from one of his students that he dismissed them after ten minutes to do research in the library. He has no alibi. When I bumped into him at the college and asked him about that, he said he guessed he forgot which day he let the class out. Strange for a memory expert!"

Pop was overjoyed to hear that. "I knew that man was a hot suspect!" he cried.

"Now," I said to Pop, "what have you discovered?"

He grinned his most devilish grin and said, "You go first. Tell me what else you know."

Well, that was not a bad idea. Then he could tell his discovery to Ted and me at the same time. Ted is the one who notices what does and doesn't fit together right away. I miss the connections sometimes till I wake up in the middle of the night.

So I told Pop about discovering Joan, and about her story of the kid who locked her in.

"Children can be monsters," he said. "My cousin Mary brought her grandson by, and he ate my Tums. Then she got mad at me. Suzie says somebody slashed your tires," he added. "That's a good sign you're getting hot."

Oh, yes, I'd neglected to tell him that, but he had Suzie on the job.

"Suzie's a fine woman," he said, "and calls me all the time." To pick his brains, I figured, and see if she knew more than I did or at least more than I told Pop.

Ted came in the front door. He always looks so great when he's been teaching. Tweedy and relaxed. He went over and hugged Pop.

"Peaches told me what you found out." Pop chortled. "Good work, Ted! Now you're just in time for some moonshine!" Pop smiled broadly. "You may get in the habit!" He reached over to the shelf in back of him and brought forth a commercial-looking bottle that said Genuine Moonshine, and in parentheses under that, *White Lightning*." A slogan across the bottle said, "Guaranteed to be less than 30 days old."

"I called the ABC store," he said, "and found out that you can buy this. It's legal! Any adult can buy it. What do you think of that?"

I was surprised.

"But I figured it might be just a bad imitation of the real thing," he said. "So I got Azalea to get us some. We'll try it."

He called to Max, who brought us glasses, and got Ted to unscrew the bottle and pour. Unscrewing is out of the question with Pop's arthritis.

We all took a sip. Wow. That stuff had the kick.

Pop said, "Whooee, get a load of that!"

Ted said, "I'm not quite sure it has the flavor of the home-made stuff we tasted, but it's hard to be sure without the other to compare."

"But you might be able to fool someone with this," I said thoughtfully. I knew what Pop had in mind. Anyone could have bought white lightning at the liquor store and filled one of the empty jars in Isaiah's pantry.

But that hardly explained why Albert Bright had lied about his alibi. Did he bring Isaiah Hubbel moonshine, or did he lie about that, too?

An odd thought came to me.

Where the moonshine came from might not turn out to be the most important question. Maybe I needed to know *why* somebody gave Isaiah Hubbel moonshine and why they gave him *moonshine*.

CHAPTER
31

THURSDAY MORNING

Yes, I drove all the way up to Linville Falls to check out the B & B. Because Joan's alibi was so fantastic. Mrs. Jackson, who ran the place in a lovely old Victorian house, was a long-faced woman who announced she was just going out. I persuaded her to give me a few minutes. Impatiently she stood and talked by the check-in desk. When she discovered I was a reporter, she first glowed at the possible publicity and then was terrified at being known as the B & B where you could get locked in.

I promised I wouldn't print the locked-in business unless it became an important element in the solution of the murder. "Which seems unlikely," I explained.

She let out a long sigh. "That boy!" she said. "He's into something every minute, and if he's angry it's locking doors. He got mad when we wouldn't let him have a puppy and he locked me in the bathroom. With five important guests about to arrive. I ought to change to inside locks, but these are original. I like to say everything in this house is original. And I never thought that boy would do it again after the spanking he got. I'd told Joan Hubbel about the bathroom thing. He must have heard me and got mad that I told. And he always gets mad about going to the doctor. He hates shots." She sighed gustily.

"I was mortified when I learned that woman was locked in all morning. I mean, I'd checked her out and told her just to leave by the back door when she was ready, since I had to go out. 'Ready' is not locked in! And then I heard her husband was killed. That was a shock. But if she'd been there with him she could have been shot, too. Why, we might have saved her life." She looked me in the eye as if to say, *So there!*

"When you got back, she was still locked in?" I asked.

"And banging on the door, screaming for help. I guess she'd heard our car or heard the front door open. Now I have to go!" she announced.

I begged to see the room. Reluctantly she agreed. Sure enough, the door had a keyhole where you could use the key from either side. The door itself was thick and heavy. Not easy to batter down. The room was pleasantly old-fashioned with a double-wedding-ring quilt in shades of rose on the bed, and flower prints on the wall. A TV on a portable stand stood where you could watch from the bed. A luxurious touch. But there was no phone.

"The TV moves," Mrs. Jackson said. "You can have it for ten dollars extra. Otherwise you watch in the parlor with me. That Joan Hubbel was a private person. Not wanting to talk. Just said 'yes' and 'no' when I tried."

The door was open to an adjoining bathroom. Lucky that was there for someone trapped.

I went over to the window and looked out. Yes, this room was too high for a safe jump. Not only was it on a high second floor, but the house was built on a slope so that what must have been the basement raised it higher from the ground on this side. There was a lawn with a line of pines beyond it. This was a private yard, but not unoccupied. A boy who looked to be about sixteen was busy mowing the lawn. Behind him near the pines was an open shed with a wheelbarrow, rakes, a ladder, and other outdoor aids.

I took a picture of Joan's room and a picture out the window. Probably a waste of time and film, but I might as well be thorough. I took a picture of Mrs. B & B. Maybe she'd locked Joan in herself and went off and killed Isaiah. She would just have had time. Maybe she was the widow of a man he'd killed in Vietnam in a drunken brawl. Life can be as unlikely as that. But, come to think of it, Mrs. B & B was too young.

I wondered where the little menace had gone off to. Perhaps he went to nursery school or to visit grandma.

I thanked Mrs. B & B and told her I'd tell folks what a lovely place this was.

The trip was a waste of time, I told myself, but I'd make the ride home useful. I'd brainstorm about all the things in this case that didn't fit together. Maybe I'd get an inspiration.

Who hit Belle over the head, and why wouldn't she tell? Was it at all possible she really ran into the branch of a tree?

Why did Albert Bright lie about his class? He said he forgot which day was canceled. I doubted that.

Why did Belle want to go see Isaiah's friend in Tennessee,

and why did she stay after he told her he wouldn't betray Isaiah's confidence?

Why, out of his whole family, did Isaiah change his will and leave everything to Maureen? Had she really been playing up to him with that in mind?

Did Jake know Brad was following us to the Opryland Hotel in time to stop him? Was Jake really a benign person trying to help, or was he manipulating *Mad Brad?*

Why did Maureen remove the dogs? Was it part of some plot?

Why did someone hide the jar of white lightning if it was a perfectly innocent birthday present?

Could there be any connection between Isaiah's murder and his time in Vietnam?

Why couldn't I make myself take down that dern poster on my bulletin board that said YOU CAN BE PERFECT? Could there be a connection between the murder of the Good News Man and the murder of Isaiah Hubbel? And could some part of me know that? At least *that* was an interesting angle.

I went straight on to the office and looked back through the stories about that earlier murder.

A young man named Kevin who wasn't even from our county had picked us to save. Why us? He'd been driving from his home in Jackson County and going from door to door, handing out religious flyers. He wasn't systematic about where he went, picking one part of the county, then another. There had been complaints, because if someone refused his flyers, he would begin to scream about how unbelievers would go to hell. But mostly people just took the flyers.

His family said he had no enemies. They said he wore a cap that said "Good News" where most caps had the name of a feed or tractor company or some such. They said he'd take the cap off and leave it at the bottom of the driveway to mark each place he went for the Lord. Then pick it up as he left.

He'd been buried in a shallow grave in the woods, and heavy rains and hunting dogs uncovered him. His cap was missing.

Kevin's family had offered a thousand-dollar reward to anyone who found his cap. Nobody had come forth yet. Now, that was odd in a poor county where such a reward was big money.

The only connection with Isaiah Hubbel was that he'd been in Isaiah's neighborhood, among others, about the time he disappeared. His car and body were found in another area, some way off.

I was mulling this over again when I got back to my desk at the office.

So maybe the Good News Man yelled at Isaiah, and Isaiah was so trigger-happy he shot the young man? And Jake the clean-up man disposed of the body? Or did Joan dispose of the body? Maybe some member of Kevin's family came and took revenge. I put that in my portable brain under "possible solutions" in the notes section.

But that didn't sound right. Because if the sheriff couldn't pin that murder on Isaiah, how would the family be so sure he did it? And would you commit murder to avenge a man who believed so strongly in the Ten Commandments that he went from door to door trying to save souls? No, I didn't think so.

Then I thought maybe a member of his own family shot Isaiah. They say that's very common. I put my portable brain away in my shoulder bag.

I keep my bag on the office bookcase in back of my desk chair. I reached back, got out my portable brain again, then punched the number for Isaiah's Nashville-Vietnam connection. The man Isaiah confided in, who was probably his best friend. Suzie said he even made Joan jealous.

Tomorrow was Isaiah's funeral, and the man would be there. I caught him, but just as he was going out.

"After the graveside service, we'll talk," he said. I hoped that would be fruitful. I put the P.B. back in my bag.

I was wondering about Isaiah's best friend when Joan came in.

She sat in the chair across from my desk, wearing a white blouse and black skirt and leaned forward earnestly. "I know you've been successful solving murders," she said. "If there's any way I can help you with this one, please let me know."

The phone rang before I could say anything. It was Pop. "Anything new?" he asked.

I told him rather tartly I'd let him know when there was. It took me several minutes to get him off the phone. Meanwhile, Joan went around in back of my desk. When I got off the phone, she was looking at the *North Carolina Gazetteer*. "Fascinating book," she said. "Did you know that Dead Squirrel Ridge is near Dog Jump Hollow?"

The phone rang again. It was the president of the garden club wanting to tell me about the club's new beautification project downtown. She took her time.

Joan came back around my desk. "We can talk later," she said. "I just wanted you to know I stand ready to help."

I thanked her. I was tired and ready to go home. I checked tomorrow's list and gathered my things to go home. Jacket, shoulder bag.

Shoulder bag! I caught my breath. She'd been in my bag. She took my portable brain! That's what I thought. She could have been doing that in back of me. With a shock I realized I had forgotten to protect my latest notes about suspects with a password. I grabbed my bag and opened it, quick as I could. Whew! My portable brain was still in the side pocket where I keep it.

I sighed with relief. *You're getting paranoid,* I told myself.

CHAPTER
32

FRIDAY

Lee Fortune Roberts from Nashville had said he would meet me at the graveside service and talk to me afterwards.

I arrived at the cemetery early and followed a drive that curved through the rows of graves. The stones were mostly shiny marble, unsheltered by trees, except for a few older stones in the middle under four maples. The new stones seemed unprotected under that broad sky, row after row of them. Of course, to true believers they might seem more open to heaven.

I found the one newly dug grave with a temporary tent over rows of folding chairs. Family members arrived and sat in the front row. I recognized Jake and Joan and *Mad Brad* and Maureen. There were several others I hadn't met. Several little girls. All the chairs were taken, and the minister said a few words over the gaping grave. Jake Hubbel threw in the first handful of dirt. Then the family members left. They had eyed me like the outsider that I was. Like the observer-spy I was, as I noticed how grief-stricken Joan and Jake seemed to be. She used up three handkerchiefs. He seemed gray with grief. They spoke briefly to a man who seemed to be about Isaiah's age. He remained after they left, standing with his head bowed, plainly disturbed. He was almost bald and had rugged features in a long, oval face. I walked over to him. "You must be Lee Roberts, Isaiah Hubbel's friend from Nashville," I said. "I'm Peaches Dann. I work for the paper here. I'm sorry for your loss."

"Thank you," he said. "Let's walk."

We left the funeral-home people behind and wandered among the stones. Almost every one had two small vases of plastic flowers affixed at each side. We were in a bright and shiny plastic flower garden. I was not in a shiny mood.

"I don't believe my old friend Belle Dasher killed Isaiah Hubbel, but she's a suspect," I told Lee. "Belle visited your shelter, and I gather she did volunteer work, so you know her."

He smiled, a warm, listening smile. "She was determined, but I can't believe she was a killer," he said.

In the distance, birds were calling, cheerful as the plastic flowers. This was a place for thinking positive. We stood by a twin stone. One half said, "Robert Malcomb, 1946-1998." The other half said, "Susan Malcomb, 1948–   ." In other words, she was still alive. So what if she married again? Is love set in stone? Did Joan still love Isaiah after all those years on the mountain? When he kept a gun in every room? When he managed to have at least one girlfriend, maybe more?

"You talked to Isaiah every day, I understand, at least by E-mail," I said to his friend.

"Yes, I should have prevented this."

"Why do you think you could have prevented it?" I asked.

"He told me he was scared. I thought it was just his usual fears taking a new form."

"Scared of what?"

"He said he'd done a wicked thing. That God would punish him. But he couldn't tell anyone or he'd get some other person in terrible trouble. He couldn't tell me because I'd have to tell the sheriff."

There was something about Lee Fortune Roberts that made me want to trust him. Maybe it was his direct look. Why wouldn't Isaiah trust his old friend more?

"You see, Isaiah had totally unrealistic ideas about how good he should be," Lee said. "That was part of his trouble in Vietnam. He thought he ought to be a model soldier, but he watched such horrible things happen, he almost couldn't fight at all."

"For example?"

"One day near a village, he saw some of his unit playing kickball."

That didn't sound too bad.

"He looked more closely, and the ball was the head of a Vietcong boy." Lee Roberts watched me to see how I'd take that.

I found it sickening. "He had to go on fighting beside those men?"

"Of course," he said bitterly. The birds went on singing.

"Do you think what's happened here is related to Vietnam?"

"I think it was related to Isaiah's state of mind. I don't know how."

He ran his hand along the top of a smooth marble stone. "My head got screwed up, too," he said with a frown.

"Don't think it was only Isaiah. I killed a man in a fight in a bar. If you check on me you'll find I've served time."

"From a fight in a bar to running a shelter for the homeless?" That seemed a long jump.

He nodded. "It fits. I need to do something that makes me feel I have a right to be alive when the man I killed is dead. I'm actually a minister now. The shelter is my ministry. And I kept in touch with Isaiah. He needed that."

"Was he there when you killed that man?" I asked.

After a full minute of silence, he said, "Thank God he wasn't. That was the most shameful and foolhardy moment of my life. But you want to know about Isaiah."

"Yes," I said. "When did he begin to act more paranoid?"

"Around the end of March. He asked me to pray for forgiveness for him, but he wouldn't say what for. He sounded sick. Two days later, I found out that Joan was gone. I couldn't get an answer by E-mail. I called him on the telephone. He said he was scared he'd never see Joan again. But when I asked him why, he sounded so strange. He said he didn't know where she was. He said if something upset her, she would take off and ride around until she felt better. He'd never told me that before. He said that one time Joan went to South Carolina, and once she went to Kentucky. When she felt better she came back.

"So I said, 'Good. She'll come back.' Then he wept."

"He was up on that mountain by himself?"

"Not entirely. His brothers came to visit, and his nieces and nephews. After a week or so he seemed to have a routine. He spent a lot of time in chat rooms, talking about the war, I think. He planned his garden. But he had panic attacks. I should have figured how to get away and see him, and find out what was really wrong. Once he said he knew he'd be struck down. That sounded so dramatic, I thought his fears were just worse because Joan was gone. But I didn't go to him. It's not easy for me to get away from the shelter. Now it's too late.

Tears ran down his rugged cheeks.

"I'm sorry," I said.

"When Belle showed up at the shelter, so sure that Isaiah had killed Joan, I let myself wonder. I'm ashamed of that now. But he had fits of rage, being cooped up on that mountain. I couldn't talk to Belle about that. I hope she didn't . . . No, I'm sure she didn't . . ."

"I'm sure Belle didn't kill him," I said. But I wasn't absolutely sure.

"One other thing," I said, quick before I forgot to mention it. "Why would someone think moonshine was the right present to take to Isaiah Hubbel?"

Amazingly, Lee Roberts leaned on a tombstone and laughed.

"Even a good boy has to rebel in some way, right?"

"And that was how?"

"All his life, Isaiah heard his mother talk about the evils of making moonshine. I heard her myself, going on and on, when we were kids. But his ancestors had done it back at least to the time of the Civil War. Moonshiners around here sold to both sides."

"Without getting killed by either one?"

"Well, not often. They had lookouts posted so the young men could hide when recruiting parties came through, and the old men sold the soldiers whiskey. That's well known in Monroe County. It took a family network, then and later, especially after Prohibition. Some members made the whiskey, young men were transporters, and Isaiah's great-grandfather was the contact man. He was the arranger, who sold to tourist hotels in Asheville, to the brass who ran the railroad, and anybody who would pay for good corn liquor. The Hubbels did take pride in their product when some didn't."

"Isaiah knew all that?"

"Isaiah had cousins who told him, and poked fun at his mother for being so strait-laced."

"She said his forebears were in hell?" I had neighbors who believed that drinking whiskey was the road to hell.

"The only story she would ever tell was how Isaiah's great-grandfather, the contact man, picked up the money for a delivery in Asheville and drank some of his own liquor to celebrate. On his way home, drunk, he fell off his horse into the snow and froze to death."

"And that could inspire someone to give Isaiah moonshine for his birthday?" I was horrified.

He shook his head no. "Not that. The first time Isaiah tasted moonshine whiskey, we were together. It was a lark. After the first sip he gave me a big smile. 'This is what I come from,' he said. 'And it's good!' So it became his secret sin. Not that he drank a lot, but he enjoyed it fiercely. Sometimes I think a man needs a secret sin to feel whole. I shouldn't think that, should I?"

"I think you must be a great comfort to strugglers," I said. "And nobody's perfect."

"After his mother died, his thirst for moonshine wasn't secret. But I think it still felt to Isaiah like a secret sin."

"And somehow," I said, "moonshine was mixed up with his death." I told Lee how a jar of white lightning was near Isaiah's hand when he died.

He frowned. "Very strange," he said. "And so sad." Then he smiled. "But I bet you'll find the answer."

CHAPTER
33

I sat at my desk, clearing out the stuff that was done—putting some of it in the file basket and some in the waste-basket. I had started a to-do list for the next issue, attached to the large clipboard, which is hard to lose.

Isaiah Hubbel was buried. A picture of the graveside service was too late to get on the front page. *Whodunit?* was still the number one ongoing story. An unopened envelope caught my eye. I hoped I hadn't missed a news release.

I slit open the envelope, and there was a fan letter! How nice! "Dear Ms. Dann," it said. "Since major surgery, I have a terrible memory. Your tips and jokes are just what I've needed. Thank you so much. I used to be a safety engineer and teach industrial safety, so I thought the old sock-on-the-television principle might be a help to you."

The what? I'd certainly never heard of that.

The letter went on: "Things left out of place can be a real safety hazard in some kinds of factories. So we tell students that anything that stays in a place for three days tends to vanish, even an old dirty sock on top of your television."

Well, I might notice that, but I could see what he meant.

"Therefore it is important to remove something out of place right away before it's just part of the scenery."

But what did this have to do with memory?

"The same thing is true with stick-'em notes. If you leave a note by the front door to remind yourself to turn the lights out, after three days you probably won't notice that note— at least, if your memory is as bad as mine."

It was, or rather is, and that's how I had forgotten the dentist appointment, even though there was a note on my computer.

"So stick on a different-colored note after three days, and that will jog your memory."

Good idea. I had tan stick-it notes on my desk to use for constant reminders, but I remembered there were neon-pink ones in my drawer. I pulled them out to switch all my reminders.

But wait. I needed to keep my mind on who the murderer was. There were still a lot of silly-seeming unanswered questions. For instance, who really put the jar of moonshine next to Isaiah Hubbel, and why did somebody hide it? Because if Albert Bright lied about his class being canceled, he could have lied about putting the jar there. I couldn't believe he would have said he put it there if he actually did it the day Isaiah was killed. He was protecting someone. His sister? But I'd checked out her alibi.

I saw the room at the B & B in my mind again. Saw how very high that window was. And she hadn't known how important it might be to get out.

Get out. I needed to get out and do something to solve all this. I looked at the clock on my wall: 3:40. I was expecting Deputy *Why Not* at 4:30, but I had time to pay a visit to Jeeter the moonshine man.

Because suddenly it came to me: Jeeter couldn't remember faces, but he could remember other things. He should be able to remember eyeglasses! Especially unusual eyeglasses such as Joan's with the rhinestones across the top or Albert Bright's with the macramé chain. I could describe those.

I decided to leave *Why Not* a note in case I was a few minutes late. On my desk full of papers, a regular note would certainly vanish, no matter how many days it sat there. So I wrote a neon-pink stick-on note: "Gone to see Moonshine Man." I put that in the middle of my desk. Next to it, I put a note that said, "If not back by 4:30, I've been kidnapped." I meant that as a joke. I also told Pat where I was going, but she might get busy and not notice when the deputy came. Martin was out.

Without really noticing what I was doing, I stuck what was in my hand in my pocket. O.K., I do that. Sometimes it causes trouble.

I went out to the car, pulled my portable brain out of my shoulder bag, and carefully followed the directions I'd noted to the moonshine man's place.

Almost as soon as I set out, I had a feeling someone was following me. It wasn't Jake's white pickup, or any other car I recognized. It was a sleek dark car that could have been brand new. It drove erratically faster, then slower, as if the driver was drunk.

I didn't worry too much on the main drag. Lots of cars went in my direction through town. But when I turned into the back road where Jeeter had his moonshine museum, I hoped to goodness the car didn't follow. The road curved so much that I couldn't see behind me. I pulled into the yard near the shed with the transporter's car in it.

I called out hello. Jeeter got up from a rocker on his porch and came toward me. He wasn't wearing his black felt moonshiner's hat. I'd forgotten how ancient he looked— lined, frail, and today he seemed gray. But he smiled as if he was glad to see me. Then he frowned. I turned and looked behind me. The dark car had pulled into the yard. My heart raced. Jake Hubbel got out of the car that had followed me. He moved jerkily and in slow motion. He was holding a gun.

"I need to take this girl to Indian Head Rock." His words were slurred.

"It's good to see you, Cousin Jake," Jeeter said in a creaky voice. "What can I do for you?" Could he mean that?

"Keep going," Jake said, keeping the gun pointed at me as we walked toward the building with the still. I was terrified. Jeeter seemed confused, but he came along. "You have a key?" Jake asked him, and he pulled one right out of his pocket.

"I have to leave her here a minute," Jake said.

This might not be too bad. I might be able to find a way to get out of that building. It was old and maybe not strong.

I went inside and heard the padlock click behind me. I had no idea if Jake would be gone for a minute or an hour, or why he'd left.

If he came right back, I needed to leave traces. I'd left a note on my desk saying I'd be here. I needed to leave a clue to the next place. What incredible luck he was drunk enough to let that slip. Unless he said something that wasn't true, as a trap. I had to hope not. I looked in my shoulder bag. I found a pencil but no paper except an old bill and a grocery tape. No one would notice those.

I searched my pockets. I was in luck. There were my neon-pink sticky notes. Now, where to stick them so Jake wouldn't notice but anyone who came to look for me would? And I had to do this fast. I looked at the assortment of objects on Jeeter's cupboard where he kept the jars of moonshine. Two blue mugs had joined the collection of objects on top. Near the package of Kool cigarettes. I had a feeling they meant something. No time to wonder. I wrote "Help! Indian Head Rock" on a pink note and "Jake H" on another and I put the slips on the cupboard top behind the cups. I stuck notes on the far side of the still where you couldn't see them from the door to the shed. It was like a game I played as a kid, except this was serious.

I had hardly stuck the notes in place when I heard a key in the padlock. I braced myself. Jeeter hurried in.

"Come on, quick," he said. "Jake's in the house."

Was Jeeter on my side? I had to take the chance. Outside I reached behind me and attached two of the neon notes to the door. Jake might see that, but if he chased after us he might not. We ran back toward the cars. Jeeter tottered, but he tottered fast. I was heading for my car, but Jeeter said, "No. This one is souped up. It might could beat a Ford Mustang G.T." He waved toward Jake's car. "Get in," Jeeter said as he jumped into the driver's seat of the transporter car. I prayed I did the right thing as I jumped in beside him. He turned the key, and the engine roared. Jeeter's face exploded with delight. "We'll beat him," he sang. "You're with the best transporter in all these coves—at least, I used to be!" The joy on his face made him look ten years younger.

As we sprang forward, Jake ran out of the house to his car. He took a couple of shots but evidently wasn't sober enough to hit a moving target. He jumped into the Mustang and took off after us.

Jeeter squealed around the curves. "Why, when I was young, I could wear out a set of tires in two months," he said happily. Even his voice was less creaky. I hoped his reflexes were still good enough to keep us on the road.

We squealed right past the big gnarled tree and then took a left past the sagging barn. When we were almost at the main road where ours dead-ended, he called out, "Indian Head Rock! He said he'd take you-uns to Indian Head Rock. We'll go the other way!"

He swerved around the corner onto the road, and a car he hadn't seen jammed on its brakes with a screech that made my skin crawl and my heart pound. I could hear Jake behind us, drunk enough to have no fear.

Once we were on the larger road, it was clear Jake's car was faster. Trees rushed by, but Jake was gaining on us. We whooshed around a curve so fast we were on the wrong side of the road. A red pickup came directly at us. I said my prayers. But Jeeter slipped around that car as smoothly as water.

Now Jake was only a few hundred feet behind us. Jeeter laughed. "I bet he can't do this!" I can hardly even describe what the old transporter did, but somehow he got that car to buck up on its back wheels and flip around. Now we were driving in the other direction. I gripped the seat. No seat belts in this old baby. That wild maneuver gave us a little lead since Jake had to turn around in the usual, slower way.

He began to overtake us again, and now we headed away from town.

"Don't worry," Jeeter said with a delighted grin, "we'll drop a little oil."

He pulled out a plunger on the dashboard. I couldn't see

exactly what happened behind us, but Jake's car began to spin all over the road.

Jeeter laughed with glee. "I never thought I'd get to do this again," he chortled. "Oh, this is fine!" His happiness was so contagious I found that I was laughing, too.

"Now, down by your feet," Jeeter said, "there's a bucket of nails. Throw some out, and if he goes on spinnin' around he may hit some and get a flat tire."

But Jake seemed in control again. He missed our nails.

"I should have topped that oil up," Jeeter said sadly, "but the only place I ever drive this car is the Fourth of July parade. I can't drop oil there."

Our tires still squealed on the curves, and I prayed someone had seen or heard us and called the sheriff, but there weren't many houses on this stretch of road. I prayed Jake was too drunk to keep control of his car. But he seemed to be one of those drunks who could navigate no matter what.

Jake put on a burst of speed, and his dark car pulled up beside us. He swerved and swiped Jeeter's car. Now Jeeter was upset. "Them Hubbels are no good," he growled. But Jake had simply forced us off the road. Jeeter had to stop or hit a big rock head-on. I pulled the stick-it notes out of my pocket and held them cupped in my hand. Maybe somehow they could still help. We screeched to a standstill. I was so jarred it took me several minutes until I felt pulled together.

Jake opened my door and said, "Get out."

"Jeeter may be hurt." I remembered how frail he'd seemed before we started our wild chase. And maybe I hoped for help from Jeeter. I can't think how.

"Feel his pulse," Jake said. "He's dead. He was stone dumb to take that ride with a weak heart." I turned and felt. No pulse. No breath. Sorrow mixed sharply with my fear.

"Now, get in my car," Jake ordered. He kept the gun pointed at my chest. The car reeked of alcohol. If he tried to drive and hold the gun on me, maybe he'd be vulnerable. Unfortunately he could steer with one hand, and the left one at that—even drunk.

So we were on the less-traveled road that led to Indian Head Rock. At least it appeared we were really going where he'd said.

We passed a few houses, but no one was out in the yard, except for one towheaded girl playing on a swing. The grass around her was new and shiny and tender. She waved. We passed a field with horses frolicking around. No point in signaling them for help.

We passed a high rock cliff and then woods. I thought of the young man found dead in the woods.

Jake kept his eyes on me and the road, darting back and forth.

I said, "I don't understand."

He said nothing.

We drove a long way on this road that was traveled a lot in summer by tourists but very little this early in the spring. Suzie had brought me to see Indian Head Rock and told me that. She also told me the superstition that went with the rock. Kiss it for good luck.

The rock came into sight in the distance. When I'd seen it before, it seemed intriguing with a projection for a nose and patterns in the rock for eyes and mouth. Now it loomed, forbidding, the face misshapen, like rock becoming demon.

The mountain behind the rock opened in a V—a steep-sided narrow gap between two slopes, as if the Indian head was guarding that. A dirt road led into the woods on the other side of the road from the demon Indian, and we turned in. Jake pulled the Mustang around into a small vacant spot beside the road. It wouldn't be visible from the main road. He got out and came around to my side, keeping the gun on me the whole time. "Get out!" he barked.

I slipped out awkwardly.

"Walk in front of me," he said. "Straight ahead."

We crossed the main road and walked toward the gorge behind the Indian rock. Suddenly Suzie's words came back to me. "Upright hollow," she'd said. "That's where the sides are so steep that you can only see the sun when it's directly overhead." She'd said that no one went there except to gather ferns, and if you fell down and hurt yourself, no one would find you for a long time.

No one would find me. I shuddered. Near the side of the road stood a young tree. I managed to come so close to it that I could palm a blank stick-it note onto the trunk. If Jake saw it, would he shoot me? No, he needed me to come to this place. He was going to some trouble to bring me here. There must be a reason. He didn't see the note because he didn't expect it.

But if Deputy *Why Not* saw the note on my desk and found the ones at Jeeter's place, he'd come looking for clues, wouldn't he? All based on *ifs*. But sometimes *ifs* work out.

Ahead of me, on the mountainside to my right, a patch of trillium with its three-petaled scarlet blossoms was the color of blood. Early wildflowers to remind me of death, which I had to cheat somehow.

The walking was not easy. My shoulder bag banged on my side. Branches of small trees leaned across our path; brush and ferns grew up in our way. This was not a real path at all, just the low middle of the upright hollow. Here and there I noticed redbud trees on the mountainsides, like the one outside our office window. No baby leaves yet in this sunless place. I felt a pang. Suppose I never saw my office again? Suppose . . . ? *Stop that,* I told myself. *Concentrate on living.* But what could I do? There was no solid tree in the path to mark with a note. If I leaned over to put one on a fern, Jake would certainly see me, and maybe go back and remove the one I'd managed to leave earlier.

Small white bloodroot blossoms spotted the mountainsides. Spring telling me to survive.

We were walking uphill, with lots of rocks underfoot that I had to be careful not to trip on. There must be a stream here in a wet year, or once was. Mountain springs can dry up. My hope for help could dry up if . . .

I remembered something. Deputy *Why Not* had said, "I'll probably be over at four-thirty but I might have to do an errand on the way. Are you going to be around until five?" I hadn't dared remember that! Until now.

I'd known he might not see my note. Now I knew I couldn't count on his help if I needed it quick. Which seemed likely. Who else would ever guess where I was? Mountainsides rose steep on both sides of us. Patches of spring beauties were tiny white and pink stars. Yes, fear of death does highlight beauty. The sky far above was a rich afternoon blue with lacy leaves against it.

Nobody looked down from up there. I had to save myself.

We plowed on. Ferns were broken. Jake called, "Here we are." We came to a flat place at the end of the hollow, almost a small room, and the walls of the V closed in front of us. The remains of a tumbledown shed were near a small sluggish spring. A large flattish rock was almost like a bench in front of that. Joan got up from it.

I found myself thinking: If they kill me here, they'll have

a hard job burying me, with all these rocks. Good. Dead or alive, I wanted to be as difficult as possible.

"Why did you bring me here?" I asked. "What have I done to hurt you?"

Joan reached for my shoulder bag. She took out my portable brain. "You found out that Isaiah killed the Good News Man last month," she said. "You found out about me."

I'd made a few wild conjectures. Lord help me, I'd forgotten to put them in code. "*You* have a Palm Pilot, too," I said. So that's how she knew how to work mine. But when did she have enough time to read it? At my office, she'd been behind me, and near my shoulder bag, for several minutes. Had that given her time to read all my notes?

"You think you're so hip about technology," she scoffed. "I bet you read how to get started with this thing and skipped the rest. Or else you'd know that you can transfer the contents of one of these to another. It's easy and quick. I had mine handy in my pocket. I just had to borrow yours for two minutes."

Of course. While I talked to that dern woman from the garden club. A school kid would probably have known all about a portable brain and how to steal the contents in nothing flat. What I'd missed might kill me.

Jake kept his gun on me. I turned fast, grabbed the gun, and twisted. He was so surprised that I almost had it. Then something crashed down on my head, and everything went black.

CHAPTER
34

A FEW MINUTES LATER

When I came to, I was lying on the ground, half on my side, half on my back. My head throbbed. The stone was cold beneath the side of my face. Something bit my arm. I winced, then tried to lie perfectly still. I realized that I'd better pretend I was out cold until I knew how the land lay. At least I was still alive.

I was surprised to hear a quarrel.

"I came here when you asked me to," Joan said, "because I could tell you'd been drinking. I was scared you might do something desperate, Jake. We can't afford to make a mistake. You go weeks without a drop and then at the worst possible moment you hit the bottle. Look how you screwed things up the last time."

"I saved the day before," he crowed. "There I was in the woods, looking for that damn Good News Man's hat. I looked some every day because we had to find it. I came out from behind a rock, and there was Belle in front of me, and the cap was wedged in the crotch of a tree right in front of her. She was going to find it! Right near your place. I hit her over the head before she even saw me. That saved your skin."

"But now we're in real trouble," Joan was saying. "Why did you make me come here, and what are we going to do now?"

"I think you know." Jake's words were still somewhat slurred, but I was amazed at how logical he could sound, if in slow motion. "You've put us in a position where we have to get rid of this woman. Don't tell me you came to me for help about what to do next and didn't know this would have to be it. We have to find out what she really knows and who else she may have told and what proof there is. What that little computer thing says isn't proof. Just theories. But she has a reputation for keeping at a mystery till it's solved. That woman never lets go. That's what's dangerous."

I tried to place where they were by their voices. Joan quite close to me. Jake further away.

Joan's voice with an angry note: "Now you say kill her! Because you kidnapped her, so we can't let her go! But if we kill her, that can get us in a hell of a lot deeper."

I prayed she'd convince him of that!

"Oh, Jake," she was suddenly pleading. "I know you're trying to help me. You know I love you. But I'm scared."

"You're in deep trouble!" Jake growled.

Some bug was walking along the side of my face. I mustn't flinch.

"But I didn't kill Isaiah on purpose—you know that!" The pleading note grew stronger in Joan's voice. "When he pulled that gun on me, I couldn't believe it. Even if I had just told him I couldn't take it anymore, told him I was leaving. I wanted to help him plan some other way to get along. You know I did. And when he said he'd rather see us both dead, I still didn't expect him . . . I wasn't prepared . . ."

"So you struggled for the gun, and it went off and killed him." *Jake's voice, brutal.* "How can you prove that? Especially now that you've lied about it? And you tell fancy lies: You weren't even around. You were off somewhere locked in a room."

"Thank God," Joan said, "for the ladder."

Ladder! The picture from the window flashed in my mind, the boy mowing the grass, and suddenly Joan's earlier words—that she was so frustrated because she could see the ladder down there and couldn't get to it. Or something like that. Oh, my thick head! The boy had put the ladder by the shed. But the ladder must have been exactly in position to have been thrown down by someone who climbed in the window, someone who'd heard about the five-year-old kid and his ways, was desperate for an alibi, and locked the door herself and climbed back in the window.

I heard the whoosh of a match and then smelled a whiff of smoke. One of them had lit a cigarette.

Oh, my really thick head, of course. Joan smoked Kools. There was a partially full pack of Kools left on Jeeter's cupboard!

"So, now, how could you prove you didn't kill your husband on purpose?" Jake was demanding. His voice was deep with irony, then accusing. "And how can you prove you didn't kill that young man that Isaiah killed? You hid the body."

Was Joan like Jake? Anything to keep the family name clean?

"I was scared," she said. "And there wasn't any reason for anyone to connect that man to us. I've always done what I can to protect Isaiah. And protect you. You know I have. I called you, and you weren't there. You've said you'd always be there for me, but you weren't there." Her voice was accusing now.

A second bug bit my ankle. Did I flinch?

Joan kept talking. "Since this happened just before dark," she said, "and no one could see our house, what I did made sense: I put the body in the back seat of the young man's own car. I was careful, you know that. Then after dark I drove him off to a wood-road a half mile away and buried him. I even said a prayer."

She was some gutsy lady. Gutsy but misled.

"You didn't bury him deep enough," Jake groaned.

"I had to get back to Isaiah!" she cried. "I had to do it without being seen and carrying a shovel. You don't know what it was like. I took the nigh way, the shortcut through the woods, and walked home in the dark. Thank goodness there was a moon. And poor Isaiah. You should have heard how that boy yelled at Isaiah. Told him if he couldn't be perfect he'd go to hell. And Isaiah yelled, 'Shut up! You're like my mother.' And he shot the guy. I certainly didn't expect him to do that. Would you expect him to do that?" Her voice broke.

Jake said, "Yes. I would."

Silence. *Please argue more,* I prayed. *Don't just shoot me.*

Jake was drunk enough to do that. And to sound sorry for himself. "You don't care about me. You don't care about my reputation. If you hadn't panicked and run away, that damn

Belle Dasher wouldn't have made up that story about how Isaiah killed you," Jake snorted. "That woman is a menace. That damn story got half the people in town stirred up. They were watching us until it made my skin crawl. God knows why you couldn't have left an address, or called to check in with us. No. You just had to vanish. Now we have to pay the price."

Joan's voice seemed to move. She was going nearer to Jake, pleading. "I had to go off and think. I had to do that or go crazy. Do you know the kind of pressure I suffered from you all? Telling me this to do or that? After Isaiah killed that man, who yelled at him so about going to hell, I almost didn't blame him. But after that, I knew I couldn't handle him by myself anymore. I tried to protect him. I always have. I couldn't just leave him. But I couldn't stay. I had to have time to think. But I came back."

"You sure came back," Jake said. "And made me and your brother so nervous we almost peed in our pants. Because when you finally called, you said you'd tell him you were going to leave him. We knew he'd go wild. And you were talking about how you had to take him a birthday present, for God's sake. A jar of moonshine."

"Moonshine calmed him down," she said. "Whiskey hypes you up, Jake, but a drink always calmed Isaiah down."

"We don't have all night," Jake said. "If this comes out, we're ruined!" His voice was hot with impatience. I heard footsteps hurry toward me. He slapped me hard on the side of my face. Inadvertently my eyes flew open.

"She heard it all!" Jake snorted.

I looked up into their startled faces. I sat up, still groggy from the slap and the blow to my poor head before that. But I had to save myself. "Other people know," I said quickly.

"No, they don't," Jake said, "or you'd have put it in that thing you've got that tells everything else you know."

He leveled his gun straight at my head. I said a prayer and expected the end. I apologized to Ted in my head.

Then a dog's bark came toward us, the high-pitched, excited yapping of a small dog. Jake hesitated.

Bailey rushed up and began to lick my ankles. Jake laughed in a nasty way. He held his fire and waited. Belle came crashing through the underbrush.

"Well," Jake said, "a reunion. All the nosy women are here. Perhaps that's a good thing."

Belle said, "The sheriff is right behind me. I saw your notes," she said to me. "I called him and came."

I wondered if that was true. Or was she bluffing for time? I couldn't hear anyone else coming down the hollow.

"You haven't done anything yet except kill a man by mistake," I said to Joan. "And," I said to Jake, "all you've done is to obstruct justice. If you kill us, that's a capital offense. You could die for that. You know that."

We all stood there, seeming frozen in time. Jake had turned so that his gun was covering both Belle and me. A mosquito buzzed by. April was early for mosquitoes. Whatever the time was, it was late for the sheriff. No one came. A hawk or some such soared across the slice of sky above us. We were lost to all other eyes.

Belle said, "You aren't a killer. Not yet."

Jake's face remained stony.

Joan looked back and forth from Jake to Belle. Joan was the weak link. Not wanting to kill.

"I don't know your children," I said to Jake, "but no child wants to know that his father committed murder."

Jake's jaw was working. "Shut up," he said. "They won't know. We can't stop now."

"But if the sheriff catches us walking out of here, and then finds the bodies . . ." Joan said.

"We might as well be dead!" Jake answered.

He raised the gun again, and Belle let out a small scream. Bailey rushed at Jake, and I thought: *Poor dog! Him too.*

But in that brief moment when Jake was distracted, Joan grabbed his gun hand, and as they wrestled, I jumped up, and Belle and I helped wrestle him to the ground and hold him until Joan was able to take his gun.

"Is this how you love me?" Jake yelled. Slowly he stood up, his face a mask of rage, but Joan now had the gun pointed at him.

"I love you too much to see you convicted of murder," Joan said. "You're drunk. You're not responsible!"

She looked me in the eye. "You'll testify, won't you, Peaches, to what really happened? Because you heard it all."

"You're a fool, Joan," Jake gasped. "You'll rot in prison."

"Listen," Joan said. "Somebody is coming."

There was no silent way to get into this hollow. We heard noises in the underbrush. It could be the sheriff. It could be *Mad Brad*. Why wasn't he here?

Through the haze of leaves, several men appeared in the distance. The one in the lead was Deputy Willie Wynatt. God bless him.

Jake turned to me. "Joan lied to you," he said. "We knew you could hear."

Joan cried out, "No!"

"I killed my brother," he said, "while you fools waited

right outside the door. I used a silencer. It wasn't safe to leave him on his mountain. Joan couldn't stay. If they came and took him to some institution, that would have ripped him apart. I killed him."

He began to run straight toward Deputy Wynatt as my friend came toward us, drawing his gun. Jake was screaming, "I killed Isaiah! I killed my brother!" Jake grabbed at the gun, tussled with Wynatt and when the sheriff, who was right in back of the deputy, drew his gun and shot Jake in the leg to stop him, Jake managed to somehow get the deputy's gun turned on himself. He shot himself in the head.

I looked at Joan. "I killed him," she sobbed.

Did she mean Jake? Or Isaiah?

CHAPTER
35

AFTER THE SMOKE CLEARED

I have to admit I didn't believe Jake Hubbel. But he knew what the county would like to believe. That he killed out of compassion. I thought I could understand him well enough to know that he would far rather be dead than have an ugly trial which might end with both himself and Joan in prison. He confessed and killed himself so there'd be no trial. The sheriff's folks didn't even investigate much more, though they never found the weapon that killed Isaiah.

Jake could have killed Isaiah as he said and quickly hidden that gun in some secret spot he knew, in a hollow tree or crevice near the house, then moved it as soon as he could. Maybe the sheriff's men wouldn't have found it. They glossed over the inconveniently missing gun.

I believed the story Joan told and that she did think I was out cold. I believe she let Jake's story stand out of respect for him, and his sacrifice, and also because it saved her hide. As a newspaper reporter, I probably should have told all. But I had no real proof.

In a surprising twist, it was Joan, not Belle, who went off to work at the homeless shelter in Nashville. Belle went to work as a Monday volunteer at the Wellness Center in Asheville where many cancer patients who came to Asheville for treatment found a haven. I hoped that meant she was going to think positive.

"What really happened when you were hit over the head?" I asked Belle. Turns out she thought Brad had done it.

"But why didn't you say you thought it was him?" I demanded. She said she didn't want to rake up all that stuff about the brick and the smoke-shop window, and besides, she hadn't seen who hit her.

Now Brad was back in Broughton State Hospital. Jake had taken him there before our confrontation. Even with his medication, Brad thought I might be a spy. He had been stalking me. It wasn't my imagination. He wanted proof. He'd even punctured my tires. His sickness was hard to control, I guess. Thank goodness he hadn't been a part of the scene in the upright hollow.

George and Maureen were married in a ceremony at the Hubbel homeplace, and Belle took all the wedding pictures. I think she wanted to make amends for accusing Maureen's poor uncle Isaiah of polluting the wells and maybe causing so much sickness. Obviously the chemicals in the water went back to Isaiah's mother, who had to be sure no bug could ever live in her orchard or house. I bet there were full bags left when she died and DDT became illegal. The chemicals were a symptom of the pressures that shaped Isaiah, not proof he didn't care about his neighbors. They were a time bomb until the roof over the old dry well rusted away and heavy rains fell.

Jeeter's still was presented to the museum at the college. I went to cover the ceremony. I shook his granddaughter's hand and told her, as I had at his funeral, how sorry I was that I helped cause his death. She smiled. "You know," she said, "he went out in glory, leastways from his point of view. He loved to tell about his whiskey-running days. He relived that."

That left one intriguing loose end. What became of that jar of money that Isaiah kept hidden in his house? I figured Joan took it so that she'd have cash in case she had to stay out of sight. If you're in hiding, you don't walk into the bank and cash a check.

"So what did you learn from the Hubbel case?" Ted asked me.

"I learned that memory devices can be dangerous unless you learn to use them right. Why, even geraniums on your car aerial can make it easier for a stalker to spot your car. Life is complicated," I said.

As for Ted, my adventures didn't hurt his health. He's full of plans. The paper got a summer intern from the college, and Martin said he could therefore let me have a month's leave of absence.

So Ted and I are going on a tour of all the classic railroads of Europe and even the Orient Express. A second honeymoon, he says. Turns out Ted's grandpa was a railroad engineer. "Besides," he said, "Thank God I didn't know what danger you were in until this was all over. A railroad tour should keep you out of trouble! At least, for a month." I could see that maybe Ted had forgotten what Agatha Christie wrote about the Orient Express.